The Whitby Murders

ALSO BY J. R. ELLIS

The Body in the Dales
The Quartet Murders
The Murder at Redmire Hall
The Royal Baths Murder
The Nidderdale Murders

The Whitby Murders

A YORKSHIRE MURDER MYSTERY

J.R. ELLIS

THOMAS & MERCER

Text copyright © 2021 by J. R. Ellis
All rights reserved.

Published by Thomas & Mercer, Seattle

www.apub.com

Amazon, the Amazon logo, and Thomas & Mercer are trademarks of Amazon.com, Inc., or its affiliates.

ISBN-13: 9781542017466
ISBN-10: 1542017467

Cover design by @blacksheep-uk.com

Printed in the United States of America

To friends and colleagues who worked with me over the years in further education.

Prologue

*Right over the town is the ruin of Whitby Abbey . . . It is
a most noble ruin of immense size and full of beautiful
and romantic bits; there is a legend that a white lady is
seen in one of the windows.*

From Mina Murray's journal in Dracula,
Bram Stoker 1897

'Oh my God! You look amazing!'

Louise Oldroyd didn't smile back at her friend, Maggie Hinton.
Instead she glowered chillingly. Her face was white, and she had
black eyelashes and eyebrows and thick purple lipstick. She wore
black earrings in the shape of small spiders, as well as a black wig
with a low fringe and a short black skirt with torn black tights
underneath. Her tightly buttoned strappy top and her heavy boots
were also black.

Finally, her expression cracked and she giggled, showing black-
ened teeth and long fangs. 'What about you?' she said. 'Look at
that hair!'

Maggie was similarly attired, but her black hair was insanely
spiky, and her lipstick was bright red. She wore a long dress,
embroidered with spiders, with black petticoats underneath.

The two friends were in a crowded bar in the Yorkshire coastal town of Whitby. It was a Wednesday towards the end of October and the famous Whitby Goth Weekend was steadily building up to its finale. The bar was full of people dressed in the same goth and steampunk fashion: garish blacks, reds, purples and whites; spiders, black capes, top hats, plague doctor beaks, goggles and curly moustaches. Loud music from Bauhaus was rocking the building.

'Oh look, they're here!' Maggie pointed to a group of people making their way through the crowd. Ben, in black leathers and steampunk goggles, laughed when he saw Louise and Maggie's costumes, but was surprised to see Louise.

'I thought you weren't coming to this,' he said.

'I managed to get away from work earlier than I thought,' Louise replied, smiling at him. 'I just got here and threw my costume on. I've contacted the escape room; they're happy with an extra person.'

'Fine,' replied Ben, smiling back. He came closer to her. 'It's really good to see you.'

'I feel the same. I didn't want to miss it.'

The other two members of the party, Dominic and Andrea, were sullen and quiet. They were in a rather stormy relationship and had had a furious and rather embarrassing row in front of the others the previous night. They had almost pulled out of today's event but in the end seemed to have entered the spirit.

Andrea was dressed as a bride of Dracula in a ghostly and ragged white wedding dress spattered with blood. She had bright-red lipstick and a cobweb-like shawl, which contained very lifelike black spiders. Dominic was dressed and made up as a magnificent Count Dracula complete with black cape and red make-up round his eyes. They both seemed to warm up when the party was all together. They had a drink and started to join in the banter. The enthusiasm in the bar was infectious, and Dominic offered to get the second round in.

'No time for another drink! We're going to be late,' shouted Ben above the deafening music. He had organised the day's event. 'It starts at two.' He led the way out of the bar into the narrow rain-soaked street.

'Shit!' shrieked Andrea. 'My make-up's going to run! Quick!' She started to run down the street, splashing through the puddles in her black Doc Martens.

'It'll look even better with streaks in,' said Dominic. He opened up his cape. 'Anyway, come under here.'

'No thanks. I don't want to be bitten by your fangs,' Andrea replied, laughing, but Dominic didn't appear to see the joke.

'Suit yourself then!' he shouted aggressively, and hung at the back of the group, apparently in a sulk.

The group of friends were in Whitby for a few nights. Two of them would be arriving later due to work commitments. The group had booked an Airbnb in the town and had come prepared for a weekend of partying, dressing up and general fun. The next thrill was an adventure at an escape room, which, like everything else in the town at the moment, had a gothic theme. It was called Dracula's Lair.

As the lively group progressed down the street and across the harbour bridge to the older east side of the town, gusts of wind blew the rain at a steep angle over the yachts and boats in the harbour. On a day like this, one glance at the dark sky, the heaving grey sea and the stark ruins of the abbey above the town was enough to explain why Bram Stoker had used Whitby as the setting for Count Dracula's arrival in England in his famous novel. There had been a similar storm the day that Dracula arrived by boat, albeit one that had been intensified by the vampire's supernatural powers.

Looking at the sky, you could almost believe that Dracula was about to return, thought Louise as she paused on the bridge and caught sight of a vessel coming into the harbour. The thought gave her a little shudder. When the natural elements showed their power like this, they were awesome and rather frightening. You didn't quite know what to expect next.

'It's atmospheric, isn't it?' said Maggie, coming to stand next to her. 'Jack's missing all this. He'd have loved it.'

Jack was driving up from London and wasn't arriving in Whitby until the following day.

'He should have got himself organised and got here on time,' said Louise. 'You know what he's like. This has been arranged for so long and he still gets the dates confused and has to stay in London for a meeting.'

'I know,' laughed Maggie. 'He's good company when he's here, though. Come on; it's nearly two.'

Louise and her group had completed several escape rooms, usually solving the puzzles and achieving their escape before the time was up, though often with extra clues from the hidden controller. In the narrow streets of the east side of town, the venue took some locating. The entrance, when they found it, was, like many other escape rooms, through a poky little door down to a back yard and up three narrow stone steps. It seemed that finding the place itself was always part of the challenge.

Louise pressed the bell and a buzz indicated that the door had been opened. They pushed through to find a gloomy entrance lobby lit by candles. Everywhere was festooned with cobwebs; strange creaking and faint wailing noises formed a spooky soundtrack in the background.

'Hi,' said a young woman from behind a black desk. She was tall, powerfully built and dressed like the party of visitors in a gothic outfit with black lipstick and purple eyeshadow. Even outside the context of the game she would have cut a terrifying figure.

'Morton. Party of five,' said Ben.

'Okay. We're just re-setting everything after previous group. My name is Elaine.' She had an Eastern European accent. Was that part of the act? Dracula famously came from Transylvania in Romania. 'While you're waiting, how about photograph? If someone lends me their camera phone I'll take picture of you all framed by this.' She indicated a wall covered in lurid gothic artwork and the words 'No Escape!' in dripping blood red.

'Use mine,' said Louise. The group formed itself into a tableau of contorted positions and threatening expressions, refraining from laughter for just long enough for Elaine to take the photo.

'Jack's going to be devastated that he's not in the photo,' said Maggie.

'That's his fault; he should have been here, the idiot,' replied Ben, and he smiled at Louise, who laughed.

'Okay. I think everything will be ready now,' said Elaine as she handed the phone back to Louise. 'So, I just explain a few things. Have you all done escape room before?' They all had. 'Okay, so you know idea. You'll be locked in and you have to follow clues to work out how to access a key which opens the door at the end. I say "at the end" because this escape experience is a bit different. It has more than one room and you have to find the keys to get from one to the other. You have to move from one to the other in a certain time because . . .' She paused dramatically. '. . . Dracula is following you.'

There was a chorus of 'Oooo!' and laughter.

'Yes, for twenty minutes in the first room, you are safe. Dracula cannot enter until that time has gone, though you may hear him outside. Also, while you are in second room, he cannot open the door to reach you until another twenty minutes have gone by. If he catches you, sorry, but game is over, but you can discover things in each room that can delay him. You win if you can find key for the third room and get out before Dracula enters. There are emergency exits in rooms two and three if anything goes wrong and you need to get out quick. If anything happens in the first room just knock on this entrance door, which you can see is just by my desk. I am watching how you're doing on the monitor; each room has CCTV camera. If you need help I put some extra clues on the screen in each room. Are we all okay?'

They were, and excitement mounted as Elaine opened the door to the first room.

'As soon as I shut the door the timer starts. You have one hour to escape. Good luck!' She smiled and then left the room, closing and locking the door behind her.

The room was furnished like a study in a Victorian house. There were church-like windows with pointed arches, a fireplace with a heavy mantelpiece, a large, ornate writing desk and other items of heavy furniture. Gloomy portraits were hung on the dark walls and there was a decayed 'Miss Havisham' feel about the room. Thick cobwebs hung from the chandelier and around the paintings. The room was illuminated by medieval-style wall sconces, which held faux candles bearing electric lights. At one side of the room was an old chest and on the other a dusty bookshelf. The chest was locked with a combination padlock.

'Four numbers, Dracula's birth,' mused Louise as she read from a piece of paper lying on the chest.

'Wasn't he supposed to have been born hundreds of years ago and been undead for centuries?' asked Andrea.

Louise was looking around the room. Then she pulled a volume from the bookshelf. 'Yes, but it could be the date that *Dracula* was written. That's when he was created by Bram Stoker.' She looked for the publication date. '1897. Try that number on the combination lock on the chest.'

Ben quickly twisted the dials and the lock opened. 'Yes! Brilliant!' He flung the lid open and then jerked back. Inside was a wax model of a female corpse dressed in black lace. It was clearly meant to be a sleeping vampire with the long fangs visible and the eyes sinisterly half closed. The chest was actually a coffin.

'Bloody hell, that gave me a shock! There's a box by her head, look!' He put his hand rather gingerly into the chest and lifted out a wooden box for which they would clearly need to find a key. And so the clues, followed by discoveries, continued, and they were all thinking hard except Dominic and Andrea who kept disagreeing with each other and arguing.

'Shut up you two and concentrate; you're being a pain!' said Maggie. The twenty minutes was nearly up but they were still in the first room. They heard a voice outside.

'My friends, it is I, the count. I see you are struggling; please let me in so that I may help you and then we can . . . get to know each other.' They heard the door handle being tried. Like Elaine he spoke in an Eastern European accent. It was hammy, but curiously effective. A frisson of fear and excitement went through the group. It was like being a child when a grown-up pretends to be a monster, and says they're coming to get you in two minutes so hide!

'Quick! If he gets in we've lost,' cried Andrea.

'Okay, don't panic; we're on it!' said Dominic contemptuously.

'Oh, just fuck off!' shouted Andrea. 'I've just had enough of you today!'

Embarrassed, the others ignored them, and Louise solved the final puzzle in the first room, which got them the key to open the door into the second room.

'Lock the door behind us so that Dracula can't follow!' giggled Maggie. 'I feel like a kid again doing this.' The others laughed as Ben locked the door.

Dominic and Andrea were still arguing fiercely as they entered a room set out like a ruined chapel and graveyard. There was a broken altar and two gravestones lying on the floor. Bats hung from the ceiling. On the altar lay an open book.

'Right, where do we start in here?' asked Maggie.

'Let's start with that book. I'm sure that will contain a clue. Maybe—' She was interrupted by Andrea shouting.

'How dare you say that, you bastard!' she screamed.

'Who's going to stop me, you cow!' spat Dominic. They were now having a furious row and Andrea struck him across the face.

'Dom, Andrea, for God's sake that's enough!' shouted Ben, but Dominic wasn't listening. His face was contorted; he looked out of control with anger and hatred. To everyone's horror, he produced a knife and lunged at Andrea, who screamed again, with terror this time. She fell onto the gravestone.

'No! Oh my God!' cried Dominic. He looked around wildly at the others, his hand on his forehead as he gasped for breath. He ran out of the emergency exit, slamming the door behind him. It was over in seconds. The others, momentarily stunned, now screamed and shouted.

'Dom!'

'What the hell? He had a bloody knife. He's gone mad!'

Ben was next to Andrea when she fell. He knelt down to attend to her. There was already fake blood on her white dress but now there was more blood and it was coming out of her mouth.

'He's stabbed her! He's bloody stabbed her in the chest!' shouted Ben.

Horror-struck, Maggie and Louise looked at Andrea. Her eyes were closed and she was groaning. Her hand was clutched to her chest where the handle of a knife was visible.

'Oh my God, Andrea!' cried Maggie.

'Quick,' said Ben, 'get back to reception, tell them to call an ambulance. She's still alive, but quick!'

'I'll go,' said Louise, who still had the key. She opened the door back into the first room and dashed through. She met the actor dressed as Dracula who was waiting in there for the next twenty minutes to be up.

'What's going on?' he asked in a Yorkshire accent. Louise realised that the play-acting had stopped and the horror was now real. She explained what had happened and they hurried back to reception.

'I'll get the first aid kit,' said the actor.

Elaine was coming out of the toilet door as they arrived. She'd been away from the desk when the attack happened and had not seen it on the monitor. She immediately rang for an ambulance.

'Stay with us! Stay with us!' Back in the second room, Ben pleaded with the unconscious form of Andrea as he cradled her head. 'Do you have anything to staunch the blood?' he said to Maggie.

She ripped off a piece of her petticoat and gave it to Ben. At that moment they heard something through the emergency door. Ben looked up.

'Is that him? Go and see will you. I'll stay with her. I've done first aid. I'm checking on her breathing.'

Maggie tried to open the emergency exit. It seemed to be blocked by something and she had to push for some time before she got through. There was a heavy packing case behind the door. Dominic must have dragged it there to slow their pursuit. She found herself in another room, which was obviously used as storage. It was full of boxes and props and a big wardrobe. There was a coffin and a rail of costume items. Fixed into the wall vertically was a mummy's sarcophagus. It was dark, but across the room she could see another door marked 'Exit', which presumably led onto the street. The door was open but there was no sign of Dominic. She went through the door and out onto a narrow, dirty alleyway full of wheelie bins and rubbish. She looked up and down but it was deserted so she ran back to help Ben with Andrea. She found him still holding her but crying with his head bowed over. Her body was limp and her eyes closed. There was more blood on her chest. Louise, Elaine and the Dracula actor came into the room, the latter holding the bright-red first aid case.

'We've called the ambulance,' began Louise. 'They said—'

'It's too late,' sobbed Ben. 'I think she's gone. There's no pulse.' He looked up with a face of anguish and incomprehension. 'Did that just happen? He's killed her! What the hell is going on?'

～

The three remaining members of the group huddled together in the cramped reception area of the escape room. They had moved beyond words to a stunned silence. Louise was shivering with the shock and Elaine had given her a coat to put across her shoulders. She looked at her friends; their costumes now appeared forlorn and pathetic. The building was full of people in uniform, radios crackling, talking in ordinary voices. The artificially created sinister atmosphere of the rooms had been destroyed to be replaced by the brutal reality of actual horror.

Andrea's body had been removed by the ambulance people who confirmed that she was dead. SOCOs had taken photographs and blue-and-white incident tape ringed the spot where she'd been stabbed. Uniformed police were mounting guard here and at the entrance while detectives were beginning the investigation.

A young DC from the Whitby station came over and spoke to them kindly. 'I'm DC Hampton. I'm sorry about what's happened to your friend. We'll need you all to come to the station to make a statement, but can you just tell me the outline of what happened?'

The three friends looked at each other and Louise turned reluctantly to the officer. 'The five of us came to do this escape room puzzle. Dominic and Andrea were arguing and it seemed to get more heated. We hadn't been in the second room for very long when they started screaming at each other. Then Dominic lunged at her and stabbed her. He shouted something out like "Oh God!" and ran out of the emergency exit door. We all saw the knife in her chest and the blood on her dress. There was some blood already on her dress but that was fake; it was part of her costume.' She paused for a moment, briefly overwhelmed by the horror of it. 'I came back here to alert Elaine and she rang 999. Ben did his best to look after Andrea and Maggie followed Dominic out but he wasn't there. Then we just waited until people came. We knew she was dead.' Her voice broke a little. 'That's about it, isn't it?'

The others nodded.

'Have they been together for a while?' DC Hampton asked.

'Over a year now.'

'And has he been violent towards her before?'

The group glanced at each other.

'Not that any of us have seen, I think,' said Ben, still looking at the other two for confirmation. 'But they did argue a lot and it got very intense sometimes.'

'I see. But never physical?'

'No.'

'Did you all witness the attack?'

'Yes,' said Maggie. 'We were all in that room working on the clues. They started shouting at each other, and then he got the knife out and stabbed her. We all saw the knife in her chest; it was horrible.' She put her hands up to cover her face.

'And he went out of the emergency exit?'

'Yes,' continued Maggie. 'As Louise said, I followed him. There's a sort of storage room and another door onto the street, which was open. I had a look outside but there was no sign of him.'

'Okay, that's all for now. I don't see any reason to keep you here. My superior, Inspector Granger, will be investigating the case. She will no doubt want to interview you early tomorrow so you need to provide an address and you mustn't leave the town. We'll go to the station so you can make official statements. It shouldn't take long. I'm sorry to say that what happened seems to be fairly straightforward. I know it's a terrible shock.'

'Will you find him?' asked Maggie.

'We'll do our best. He's the clear murder suspect so we'll be pulling out all the stops to track him down.'

Louise recoiled at the phrase 'murder suspect'. It was appalling and unreal.

~

While Hampton was talking to the three remaining friends, Elaine Pesku, the supervisor, and Philip Owen, the Dracula actor, were talking in a little room behind reception. Owen seemed very jumpy. He was taking long drafts from an e-cigarette and the fragrant smoke was billowing out into the room.

'Crap! I can't believe this has happened! Everybody has fun here; we've had no trouble and then some nutter stabs his girlfriend in the middle of the game. Why did he do it here? What the hell are the police going to think?'

Elaine was sitting behind a small desk. She was calm.

'What's your problem?' she asked in her East European accent. This was genuine and not faked for the game. 'It's got nothing to do with us. It's not our fault.' She coughed. 'Can't you stop using that in here?'

Owen said nothing but put the e-cigarette into his pocket. 'I don't like the police being around.'

'Why?'

'Never you mind, I've got my reasons.' He sighed. 'I suppose we're going to have to shut for a bit now. I need the money from this job. I—'

At that moment Hampton came into the room. Owen frowned at the young DC.

'Okay,' said Hampton. 'I just need your account of what happened, please.'

Elaine looked at him suspiciously. 'Everything was going fine. I am watching on the monitor. I go to the toilet and when I get back there is screaming and shouting. I think someone has been taken ill or there is an accident. One of the group came running to the desk and said to call for an ambulance as someone is badly hurt, so I did and then I went through to see what had happened. But it was too late.'

'Did you have any idea that anything like this was going to happen? Were there any rows or threatening behaviour?'

'No, nothing.'

'And how about you, sir?'

Owen swallowed and looked as if it was a struggle to speak. 'I was doing my job, which is to follow them through the rooms and scare them a bit. Suddenly I heard the shouting and one of them, a woman, came running out of the second room, saying someone was hurt so I went straight to get the first aid kit, which is just by the entrance to the first room. That's standard procedure if there are any accidents.'

'Do those happen often?'

'Naw, there's nothing dangerous in there. Someone once fell and cut their leg and that's about it.'

'Okay. So, if you can come with the rest down to the station now and make full statements.'

Owen looked at Elaine and sighed but she only shrugged her shoulders.

~

When Louise, Maggie and Ben left the police station it was getting dark and still raining. They walked disconsolately up the hill out of the town to Pannett Park still dressed in their goth outfits, which now seemed outlandish and silly. The idea of goths and dressing up was now horrible. There were bloodstains on some of the garments but these were grotesquely real. Their Airbnb was in part of a grand Victorian terrace overlooking the park, which was now dark and wet with rain dripping off the trees.

Inside they flung themselves down on the sofas in exhaustion. While Louise was putting the kettle on, Maggie collapsed in tears again.

'I just can't believe it; it's a bad dream.'

Ben comforted her. 'I know.'

'Where the hell is he? Has he gone mad? Maybe he'll do himself in. Oh God! That'll be even worse!'

Louise returned with mugs of tea. 'Did either of you see him behaving strangely recently?'

'No, nor her. I mean, they argued, didn't they? But that wasn't unusual.'

'No.' Louise looked very thoughtful. They all lapsed into silence again for a long time until Ben suggested they order some pizza.

'Yeah, it's a good idea, but I can't eat much,' said Maggie. 'Shit! I should call Mark, but I can't do it now. I'll just break down on the phone.'

'Wait until tomorrow,' suggested Louise. 'We're all in shock now.'

The pizza arrived. They attempted to eat, without any enthusiasm. Nor could they settle to watch a film or anything on television. They remained sprawled on the sofas, stunned and quiet throughout the long evening.

Maggie went off to bed early, leaving Louise and Ben together. Ben had said the least of the three of them all evening. He was laid out on the sofa with his head facing the back.

'How are you?' asked Louise.

He turned over to face her. 'Just exhausted and shocked and, I don't know.'

'It was the worst for you, trying to save her life. I don't know how you did it.'

Ben shrugged. 'I just did things automatically. It's not long since I did some first aid training at work and it just kicked in. I wish it had been enough.' He turned away from her again and sobbed. Louise went over and put her hand on his shoulder.

'Ben, don't; you did your best.'

His muffled voice said, 'Maybe.'

'You did. I was proud of you.'

'Thanks.'

Louise sighed. 'I think maybe we should go to bed too. Do you want a drink or anything first?'

'No thanks.'

'Well, I'm off up. Don't stay up long and try not to go over it all in your mind.'

'Okay.'

Louise left him still inert on the sofa and trudged wearily up the stairs.

Later in the night she was tossing and turning in bed and unable to sleep. She wasn't surprised by this as the day's events had been so traumatic. She got up and looked out of her window. The sky was now clear and there was a full moon. Everything was a ghostly black-and-white and the street was empty. She put her hands up to her face, yawned and shook her head. Beneath the shock of what had occurred, something else was bothering her. The nice DC had said that it all seemed straightforward, and so it appeared, but she couldn't get the idea out of her head that something was not right. Something didn't ring true but she couldn't pinpoint what it was. Eventually she decided that there was only one thing to do. Early in the morning she would ring her dad.

One

This ae nighte, this ae nighte,
Every nighte and alle,
Fire, fleet and candle light,
And Christe receive thy saule.

From the Lyke Wake Dirge, *an ancient Yorkshire*
dialect song which evokes the bleak landscape of the
high North York Moors

Detective Chief Inspector Jim Oldroyd was walking to work at the HQ of the Harrogate Division of West Riding Police over the Harrogate Stray, which enclosed part of the town centre in a wide green loop. It was a bright morning and the colours around him were rich and vivid. He looked up. Against the blue sky, bright yellow and red leaves were clinging to the branches of trees or whirling down to the ground in the wind to lie in damp piles on the wet grass. He inhaled the cold air with gusto. It was very 'bracing', as they say in Yorkshire. This was characteristic of the air in Yorkshire generally but never more so than on an autumn morning like this. After pausing for a moment to take in the scene, he set off again, his shoes scrunching through the leaves on the path.

Suddenly he heard his phone ringing and the contented smile left his face. Damn! Could he not be left in peace for just a little while? Surely it wasn't work? Couldn't they wait another twenty minutes until he was at his desk? He took his phone out of his pocket and saw that the caller was his daughter, Louise. Calls from her were comparatively rare and unknown at this time in the morning.

'Hi, love, how are you?'

He knew immediately that something was badly wrong when he heard her voice: quavering and close to tears. 'Oh, Dad, something terrible's happened. I need you to come over.'

He stopped on the path. 'Where are you? What's going on?'

'I'm in Whitby and someone's been killed. And they've got it all wrong.' She started to cry.

'Hey, okay, calm down, love,' he said gently, 'and just tell me what's happened. How come you're in Whitby?'

Louise explained how she was there with her friends for the Goth Weekend. She gave a brief and rather garbled account of what had happened, which greatly alarmed him.

'That's absolutely terrible, love. Why didn't you ring last night?'

'I don't know. We were at the police station for a long time and then when we got back, we were all just so shocked and just not thinking clearly. Sorry.'

'No, don't be. It's an awful thing to have gone through. Look, I'll have to go into work and talk to Tom Walker. I'm sure he'll give me some time off. I'll be over as soon as I can, so text me your address. Okay? Just try to stay calm and wait for me. I'll be there in three to four hours' time.'

'I'll try.' Her voice sounded weak and forlorn with none of its normal confidence.

'Have you got anyone with you?'

'My friend Maggie. She's in the same state as me but we're looking after each other. And Ben too; he tried to save her life. It

18

was really bad for him. She died in his arms; he was holding her head.'

'Just try to stay calm and I'll be there soon, I promise.'

'Okay.'

Oldroyd pocketed his phone, picked up his pace and soon arrived at Police HQ. He went straight up to see DCS Walker. They'd known each other a long time and were on first-name terms. Walker was a mustachioed man in his sixties who didn't really like the bureaucracy of his senior position. He looked pleased to see Oldroyd.

'Mornin', Jim. What can I do for thi? Sit down.' Oldroyd sat at the other side of Walker's desk. 'You look worried. What's up, lad?' The two detectives liked to throw a bit of Yorkshire dialect into their conversations. It was one of the bonds between them.

'Something bad's happened, Tom, over in Whitby.'

'Oh, you don't mean that murder at one of those escape things, whatever they are? It was on the local news this morning. They showed some film of the town; it's full of those crackpots dressed up as bloody vampires and stuff.' He shook his head.

'Yes, I do mean that, but the thing is, Tom, my daughter Louise was there; she saw it all happen. It was one of her friends who was killed. She's very upset.' He put a trembling hand up to his face and only then realised how agitated he was.

'Good God!' exclaimed Walker, looking genuinely shocked and concerned. 'That's bloody awful. You must be worried sick.'

'I am, Tom, and I want to ask you a big favour.'

'You don't need to, lad. I know what you want. Get yourself over there now. I know how I'd feel if our Susan was involved in anything like that. And don't worry about being away from here. It's not that busy at the moment and we've plenty of people capable of covering for you.'

'Thanks, Tom, I really appreciate it.' He paused and took a deep breath. His heart was pounding and he felt weak. 'There is another thing. As you can see, I'm a bit shaky myself, and I'd like to take Stephanie Johnson with me. She can drive there and also I think she'll be useful with Louise, you know, a bit of woman to woman. I know it's asking a lot.'

'Not at all. You're absolutely right. You shouldn't go by yourself.'

'Thanks.' Oldroyd suddenly had to fight back tears. Whether it was because of Tom Walker's understanding and generosity or his concern for Louise, he didn't know.

'Come on, then,' said Walker kindly. 'Just take a bit of time and then get over there. I'm sure everything will be fine.' He paused. 'She's . . . She's not a suspect surely?' he said awkwardly.

'No, no, Tom, but as you probably heard on that bulletin, the killer's scarpered and he was one of her friends too, so she's deeply involved.'

'I see. Well, off you go.' Oldroyd got up from the chair. 'And, Jim' – Walker looked at him meaningfully – 'just remember: this force can never repay you for the wonderful work you've done over the years and the dedication you've shown. It owes you a few favours.'

Oldroyd nodded; he was beyond words. He left the office and had to fight back the tears again.

He went down to his office and saw the two young detective sergeants who normally worked with him sitting at computers in the main office. Andy Carter was a Londoner who had joined the West Riding Police from the Met. His partner Stephanie Johnson had joined the force from school and had worked with Oldroyd for many years. Andy looked up.

'Mornin', sir,' he said, then he saw his boss's strained face. 'Are you all right?' This prompted Steph to look round quickly.

'Can you both come in here?' said Oldroyd in a weak voice very unlike his normal one. He indicated his office. They both got up and followed him in, glancing at each other in alarm. They'd never seen Oldroyd this upset. He asked them to sit down, then explained what had happened.

'Bloody hell, sir, I'm sorry about that,' said Andy.

'Me too,' added Steph. 'How's Louise holding up?' Steph had met Louise briefly once or twice over the years.

'She's struggling as you can imagine and I need to get over there. Now let me explain what's going to happen. I've been to see DCS Walker and he's given me permission, very generously, to go over there and be with Louise. He's also allowing you, Steph, to come with me. I need some support and I think you'll be good for her too. We'll need to call home first to pack a few things; we may be there a few days.'

'Of course, sir. I'd love to help.'

'So, Andy, I want you to hold the fort here. I don't know exactly how long it will be, but report to DCS Walker directly and put yourself about, be useful. You know what I mean. That will be a big help.'

'Don't worry, sir; you can rely on me. Just get over there and be with your daughter.'

'Thank you,' said Oldroyd, and he had to turn away again. Their loyalty and concern moved him a great deal in his present emotional state. He composed himself and handed the keys of his old Saab to Steph. 'You drive. I'm afraid I might not be very good company.'

She smiled. 'Not to worry, sir. You just try to relax on the journey. We'll soon get to your place and mine, then we'll be off. I know the way.'

❧

Back in Whitby in a new detached house on the edge of the town, Alice Granger had discarded her light blue linen trouser suit, thinking it had a more weekend vibe, in favour of a grey, so-called 'work suit' from Next and was ready to leave for work.

Granger was a detective inspector at the Whitby Police HQ and was about to start work on the strange and shocking case of the murder of a young woman at the Dracula's Lair escape room. She was a well-organised, energetic woman in her forties, and she needed to be. She'd moved from the West Riding police in Harrogate to Whitby for promotion some years before and she was one of the station's few women inspectors. Although she fought against it, this situation made her feel that she constantly had to prove herself in the male-dominated force. In addition to this, she had two teenage children and a husband whose job involved regular travel to London and abroad. She was frequently in the role of single parent, as she was today with her husband in Paris. Okay for some, she thought as she tried to rally her fifteen-year-old son Ian and seventeen-year-old daughter Lesley and get them off to school.

Ian was eating a bowl of cereal at the kitchen table. He was usually reasonably well behaved. Lesley was the problem. She was surly, unkempt and kept company with a group of rather wild and unruly characters, some in her school sixth form and some, her mother suspected, of indeterminate age and from dubious parts of town. She was constantly being called into school over some disciplinary matter and Granger was afraid that Lesley might be expelled at the end of the lower sixth.

Granger was about to call her again when she slouched into the room yawning and dressed in a parody of the dress code they were supposed to follow. She'd often been sent home for infringements in her appearance. She was wearing a school skirt, but very short, with stockings full of holes; a white blouse beneath a leather jacket and a school tie wrapped contemptuously round her neck. Granger thought about advising her to change but decided she hadn't time.

'Look at you,' said Ian. 'I wish we could wear stuff like that.'

'Wait your turn,' replied Lesley. 'Little year tens have to do as they're told.'

'Don't forget to take your rings out,' said her mother. Lesley and her friends were heavily into body piercings and tattoos, but the school insisted that rings be removed on the premises. Lesley ignored her.

'It's Goth Weekend starting tomorrow; we're going down to the old town in the evening and again on Saturday.'

'Who's "we"?' asked Granger, annoyed by Lesley's blunt announcement. She never asked permission to do anything until it was all arranged and fait accompli. Even then it was usually a statement rather than a request. She was still underage to be wandering about the town at night and no doubt going into pubs. Granger doubted that pubs performed the normal ID checks in the busy chaos of Goth Weekend. She shared the police-parent nightmare of their offspring being arrested and the news being splashed across the papers.

'Amelia, Mandy, Robin and some more; we're all meeting up in our goth stuff. I hope it's as good as last year.'

Granger winced at the memory of picking Lesley up by the harbour at nearly midnight and whisking her and one of her friends away from drunken men dressed as Dracula. That had led to her daughter being grounded for a good two months. But she was a year older now, and she might be more sensible.

Granger frowned at this thought; who was she kidding?

'Well, I hope it doesn't end up like last year, but we'll talk about it later, I have to go now,' she said. Lesley was putting bread into the toaster. 'You're going to be late, aren't you?'

'I don't have anything till English at eleven.'

'Yes, but I thought the rule was you had to be there for registration at nine and then do private study?' She shook her head. 'Oh, I don't have time for this; see you both tonight.' She grabbed her bag and headed for the door.

'Bye, Mum,' called Ian.

'Bye,' grunted Lesley.

~

The Airbnb was eerily quiet. After she'd spoken to her father, Louise sat thinking for a while on the sofa in the large sitting room. It was still early and no one else was up. They were all shattered by the events of the previous day. She ought to speak to her mum soon before she learned snippets of information from the media and started to worry. Julia lived alone in Leeds. She and Oldroyd had been separated since Louise was a young teenager. Wearily she phoned her and explained what had happened. Julia had heard nothing and so was both shocked and reassured by what Louise had to say. She was just on her way to work at the college where she was a lecturer, so they planned to speak again in the evening.

Louise ended the call with a sigh. Everything seemed to be an enormous effort. She shuffled into the kitchen to make coffee and peeped into the bedroom she was sharing with Maggie to find her still asleep. There were two more bedrooms on the floor above: Ben was in one which he'd planned to share with Jack when the latter arrived; the other, now empty, had been Dominic and Andrea's room. Louise couldn't bring herself to climb the stairs and see how Ben was, in part because she didn't want to go near the vacant room. She suddenly realised that she was cold and turned the heating on. The gentle thrum of the boiler and the water going through the pipes was somehow reassuring.

She turned on the television with the volume down low and switched to the news. She was pleased that, when the item came up, there were still few details being presented and that the story only seemed to be on the local news. She knew that the profile of the case would become more prominent when the police investigation really got under way. She and the others would have to brace themselves for more intensive questioning and the media people would descend on the town. She hoped her dad could get over quickly because she was worried about how that investigation would go. She badly needed to talk to him about it.

Her phone pinged. She was pleased to get a message from him saying he was on his way. He was also bringing Steph, that nice detective sergeant she'd met a few times before. That was good.

Then the phone pinged again. She looked at the name that came up and her stomach lurched. It was a text from Dominic.

~

Oldroyd said little on the journey from Harrogate over to Whitby. For once his attention wasn't on the attractions and curiosities of the Yorkshire landscape. He texted Louise to ask if she'd contacted her mother and received an affirmative answer. He then rang his partner Deborah, a clinical psychologist, to briefly explain what had happened and that he might be away for a few days. She was her usual understanding self and said she would call him in the evening.

It was only when they'd passed the natural amphitheatre of the Hole of Horcum and the RAF station on Fylingdales Moor that he started to notice his surroundings. He pointed to the strange pyramid of the current radar system.

'Do you remember the golf ball radomes that used to be there?' he said to Steph.

'Yes, sir. I remember passing them whenever we came to Whitby for the day on the coach when I was a small kid. We used to be glad to see them because it meant we weren't that far away and we'd soon be on the beach. If it wasn't chucking it down, that is.' She laughed. 'Happy days. My mum didn't have much money after my dad left us, but she always made sure we enjoyed ourselves.'

'You always do your best for your kids whatever the circumstances.' He was starting to think gloomy thoughts again, but he caught a glimpse of the sea, which raised his spirits a little. He too remembered coming to Whitby when Louise and her brother Robert were small, to play on the beach and eat fish and chips. How odd to be coming back to the town now in these circumstances. But his daughter needed him, and he was glad to be there for her.

At the Airbnb, they were greeted by a clearly relieved but subdued Louise. She gave Oldroyd a big hug, saying, 'Oh, Dad!' but nothing more.

Oldroyd was shocked by how pale and drawn her face was. Her eyes were red; she had clearly been crying. She turned to Steph and hugged her too and then led them into the sitting room, which was still empty. Louise had heard noises from the bedrooms but neither Maggie nor Ben had appeared, even though it was nearly midday. Steph sat on the sofa next to Louise and Oldroyd sat in an armchair opposite. Louise looked bewildered, as if she didn't know what to say. She held up her phone.

'I've had a text from him. I still can't believe he did it.'

'From who?'

'From Dominic. He says he's sorry, but I know him. He . . .' She burst into tears.

'Okay, love. Take it steady. Go back to the beginning and tell us what happened.'

Between sobs, Louise went yet again through the events of the previous afternoon. She calmed down as she talked.

'So you saw him stab her?' asked her father at the end of her account.

'I saw the knife in his hand as he lunged at her. And then she screamed and the blade was sticking out of her chest. There was blood.' She shut her eyes.

'And there was absolutely no doubt that it was him?'

'No, we were together the whole time. Nobody could have been pretending to be him or anything. I've thought of that. And if it wasn't him where did Dominic go? It was definitely him when we went into that place.'

'Right.' Oldroyd sighed and glanced at Steph. 'In that case it's hard to see round the facts, love.'

'I know, but trust me, Dad, I've been over it a thousand times. It's driving me mad but something's not right. For a start, I just can't believe that Dominic would kill anyone, let alone Andrea. He's not like that. He did care about her.'

'What do you think the average murderer is like? Most are ordinary people whose feelings get out of control: anger, jealousy and so on, and then they do something out of character. That seems to be what happened here. There was probably something going on that you didn't know about.'

'He wouldn't do it; I know it.'

'You say they argued quite a lot.'

'Yes, but they always made up. I told the detective. There was never any violence. No one ever thought anything like this would happen.'

Oldroyd frowned and shook his head. 'But he'd brought a knife with him, which seems to indicate that he'd planned what he was going to do.'

'No, Dad, no!' Louise was getting increasingly agitated and her voice was getting louder.

'And what about this text you've had? You say he's sorry for what he did. Let's have a look.'

Louise handed him her phone. Oldroyd read:

OMG what have I done? cant face u all, please forgive me.
Dom

'It sounds as if he's in a terrible state, but he does seem to be admitting responsibility,' said Oldroyd gently.

'But it's all so weird. Where is he? He runs away and then sends a text?'

'He must be in shock himself. If he's hiding somewhere the police will find him.'

Louise put her hands up to her face. 'And what then? I can't bear it, and I tell you there's something weird. I was awake all night thinking about it, but . . .' She burst into tears; Steph put her arm around her shoulder.

Oldroyd was used to his daughter being feisty and strong. He hadn't seen her so troubled and upset since she was a child. He wasn't sure what to say next.

Luckily Steph knew what to do. She spoke gently to Louise. 'It's been terrible to see your friend stabbed to death like that, and by another of your friends. You must still be in shock and maybe not seeing things clearly. It's such a big thing to come to terms with that it would be natural to feel you want to deny it. It doesn't feel real; in fact, it's all weird as you keep saying.'

Louise wiped her eyes with a tissue and sighed. 'Yes, I hear what you're saying; you think it's all in my mind and I'm in shock.' She shook her head. 'And I know it looks like one of those open-and-shut cases, but it's not! I'm sure of it. I'm not saying this because I'm feeling emotional or because I'm in denial.' She looked at Oldroyd with confidence and determination.

She didn't look like someone whose thinking had been overcome by hysteria. Oldroyd thought about how often he'd listened to his instincts about a case when the facts apparently pointed to a certain conclusion, but he felt there was something wrong. It was a piece of advice he was constantly passing on to Steph and Andy. Had his daughter somehow inherited the faculty? A sort of sixth sense? That was a little fanciful for a rational thinker like him, but he found it hard to ignore her. He shook his head again but smiled this time.

'What do you want us to do?'

'Can't you help the police here?'

'Hmm, you know that's not straightforward. Whitby's not even in the West Riding police area; I've got no right to interfere. And then my own daughter's involved in the case. The whole thing's a minefield for me.'

'But, Dad, you'll find a way; you always do. And you know you're bloody brilliant at solving these puzzling cases.'

Steph laughed.

'Whoa, wait a minute! I think Steph is right; the problem is more likely to do with you and the state you're in. But if it makes you feel better I'll make a few enquiries and see what I can do. I know the inspector you mentioned: Alice Granger, she started out with us and became a detective sergeant before she got the job over here. She's very good and I don't think she'll mind me being around.'

'And can Steph stay to help you? I'd like that.'

It was like a request from a child; very needy and again most unlike her. He realised how shaky she was and in need of emotional support.

'That's asking a lot. I'd have to clear that with DCS Walker and I'm not sure he'll like the idea of two of his officers away working for another force.'

Louise didn't say anything and he noticed she was holding Steph's hand while the detective's other arm was still around her shoulder. How could he say no?

'I'll see what I can do.'

❧

Inspector Granger arrived at the escape room to view the murder scene. She'd received brief reports from DC Hampton, who was with her now, that suggested that the case was uncomplicated, but she was intrigued by the unusual setting. She'd heard about escape rooms from her teenage daughter but had never been in one. They stood in the mock graveyard where the crime had taken place.

'It's a ghoulish setting for a murder, isn't it?' she said, looking round the gothic decor and then at the still-taped-off area where Andrea had been stabbed. 'So the victim was attacked and fell here?'

'Yes, ma'am.'

'And the assailant ran out through there?' She pointed to the emergency escape.

'That's what all the witnesses agreed, ma'am.'

'Right, let's have a look. You didn't find anything?' she asked as they walked through.

'No, ma'am, we had a careful look through all this stuff.' Hampton indicated all the cases and boxes in the storage room. 'We looked in there too.' He pointed at the sarcophagus. 'The lid opens but it was empty inside. We went out into the street, but there was no sign of anything or anybody.'

'Hmm.' Granger went over to the strange construction and opened it. It was a good place in which to fit a body, but it was most emphatically empty. She wondered why it was fixed upright onto the wall. It looked like the kind of sarcophagus that a mummy might walk out of in some corny Hammer Horror film.

'That puzzled me, too, ma'am. I asked the woman who was on duty that day.' Hampton looked at his notes. 'Ms Elaine Pesku, Romanian. She said the owner, a Mr Hugh Preston, is intending to expand things by adding this room to the game. He's storing the stuff in here until he's got everything. He must have picked it all up from various places.'

'Where is he?'

'In Sheffield apparently. He owns a number of these escape rooms in different cities in the north. We've tried to contact him but not managed it yet.'

'Keep at it, and contact Sheffield police to see if they have any leads. Mr Preston might have some useful information.' Granger looked around both rooms again and frowned. 'Well, I agree with you that it looks pretty clear-cut. Have we had a forensic report yet?'

'Yes, ma'am. The victim died of stab wounds as we expected. Also, there is a CCTV video of the murder, which we are acquiring.'

'Good. Hopefully that will confirm what the witnesses are saying. We've got officers out doing a search and messages out to the public to report anything suspicious. So we need to interview all the witnesses more thoroughly but apart from that I think—' At that moment her phone went off. She answered it and heard a once-familiar voice.

'Now then, Alice, how are you?'

Granger's face lit up. 'Chief Inspector Oldroyd?'

'That's right. I got your number from HQ. I'd like to come and talk to you about this escape room murder, if that's okay with you and your superiors.'

'I'd be delighted, sir, but why and what on earth are you doing here?'

'Ah, that's a bit of a story, Alice. I'll tell you all about it when I see you. I'll come down to your HQ in half an hour or so, okay?'

'Yes, sir, I'll see you there. I'm on my way back anyway.'

Granger ended the call and smiled to herself. DCI Oldroyd was her mentor; the man who'd taught her most of what she knew. It would be great to work with him again. Not least because when he was around, things often turned out to be unexpectedly interesting.

~

'I couldn't call you before now. I was absolutely knackered last night when we got back. I went straight to bed. I hardly slept until about three this morning; I've only just woke up.'

Maggie was in bed, speaking to her boyfriend, Mark, on her phone. Her head was laid back on the pillow.

'Yeah, I know . . . I'm sorry you had to see it on the news first, the media don't waste any time . . . It was bloody awful, Mark . . . Yeah, I'm all over the bloody place . . . It would be great if you could come up . . . Oh my God!' She burst into tears as she remembered the horror of what had happened. 'No, it's fine; we're helping each other . . . We'll be interviewed again no doubt . . . Yes . . . Can't wait . . . Love you.'

She put the phone on the bedside table and pulled the duvet back over her. She ought to get up, but she didn't feel as if she had the energy. She'd heard voices in the living room; Louise was up and had been talking to someone. She looked at her phone. Shit, it was twelve o'clock! The detectives might come round; she'd better get dressed. She didn't want to get on the wrong side of the police. She got out of bed and suddenly realised she was desperate for some coffee. She pulled on her dressing gown and went downstairs to the kitchen.

'Maggie? Come in here, will you?' It was Louise's voice. Maggie went into the living room where she was surprised to see two strangers. Louise introduced her to her dad and his colleague Steph. 'I asked him to come over to help us, because I'm worried about it all. I hope you don't mind.'

Maggie was a little taken aback. She knew Louise's father was a detective, but she hadn't expected him to appear like this. She would have liked to have been consulted before more police were brought in, even if they were there to give support.

'No,' she said, sounding uncertain and looking at the detectives with suspicion. Oldroyd responded.

'We realise it's a bit of an imposition, Maggie, but I'm sure you can understand that I felt I had to come over as Louise is involved in these awful events. We won't interfere with anything. We're just here to give you any help or advice you might need.' He wanted to ask her about what had happened and what she thought about it all but decided this was the wrong time.

'Okay, well, thanks. I'm making coffee if anyone wants some.' Oldroyd and Steph declined.

'We need to go,' said Oldroyd, and he and Steph got up. 'I called the detective in charge of the case. We're going to meet her at police HQ. Now, I think she'll probably be getting you all in to the station for an interview this afternoon so we'll come back later on. It would be inappropriate for us to be there when you're interviewed. Just be absolutely straight with her and tell the truth, okay?'

'Okay,' said Louise, looking anxious at their departure.

Maggie simply nodded.

~

'Seen anything of Ben?' asked Louise when Oldroyd and Steph had gone. 'Oh, talk of the devil.' At that moment Ben came down the stairs dressed in jeans and t-shirt with his hair dishevelled.

'Hi. God I've got a terrible headache. Any coffee going?'

'I've just made some,' replied Maggie. 'You've just missed Louise's dad and his sergeant.'

'What?' Ben was very surprised and suspicious like Maggie.

'I asked him to come over,' said Louise. 'I thought it would be good to have him around, if things get difficult.'

'Fine,' said Ben. 'But do you honestly think they will? I mean, come on. We didn't talk about this last night, and it's bloody awful, but he stabbed her. I hate it and I can scarcely believe it, but he stabbed her. We all saw him. I've been thinking, maybe he has lost his balance as you said. Looking back, I think he's been behaving oddly for a while.'

'Has he?'

'You must have noticed. He's been moody, quiet and he's started rows with Andrea. He hasn't been himself.'

'I don't know. Where do you think he's gone?' asked Maggie.

'Oh, I forgot; I got a text from him,' said Louise.

'What?'

She showed them the text. Maggie put her hand over her mouth.

'Oh my God! That's terrible. I can't bear it. He must be in a horrific state; where the hell is he?' She collapsed in tears again.

Ben took the phone and read the text again. 'He has to be out of his mind. He must be hiding somewhere; the police will find him, won't they? And then what?' he said, echoing Louise. He put the phone down and shook his head. 'I don't know what to say.'

'Maybe we should try to find him before the police do,' said Louise.

'What?' replied Ben. 'But how?'

'I'm not sure yet, but I'm not convinced that the whole thing is as simple as you say. He might be able to explain things.'

'What things? You mean why he stabbed her? Okay, maybe he can, but the fact is he still did it,' continued Ben.

'Oh, please shut up!' shouted Maggie. 'I can't cope with any more of it.' She covered her face with her hands and slumped sideways onto the arm of the sofa. The doorbell rang and Maggie sprang up again. 'Oh God, that's the police! I'm not even dressed.'

Then they heard a voice calling: 'It's me. Jack.'

'Oh, that's a relief.' Maggie relaxed again and Louise let the newcomer in. Jack was dark-haired and tall, wearing jeans and a coat. The others got up and greeted him and Louise brought him coffee. He sat down, holding the cup as if he didn't know what to do with it.

'I don't know what to say. I set off at six this morning. Then I got your text.' He nodded at Maggie. 'It's just awful. I can't imagine what you've all been through. I feel bloody awful about not being here. Tell me exactly what happened. Maybe I could have done something.'

'You couldn't have,' replied Ben. 'It happened so quickly. Needless to say we weren't expecting it. They had a furious row in the escape room, and Dominic stabbed her. Then he ran out of the building through an emergency exit.'

'Bloody hell,' said Jack, shaking his head. He put his undrunk coffee down on the coffee table.

'I know it sounds unbelievable but that's what we saw happen.'

'So you say they were having a row . . . ?' Jack seemed lost for words.

'They were arguing, but you know what they were like,' said Maggie. 'It was no worse than we've seen before.'

'Right. And has he just disappeared?'

'No, he's around somewhere,' said Louise, and she showed him the text she'd received earlier.

Jack stared at it. 'It's a bloody nightmare, isn't it? It's the kind of thing you watch on telly but you never imagine happening to you.'

There was silence. No one could disagree.

'So what are we going to do?' asked Jack.

'We're waiting for the police to arrive,' replied Maggie. 'I thought you were them. They'll want to interview us. What we do after that I've no idea.' She sounded desperate.

~

Oldroyd, Granger and Steph watched the smudgy black-and-white images of the CCTV record of the murder. As the five people in the pictures were all dressed in goth costumes, the whole thing looked like some amateur horror film shot amongst the tacky gravestones and broken altar. Nevertheless, it was very chilling because of the terrible events at the end of the sequence. Several times they watched Louise and the others come into the second room and start to look for clues. Then the camera was partially obscured as the commotion took over. The figure of Dominic ran out of view and Andrea fell to the floor at the bottom of the picture. Maggie could be seen with her hands over her mouth, while Ben was crouched over Andrea with his back to the camera. Maggie then disappeared, presumably into the next room, pursuing Dominic. Louise and the actor came into the room and Maggie returned. It all seemed to happen as described by the witnesses.

'Hmm,' mumbled Oldroyd, frowning. 'It seems to confirm what they all said.'

'It does, sir,' agreed Granger, thrilled to be working with Oldroyd again.

'It's weird watching it on the screen,' observed Steph. 'It makes it all seem like a black-and-white horror movie.'

'That's what I thought, and in those costumes they look like actors.' Oldroyd sighed and frowned. The annoying thing was that despite what he'd just said, he was starting to feel, like Louise, that something wasn't right. But was that just a feeling in sympathy with her? Could he trust it? It was hard to be objective when someone so close to you was involved. Maybe it was sensible to go with what the other two thought.

'Is it our conclusion that the film confirms the witness accounts?' asked Granger.

Oldroyd and Steph agreed; Oldroyd with great reluctance. 'Is there any news of the fugitive's whereabouts?' he asked, wondering straight away what was stopping him from saying 'killer'.

'None yet, sir, but we've got several officers on the search and I'm expecting results soon. He sounds desperate judging from the text he sent to your daughter and he can't have got far. He may be hiding in a boat or someone's garage. It's often the public who discover these people in the end. He must be still in a goth costume unless he had clothes hidden somewhere, but of course he won't stand out in the town at the moment dressed like that.'

'There's always the danger that he'll do himself in,' added Steph.

'Yes. I didn't want to say that to Louise, but it's a distinct possibility. How are you handling the press by the way? Have you . . . ?' Oldroyd stopped himself and shook his head. 'Look, I'm sorry. I don't mean to take over your investigation. You'd be quite in order to tell me to shut up.'

Granger laughed. 'Don't worry, sir, it's great to be working with you again. I've checked with DCI Garner and he's fine about you both being involved. Why wouldn't he be, getting such wonderful assistance free of charge? As long as you're not involved too directly because of your daughter, you know. I want to clear the air with you about this at the beginning. We have no reason to suspect her of any involvement in anything criminal in relation to what's happened. If at any stage that changes, I would of course ask you to stand down from the case.'

'Absolutely understood,' replied Oldroyd. He saw that Granger was heaving a quiet sigh of relief. It clearly hadn't been easy to say that to her old boss, but he respected her for having done so. 'And you were right to say it,' he added and then turned to Steph. 'This,' he said, indicating Granger, 'is the type of detective that you and Andy can become. I'm training you two in the same way.' This was said in Oldroyd's genially bumptious manner and both women laughed.

'You're embarrassing me, sir,' said Granger.

'Not at all. I'm proud of all of you and I know DCS Walker is too. By the way, he's been very generous and understanding, but I don't know for how long he can spare us.'

'I remember DCS Walker; he was a good person to work for. You always felt he understood the job.'

'That's because he did it for more years than any of us have,' replied Oldroyd. 'People like him make the best managers.'

'To answer your question, sir,' continued Granger. 'I'm speaking to the press later. I'll obviously stress that we're looking for the suspect, and any information, etc.'

'Good. I take it you'll want to interview my daughter and the others.'

'Yes. I think it will be better here at the station. I understand they live nearby so I'll send a car to bring them down.'

'Fine. I'll text Louise telling her to expect you and then Steph and I will get out of your way. Is it okay if I go to look at the crime scene?'

'Yes, sir. I'll tell the officers there that you're on your way.'

～

Louise, Ben and Maggie were sitting in the back of a police car with two uniformed officers in the front. It felt a bit cramped but it was a short journey.

'I'd never been into a police station before this happened,' confessed Maggie. 'It makes me nervous.'

'Don't worry,' replied Louise. 'Dad said that the inspector in charge of the case is nice. She's a woman: Inspector Granger.'

'What is she going to ask and what shall we say?' asked Maggie.

'Just the truth,' said Ben, who appeared very relaxed. 'We've already told everything we know to that other detective, so this will just be to confirm it.'

'Oh, it sounds very formal,' said Maggie, looking anxious. 'Things like that freak me out.'

'Don't worry about being questioned. It's not about being intimidating anymore. They don't shine bright lights in your face and shout at you. They want to put you at your ease,' said Louise.

'Then you get too comfortable and let things drop,' said Ben, before correcting himself when he saw the look of alarm on Maggie's face. 'No, I'm only joking, I'm sure it will be fine. What happened was pretty straightforward, wasn't it?'

'Yeah, I suppose so.' Ben made the whole thing seem very simple, but Louise remained unconvinced. Simplicity was the problem: it just seemed too easy.

'They'll want to know about their relationship as well, won't they?' asked Maggie. 'They'll be trying to establish Dom's motive. We'll have to tell them that they argued, but even though they did, I'm not going to make it sound worse than it was. I still never thought it would come to this, did you?'

'Of course not,' replied Louise as they reached the station. As they got out of the car and walked in she felt that she was being swept along into the official investigation, which was quickly going to conclude that Dominic murdered Andrea: period. She hoped her dad would come to see things from her point of view and that he would be able to do something to change it.

When they left the police station, Oldroyd and Steph headed down to the harbour and across the same bridge, towards the older eastern part of the town, that the group of friends had crossed in such high spirits the day before. Today the sky was clearer although a fresh wind was blowing in from the sea sending seagulls wheeling and calling over the water. Oldroyd paused on the bridge, as Louise and Maggie had done, and took a deep breath as the wind ruffled his hair.

'It's lovely to be at the sea again and breathe in that air. I don't get over here often enough.'

'Me neither, sir. It brings back a lot of memories. You appreciate it more when you're older though don't you? It's not all about being on the Sands, building castles and going in the sea anymore.' They laughed.

'You're right. You're not interested in views when you're a kid. Come on, though, we can't behave like day trippers; we'd better take a look at this escape room.' They set off into the east side of the town. 'Do you know anything about those things?'

'Escape rooms? Oh yes, sir, they're great fun; Andy and I have done a few in Leeds with our friends: The Underground Bunker, The Psychopath's Trap, The Mummy's Tomb. They're always on a theme. We prefer the scary ones; they give you an extra thrill. It sounds like Louise and her friends were the same.'

'I see. Obviously not enough excitement in the job. I'm sorry we're boring you.'

Steph laughed. 'It's not boring when we're out on a case like this, sir, but unfortunately we have to spend a lot of our time at our desks on the computer writing stuff up and it can get tedious.'

'Yes, tell me about it. It's the same for everybody these days. Anyway, how do they work?'

'You're locked into the room and you have clues which you have to solve in order to find the key, which will get you out. Stuff is hidden in the room and you have to find it; there's often more than one room. You normally have about an hour. It's a great challenge pitting all your wits against the clock and seeing if you can get out before the time is up. Usually, if you're running out of time, the controller will put extra clues up on a screen.'

'Right. Well, here we are. See what you make of this one.'

They'd made it to the dingy entrance. They showed their identity to the constable on guard and were let in. There was no Elaine at the reception desk. They walked into the first room and looked around.

'I must say, it's all a bit tacky,' remarked Oldroyd as he surveyed the cobwebs, the chandeliers and the coffin.

'All part of the atmosphere, sir. The whole of the Goth festival is like that; it's all deliberately over the top; that's the point. And I suppose Whitby wants to make the most of its Dracula connection throughout the year.'

'Yes. Well, let's see where it all happened.'

They progressed into the second room to find another constable by the cordoned-off section of the floor where Andrea had died.

Oldroyd examined everything. 'I presume, after the attack, the suspect went through that door?'

'That's right, sir,' said the constable. 'There's another door into the street from there.'

Oldroyd and Steph wandered through. 'Seen anything so far?' he asked.

'No, sir.'

'Me neither.'

The clutter of the spare room was all there. 'Granger said that the owner is going to convert this into another part of the game. It looks about as tatty as the rest of the place.' Like Hampton and

Granger before him, he opened the coffin and the wardrobe and inspected the interiors carefully.

Then his attention was caught by the sarcophagus. 'I didn't know there were mummies in the Dracula story. They're getting their horror fiction mixed up.' He opened it and then stood back and peered at it with his head on one side. 'Why has it been built into the wall like that? It's odd.' Suddenly his face changed and took on an alert expression. 'Hang on a minute, I know what's going on here. Let's see if I can find it.' He felt around the edge, and there was a click. Oldroyd pushed at one side of the sarcophagus and it spun round to reveal another, identical to the first which came to rest in the same position.

'Wow, sir, well done. What's all that about?'

'The owner, whoever he is, has acquired this from an illusionist. It's a simple trick, a bit clunky. Someone from the audience checks there's no escape from this casket; then the illusionist's assistant gets in and the door is shut. They draw the curtain across and while it's all covered up, they spin the whole thing round, the empty casket comes to the front and when they open it the person seems to have disappeared. Of course it's easy to reverse the procedure and bring them back again. He must have created a stud wall here and incorporated this into it; there will be a cavity behind here. This will be the centrepiece of his new room.'

'I imagine that someone will hide in there dressed as Dracula or something and scare the players or there may be a clue in the fact that there are actually two caskets,' added Steph.

'Yes. But it's making me think; let's have a look inside the one that was concealed.' Oldroyd looked closely at the curved surface and then called Steph over.

'I think that small stain there might be blood.'

Steph had a look at the red mark. 'It's not much, sir. What are you suggesting?'

'I'm not sure, but it makes me uneasy. Let's have a look at the outside door.' The door was locked but the constable opened it. Oldroyd strolled into the alleyway as Maggie had done. So this was where Dominic Holgate had supposedly run out. Or had he been hiding in that sarcophagus? He went back inside. 'Do you know what?' he said to Steph. 'I think I'm starting to agree with my daughter: there *is* something fishy about it all. I think we're going to be here in Whitby for a while yet.'

~

Jack met the other three in a pub in the late afternoon after their interviews at the police station. The cramped old bar was on the west side of the town up a street that rose steeply from the harbour. It contained a fair number of people in goth costumes as momentum continued to build for the coming weekend. On a long window ledge was a line of bottles streaked with candle wax and festooned with white cobwebs.

'How did it go?' he asked as he brought back a round from the bar.

'Fine,' replied Maggie. 'We all just told them what we'd seen, which was fairly straightforward. They talked to us separately; I don't know if they were looking for differences in our stories as if they think we had something to do with it.'

'They always do that.'

'They asked us more about their relationship,' continued Louise. 'I suppose they're looking for reasons why he would stab her.'

'They did get a bit mental with each other,' said Ben, drinking from his pint. 'All I can think of is that he just lost it with her.'

'How come he had a knife?' asked Jack.

'I don't know. Maybe he often carried one around.'

'What, like a boy scout or drug dealer in a tough area?' Maggie sounded very doubtful.

'Perhaps, or it could have been part of his costume.'

A sceptical silence greeted this suggestion.

'Anyway,' said Ben, speaking to Louise, 'what's your dad going to do while he's here?'

Louise looked around the group a little nervously. She had foreseen that Oldroyd's presence might be treated with a measure of surprise if not suspicion by the others. It was also time for her to declare her feeling that the case was more complicated than it appeared.

'He's going to help the police here. He's very experienced. I asked him to come over because I think there's more to what's happened than we think. I don't trust the local police to look into things deeply enough.'

'How do you mean?' asked Jack.

'I don't know. It's frustrating; I can't explain it, but don't we all think that it doesn't really add up? Would Dominic just stab Andrea and run off?'

Maggie sighed. 'I'm sure he didn't intend to kill her.'

'They cared for each other; I know they did. Even if they argued a bit,' insisted Louise. She took a drink from her glass of wine. Her hand was shaky.

'It was more than a bit, to be honest, and the thing is,' said Ben, 'we all know what we saw. There's no getting away from it. I wish we could.'

'That's what my dad and the detective sergeant said. They think I'm emotional about it because of the shock and I'm not seeing things clearly. They could be right, I know.'

'Oh, I don't know what to make of it all,' said Maggie with a big sigh. 'But I don't want to leave here until they find him.'

'Why?' asked Jack.

'I don't know. It doesn't feel right somehow. Mark should be here soon. I'll feel better then.'

'What about you?' Jack asked Ben.

'I'm going to stick around too. I want to see how Louise's dad gets on; see if there are any complications; I can't see any myself.'

'Right. Well, I suppose I'll stick around to keep you company. I was supposed to be here all this weekend anyway. I'm the only one who hasn't had a chance to dress up yet.' Jack drained his glass. 'Your round, Ben.'

Louise was looking at her phone. 'I've got a text from Dad. I'm going back to meet him at the Airbnb. He says he's found something.'

~

'So, I think it's time you told me about everyone involved in this, including the bloke who arrived today.'

'Jack?'

'Yes, everyone.'

'Why? Do you suspect someone of something?'

'Not at the moment, but if Steph and I are going to look into this we need to know everything. It's often some detail which you think is unimportant that turns out to be crucial.'

It was early evening and Oldroyd, Steph and Louise were back in the living room at the Airbnb. Oldroyd had brought some take-away vegetarian curries. Louise's friends had stayed in the pub and were going to eat out later. Oldroyd had told his daughter about the sarcophagus trick and that he now felt that there were things worth exploring. He sat and munched a samosa as he listened to Louise. Steph was eating a bowl of butternut squash curry with rice.

'Okay. I'll start with Dominic and Andrea. I knew Andrea – her surname's Barnes – at college in Leeds years ago, but I met her again in London when I was working in the refuge. She was going out with Jack Ryerson at that point but she left him for Dom who was a drama type like her. She'd done drama at one of the drama schools and she was working with a women's theatre group, which did plays about abused women and stuff like that. She was still working for them as far as I know. They came to perform at the refuge. Dom didn't do drama like her but he was interested in theatre and was in student productions and stuff at uni. He was working for some kind of media company. I think he still does that kind of work. It was always a bit of a fiery relationship, as we've told everybody, but I'm sure they cared about each other. I've known them as a couple for a while.'

'What did they argue about?'

'Oh, anything and everything. They were both very extravert confident types who liked their own way. They always made it up though. One of the worst rows they had was about Andrea's inheritance. She had an aunt who died and left her a lovely flat in Leeds. It's in one of those early Victorian stone buildings out in Far Headingley near the Cottage Road cinema. Andrea loved the place partly because she had so many fond memories of visiting her aunt. Anyway, she was keen to move up from London and live there but Dominic's a Londoner and he wouldn't consider it; didn't want to give up his job and come up north.'

'So what happened?'

'They couldn't agree. The aunt left the flat fully furnished. It's beautiful; I've seen it. I used to go with Andrea to see her aunt in the old days. It's just there empty most of the time at the moment. Andrea comes up for weekends sometimes to see her old Leeds friends. I think she was going to rent it out soon unless she could persuade Dom to change his mind. Meanwhile they live in Tower Hamlets somewhere.'

'And what about Ben?'

'Ben Morton; he's an artist and lecturer. He studied Fine Art in London somewhere. He's a friend of Dominic's; that's how he came into our group. He does a bit of teaching to supplement his artwork I think. He's a few years older than the rest of us.'

'How did Dominic get to know him?'

'I'm not sure. I think they may have shared a house together when they were students or at least when Dominic was.'

She stopped to eat a bit of her curry but didn't have much appetite.

'Go on,' said Oldroyd, filling himself a bowl of spinach and potato curry and breaking off a piece of naan bread.

'You've met Maggie Hinton before. She came up to Harrogate once and stayed with us. She was at Oxford with me and then we both went to work at the refuge. She's travelled in Thailand and Australia for a while. Now she's working in a coffee shop and still trying to work out her next move I think.'

'Not unlike a lot of people of your generation.'

'No. Last there's Jack Ryerson. As I said there's a bit of history there: him and Andrea were an item a while ago. But it all ended amicably and he stayed in our friendship group. I don't know where Andrea originally met him but he works for a publishing company in London.'

'I see. Why has he only got here today?'

'He said he had work to do or a meeting or something so he had to miss yesterday. I suppose I ought to mention Mark. He's Maggie's boyfriend and he's going to arrive soon; tomorrow, I think. He's not really part of our group but he comes along to do stuff with her occasionally. He works in personnel. They moved in together recently.'

'Does he have any connection with anybody else you've mentioned?'

'Not particularly. I think he was at college at the same time as Andrea and Dom but he didn't really know them.'

Oldroyd glanced at Steph, inviting her to ask a question.

'Could Jack have harboured any resentment against Andrea and her new partner? That's the only possible motive I can see in what you've told us,' she asked.

Louise put down her fork and took a sip of water. 'I never saw any sign of it. But anyway, how can Jack be a suspect when he wasn't even there when Andrea was stabbed?'

Oldroyd shrugged. 'I've no idea, but talking about that moment and what happened afterwards, when Dominic went out of that room, did you hear anything else? Did you hear him open the door in the other room to the outside? Maybe there was traffic noise or something.'

Louise furrowed her brow. 'It all happened so quickly and people were shouting and screaming and he was in the next room. I didn't hear anything.'

'Okay, not to worry. It was just a thought.'

Louise lay back on the sofa. 'God, I'm exhausted again. It's been another long stressful day.'

'Yes, well, Steph and I will be off soon. There are a couple of things I want you to do for me. First, can you ask Ben and Maggie about Jack and whether they saw any sign of hostility to Andrea and Dominic? They're not to mention anything to Jack. Okay?'

Louise looked uneasy. 'Okay.'

'And then I want you to ask them if they heard anything from that room where Dominic went after he stabbed Andrea. Okay?'

'Yes. I don't like this, though: asking questions and being secretive.'

'No, I understand, especially when they're your friends.' He smiled. 'But you asked for this, so you'll have to help.'

'All right.'

'Also, you must remember that everything we find out has to go back to Inspector Granger. You understand? She's in charge of the investigation and none of us can keep any relevant information or evidence from her. I would be in big trouble if that happened.'

'Yes.'

Oldroyd stood up. 'Right, love; we'll leave you in peace now. Give us a hug. How are you feeling now? You look better than when we arrived this morning.'

'I do feel better, thanks. I'm sure it's not just my imagination. Do you think you're on to anything?' she asked as she embraced him.

'It's too early to say and Steph will tell you that I don't like sharing theories until I have evidence to support them. Let's just say I have questions in my mind.'

Louise nodded. 'Good.'

~

Oldroyd had booked rooms for himself and Steph in a small hotel. As they walked back in the dark, they discussed the case.

'I presume you're thinking the sarcophagus has some significance, sir?'

'Yes, we'll get Granger to call her forensics people in to analyse that stain.'

'Do you think someone could have hidden in there?'

'Maybe, though I'm not sure who. Dominic may have had an accomplice or he may have gone in there himself, hid, and got out later. That's why I was asking if she actually heard him leave the building. He may have cut himself on the blade he used. That often happens with knife assaults.'

'But why would he hide in there instead of just going straight out of the emergency exit door?'

'I don't know. But if he did, that's clear evidence of premeditation. He had to know that the sarcophagus had two parts. Louise won't like the idea, but that together with the fact that he'd brought the knife points to the attack being planned.'

'Hmm,' murmured Steph. 'It's not a very good plan though, is it? Murder someone in a room full of other people and then bolt for it? It makes more sense if he just lost it and stabbed her in anger, but then you still have to explain why he had the knife.'

'You're absolutely right, and it's what makes me think we've got more to find out yet. At the moment it doesn't really make complete sense either way.'

'Where do you think he is?'

'I haven't a clue, but I would expect him to be found before too long. Anyway, here we are.' He stopped at the hotel entrance and they checked in.

'Tell Andy we're enjoying the seaside. We should send him an old-fashioned postcard saying "Wish You Were Here".'

Steph laughed. 'I don't think he'd particularly want to be here, sir; especially at this time of year. He likes the countryside and the villages a lot more since he joined us from London, but a little coastal town like this at the end of October is probably not for him.' They laughed and went their separate ways. Steph's room was on the ground floor.

As he ascended the stairs, Oldroyd felt tired. It had been a long day. It was still quite early but he decided to go to bed. Before he did, he spent a few minutes looking out from his window which had a view over the River Esk. It was a moonlit night with ragged clouds moving across the sky and stars above the dark mass of the abbey on the hill opposite. On a night like this it was easy to see why Bram Stoker had chosen the town as a setting for his gothic novel. And now the town was full of people dressed like characters from that style of fiction. Was there some clue in all this? Why did

Dominic attack his girlfriend in that Dracula-themed escape room? Steph was right; it was strange. As yet, he had no answers. But more and more questions were entering his mind.

～

Louise sat on the sofa trying to relax, waiting for the others to return. Her dad was a reassuring presence, but the events of the previous day were still raw. She would never forget Dominic lunging forward and Andrea's scream. She was sipping tea and beginning to doze off when suddenly there was a commotion outside and the door crashed open. Maggie came in looking highly agitated followed closely by the others.

'Louise, it's him again. Dominic! He's texted me this time. And look what he says!'

Louise grabbed the phone and read:

Meet you by the church near the abbey 11.30 tonight. I'll explain all. Dom

'He wants to meet you?! What the hell?!'

'I'm not going by myself,' said Maggie. 'I still think he's mad. He might attack me.'

Jack looked at the message. 'What does he mean, "explain all"? What is there to explain?'

'Why he did it? Maybe he was forced to somehow,' replied Louise.

'What does he expect us to do?' asked Ben. 'He must know that you'd tell us about the text. It sounds like a plea for help.'

'I don't know,' replied Louise, looking very thoughtful. 'But surely we have to respond. Whatever's going on, I'm sure he's in a very bad way.' She looked at her watch. 'Let's go, now. It's nearly time.'

'Hold on,' said Jack. 'Maggie's right. He could be dangerous. You all saw what he did. I'm taking this stick.' He picked up a heavy walking stick, which was by the coat stand in the hall.

'You're right,' said Ben. 'Well, I'm taking a knife.' He went to the kitchen and came back with a small but sharp knife.

'Oh no, not a knife again,' wailed Maggie. 'For God's sake be careful with it!'

'Look, it's just a precaution, okay? I don't think for a moment he'll be any danger to us, but we can't risk it after what happened.'

'Ben, you can't take that, it could just make things worse,' said Louise. 'It's illegal to carry a knife.'

'Is that what your dad would say?' asked Ben with an edge of contempt in his voice.

'Yes, but it's true,' insisted Louise.

'Okay,' replied Ben, raising his hands in a sign of defeat as he took the knife back to the kitchen.

'We should just make it over there by half eleven,' continued Louise as she put her coat on and the group left the house. She thought about telling her dad but decided against it. He would definitely tell her not to go, but this was important. If Dominic needed them, they couldn't let him down.

Two

There was a bright, full moon with heavy black driving clouds, which threw the whole scene into a fleeting diorama of light and shade as they sailed across.

From Mina Murray's Journal in Dracula

The streets around the harbour were still noisy as revellers, many in goth costumes, left the closing pubs. A figure wearing a mask, steampunk goggles and the sinister beak of a seventeenth-century plague doctor stumbled into Louise and then fell onto the pavement. It was pulled up onto its feet by two grinning skeletons in black costumes painted with white bones.

'Get up, you drunken sod!' laughed one of them.

As they progressed down Church Street, it became quieter and, when they reached the famous 199 steps up to St Mary's Church and the ruined abbey, there was no one ahead on the steep climb up the hill.

'Where is he going to be, do you think?' asked Maggie as she looked nervously up towards the abbey over which a purple searchlight raked the sky. This was another way in which the town created an atmosphere for the Goth Weekend.

'Who knows?' replied Jack, gripping his stick. 'No doubt he'll see us coming up from wherever he's hiding. There's a scene in *Dracula*, isn't there? Where he's seen with a victim near this church?'

'Stop it!' said Maggie. 'You're freaking me out even more.'

They reached the top of the steps and saw the dark mass of the church with its wide, squat tower ahead to their left. The churchyard was full of gravestones and monuments. It all felt very sinister in the darkness.

'Oh God! Where is he?' whispered Maggie. They all looked around keenly in every direction. There was no sign of anybody.

'Let's go round the church; stay together,' whispered Ben.

They explored the dark path by the church entrance and then moved slowly around towards the graveyard.

Suddenly Louise exclaimed in a loud stage whisper: 'Over there! Look! Someone's sitting on a gravestone; right in the corner.' The others looked over to where she was pointing. It was difficult to pick out in the gloom, but there was a figure dressed in black sitting with its back to them. It was very still.

'Shit! Is that him?' said Ben. He called out. 'Dom? Is that you? It's us. We're here.'

The figure stood up and turned towards them. It was too far off for them to make out any features, but the face was white and apparently made up like Dracula. As they watched, an arm came up slowly and waved at them, but then the figure turned and walked rapidly towards a gate out of the graveyard and quickly disappeared from view.

'Dom! Is that you? Wait!' shouted Jack and he ran across the graveyard in pursuit of the strange figure. The others went over to where it had been sitting.

'That was creepy as hell,' said Maggie. 'The way his arm came up. I don't like this at all. Oh God, what's that?'

There were things lying on the gravestone. Louise picked them up as Jack returned out of breath.

'I couldn't see anyone,' Jack said. 'There are paths off into the fields. He could have gone anywhere. What have you got there?'

'This is Dominic's watch; I recognise it. So it *was* him. And this' – Louise was holding something round with a papery skin; a piece of vegetation – 'looks like garlic.'

'Garlic! He really has gone mad.'

'Maybe, but he could also be sending us a message. He's telling us that it is really him by leaving his watch. And this' – she held it up – 'is what is used to deter vampires, isn't it?'

Jack shrugged his shoulders. 'Yes. But I don't get it. What have vampires got to do with Andrea's death and Dom's disappearance? And why couldn't he speak to us instead of leaving stupid stuff like that?'

Louise looked over the deserted graveyard and up at the clouds racing across the sky. She shuddered.

'I don't know,' she said. 'The whole thing just seems to get weirder.'

~

'Well, I must admit it's getting a bit more interesting, sir.' Inspector Granger smiled at Oldroyd. 'But I'm not sure where it leaves us.'

Steph and Oldroyd were in Alice Granger's office as the three of them assessed the new information in the case. They were drinking the good coffee from the inspector's coffee machine and eating chocolate brownies that Steph had allowed Oldroyd to indulge in on this occasion. Due to his and Andy's struggles with their weight, all cakes and biscuits had been banned from his office in Harrogate. Steph supervised this. Granger had been informed about the true nature of the sarcophagus at the escape room and Oldroyd had given her an account of what had happened to Louise and the others the night before. Louise had called him early in the morning and told him about the strange encounter at the abbey church. His first instinct had been to be angry with her for taking such a risk, but she persuaded him that it was not really dangerous as there were four of them. He'd made her promise to inform him immediately if further messages came from Dominic.

'As far as the sarcophagus is concerned . . .' began Oldroyd, who paused to enjoy his brownie. He glanced at Steph as he bit the crumbly, cakey chocolate treat and she raised an eyebrow. He was revelling in a break from the strict regime. 'It could have been used by the assailant, Dominic Holgate, to hide in, instead of going through the door onto the street. If that's what happened, it means that he somehow knew about the sarcophagus and that the attack was planned.'

'And later on he left the building through that door?'

'Presumably.'

'I'm wondering why bother? If you're going to go out of the building later anyway, what do you gain by hiding in there for a while? In fact, later on people are on the lookout and it's harder.'

'I agree, but I'll be very interested in what forensics have to say about that stain.'

'You really think it's blood?'

'My instincts say yes, but it could have been there a long time and may have nothing to do with this case. If it's more recent, it could be that Holgate cut himself when he stabbed the victim. We could prove that he did hide in there. In itself that might not take us very far, but I find it difficult to accept that the sarcophagus illusion just happens to be in the next room to the murder.'

'But, sir, you've said to Andy and me several times in the past that coincidences do happen and they're not as unlikely as people think,' said Steph.

'You're right and I might be on the wrong track completely. We'll see.'

'This business last night,' said Granger, moving on. 'I'm sure you've emphasised to your daughter and the others that what they did was very risky.'

'I have and they won't do it again.'

'Good. The whole thing is very odd though, isn't it? Apparently he arranges to meet them and then as soon as they see him he disappears, leaving the suspect's watch and some garlic. What do you think's going on?'

'It doesn't make much sense. They didn't get close enough to see his face, which from a distance seemed to be made up to look like a vampire, or hear his voice, so there's no proof it was actually him.'

'I presume the watch was designed to convince them that it was him?'

'I would have thought so.'

'What about the garlic?'

Oldroyd raised his arms in a gesture of incomprehension. 'We all know that in the legend, garlic is supposed to deter vampires. Is it some kind of cryptic clue?'

'It would be consistent with the meeting point up on the dark hill above the town and in a graveyard. As if someone's trying to create a gothic atmosphere for some reason,' suggested Steph.

'A clue to what?' asked Granger. 'It's Goth Weekend here and the murder took place in a Dracula-themed escape room . . . But apart from that I'm not sure how all this vampire stuff is really relevant.'

'Maybe it was significant that he murdered her in that escape room while they were both dressed up in gothic costumes, ma'am,' replied Steph.

There was a pause. No one could add anything to that suggestion.

'I take it you've had no information about where Holgate might be?' asked Oldroyd.

Granger shook her head. 'No, and it's not what I would have expected given that I understand he didn't know the area so he wouldn't have had any hiding places ready. I thought he would have been spotted by now, especially if he's in a distressed state.'

'Unless he had an accomplice, ma'am,' offered Steph.

'Yes, but we've no evidence of that yet, have we?'

'No, ma'am, but I agree with DCI Oldroyd that things appear to be getting more complicated.'

Granger continued. 'We've spoken to the woman running the escape room, Elaine Pesku. She's Romanian; she confirmed the account given by the others. She missed the action as she'd gone to the toilet. She encountered Louise and the escape-room actor, and then dialled 999. She told us all about that spare room and confirmed there was no other way out. The owner, Hugh Preston, told her he was going to convert that room into part of the game.'

'How long has she been working there?'

'She said for just over six months. We can't confirm that, or the business with the sarcophagus, until we find the owner . . . which we haven't done yet. The only other person present was the actor playing the part of Dracula.' She looked at her notes: 'Philip Owen. Again, he confirmed the story that everyone else told us. His job was to add to the tension by following the players through the rooms. As soon as he knew something was wrong he went in to help them. He went back to reception with Louise and then got the first aid kit. But it was too late.' She put down her notes. 'There are no inconsistencies in the witness accounts. I've got forensics onto that sarcophagus thing, and the blood stain. Other than that, we'll just have to wait until we find Holgate or see if he texts again. If he does, and tries to arrange another meeting, we'll be ready for him this time.'

'Good,' said Oldroyd. 'In the meantime, if it's all right with you, we'll go back to Leeds with Louise and have a look at this flat that the victim had. There might be something interesting there. Maybe you could get the Met to look at the flat they shared in Tower Hamlets.'

'Yes, I will. Also we've examined the victim's phone, which was in her bag at the escape room reception, but there was nothing unusual in the messages or recorded calls to suggest what was going to happen.'

Granger smiled at Oldroyd. 'By the way, sir; I remember how you used to give murders acronyms like MOTA: Malignancy of Time and Place, for an unfortunate victim of a serial killer. How would you describe this one?'

'Oh yes, I still like to do that. If we confirm that it was Holgate and the case is closed then depending on the circumstances, it could be an "O" for Othello. He killed the person he loved. In this case it seems it was done in anger and not out of jealousy as in the play, but, like the Moor, he seems to have immediately regretted it. However, if it turns out that there's more to it than meets the eye, then I'll say it's NRTJ.'

'What's that, sir?'

'Never Rush To Judgement.'

Granger laughed and then sighed, as she faced the hard reality of police work. 'By the way, her parents have arrived and I'll have to speak to them. Never an easy job.'

Oldroyd agreed; he was glad at this moment not to be in charge of the case.

'Oh shit, I'm not sure I can do this!'

Steph and Louise, wearing plastic gloves, were about to enter Andrea and Dominic's room in the Airbnb. No one had been in there since the horrific events of Wednesday.

'You can with my help,' said Steph encouragingly. 'We need to see if there's anything in there that could be important evidence in the case and we also need to get the key for the flat in Leeds.'

'That means going through Andrea's things.' Louise gave a deep sigh. 'Okay. Let's get it over with.' She opened the door and they crept in slowly as if they might disturb someone in there. The curtains were drawn back and the room showed signs of having been recently inhabited. The bed was roughly made. On one side were some of Dominic's clothes in an untidy pile, on the other a suitcase containing Andrea's clothes. She had died in her goth costume. Louise leaned down and picked up a burgundy-coloured top. 'I bought her this for Christmas last year. It really suited her.' She put the top back down, sat on the bed and sobbed. Steph put her arm around her.

'Look, just sit in that chair and I'll ask you about things if I need to. I know this is really difficult. Can you see a handbag? She only had a small bag with her at the escape room with not much in it apart from her phone so there must be another one.'

Louise pointed. 'It's that brown leather bag there on that chest of drawers. She had all her keys and stuff in there and she said she was going to call at the Leeds flat before returning to London.'

Steph opened the bag and found a number of sets of keys, one of which was marked 'Cornwall Avenue'. Louise identified them as the correct set. Steph continued with the search through wardrobes, drawers and clothing. She found supplies of a contraceptive pill and also a blister packet of capsules.

'Do you know why she took these?' she asked Louise, indicating the capsules.

'I think they were for heartburn or something. She had a few stomach problems.'

On the dressing table Steph found a necklace made in silverwork with a shiny black stone at its centre. 'That looks like Whitby jet.'

'Yes,' replied Louise. 'She got that recently, I think. She was very fond of it.'

'Did she buy it here? Or maybe someone bought it for her?'

'I don't know.'

Steph continued the search, but the only unusual item in the room was a small bottle, which, according to the label, contained fake blood.

'That was for her costume,' Louise said. 'I think she got it from some kind of joke shop. She had this Bride of Dracula outfit that she splashed with fake blood.' Her voice faltered. 'She didn't know that there would soon be real blood on it.' She burst into tears again.

'Okay,' said Steph, holding a plastic bag containing a few items including the blood. 'Just sit down. I'll have a look through Dominic's stuff.'

Steph sorted through some clothes and then looked into his case. Here, concealed under more clothes, she was surprised to find a gun holster. There was no gun but there was a small metal container which was clearly an ammunition box. There were some bullets inside.

Steph showed this to Louise. 'Did you know he carried a gun?' she asked.

Louise was shocked. 'No. What the hell did he have that for and where did he get it?'

'Maybe to protect himself. Did he have any reason to feel threatened?'

'Not that I know of. I don't know of anyone who would want to harm him. God, this whole thing just gets worse! Does this mean he's got the gun with him now?'

'It would seem so.'

'Why? I don't get it. This is all just a nightmare.' She burst into tears again.

'Okay,' said Steph, putting an arm around Louise's shoulder. 'I think we need to go down and tell your dad.'

~

While Louise and Steph were upstairs, Oldroyd stood in the entrance hall and took a call from his ex-wife, who naturally sounded very concerned.

'She's okay, Julia . . . Yes, I'm here. There's no need to drop everything and come rushing over. We're coming over to Leeds tomorrow . . . Yes, Louise too. We need to look at the victim's flat . . . No, we haven't caught the killer, but I can't see there's a threat to anyone else. He's a friend of Louise's; it looks as if it was a row that went wrong . . . Yes, terrible, isn't it? They were a couple . . . No, it was unexpected . . . She's had a shock but she's fine. She's still with her friends. Maggie. Remember her? . . . Yes, and some others . . . They're all helping each other . . . Tom Walker's been very understanding. I'll have to return to Harrogate soon, but I'm hoping to get back . . . Yes, I'm helping the police here; the inspector used to work for me. Okay, I'll probably see you Saturday.'

Oldroyd ended the call to his wife, feeling relieved. He'd found her difficult to relate to since they'd separated, though they'd always remained in touch. Clearly she wanted to see Louise, but he didn't think her coming to Whitby would help the situation. There wasn't much she could do and he would find her presence very off-putting.

Much better for her to see Louise when they were over in Leeds. It would be the weekend so she would be off work. It was bad enough that their daughter was involved in this; he didn't want to have to deal with any marital stuff as well.

He went back into the apartment and looked round the living room. Mark Garner, Maggie's boyfriend, a handsome blonde-haired young man, had arrived. They were sitting together on one sofa and Maggie's head was resting on Mark's shoulder. Jack Ryerson, the late arrival at the doomed weekend away, was sitting in an armchair looking at his phone. Ben was in another armchair reading a magazine. They looked at Oldroyd and he felt their embarrassment at his presence but before he had time to say anything Steph and Louise returned from the bedroom and Steph showed him the holster and the ammunition box. Oldroyd examined them and then turned to the others.

'Did any of you know that Dominic carried a gun?'

'A gun!' exclaimed Mark. 'No!'

'Why would he need a gun?' asked Ben. He seemed to think this over for a moment. 'Ah, but wait a minute, he once told us his uncle gave him a gun. Jack, do you remember? In the pub that time? We were talking about weird stuff people have in their attics. There must have been something on the telly, and he said he had a gun hidden away.'

Jack nodded. 'Yeah, he did. And didn't he say his uncle was in the army, in Afghanistan or somewhere, and he'd kept some weapons when he was discharged?'

'Yes, and that wasn't legal so he kept the gun secret.' Ben turned to Maggie. 'I'm sure you were there that night, Maggie?'

'Yes, I was,' said Maggie. 'He was very fond of his uncle. Didn't he keep the gun as a memento? But why would he bring it up here? Bloody hell! Whatever next?'

'Was there anyone who had threatened him in the past? Anyone whom he might have reason to fear?' asked Oldroyd.

They all looked at one another and shrugged their shoulders.

'Everyone liked Dominic; he was a nice guy, even if he had a bit of a stormy relationship with Andrea,' said Ben.

Oldroyd frowned. This was another odd development. The gun had been there for a reason and the fact that it was out of character for Dominic to carry it suggested that he'd been expecting trouble. He knew it was illegal, but he still had the gun with him. Was Andrea's murder connected to this? How? He hadn't shot her, but presumably he had the gun with him now so he must have been carrying it that day. Or had he hidden it somewhere? Oldroyd didn't know the answers but, more and more, events were suggesting that Louise was right: this was not going to be an open- and-shut case.

~

Andrea's parents were brought into Granger's office. They seemed much older and more fragile than they probably were as they shuffled in, bent over with their grief. The mother's face was dazed and blank with the shock; the father's tight with anger. Andrea had been their only child.

Granger expressed her condolences to them and explained what the police knew about their daughter's death. The mother said nothing but started to weep quietly.

'I never liked him, that Holgate,' declared the father in a pronounced Yorkshire accent. 'He was a smooth-talking southerner type; he never looked after her. We heard them arguing when they came to stay with us, didn't we, Joyce?' He turned to his wife, who nodded but remained silent. He turned back to Granger and shook his head. He wasn't far from tears himself. 'What can you do? You can't tell your children who to go out with, can you?'

'No.' Granger smiled sympathetically, thinking about her own problems with Lesley.

'Are you going to catch the bastard?' the father blurted out, caught between grief and anger.

'I'm sure we will, Mr Barnes. I've got lots of officers on the case and they're searching everywhere.'

'Good. Don't let me near him when you find him or . . .' He looked away, unable to finish his sentence.

'You say you heard them arguing. Was Holgate ever violent towards her?'

'Not when I was around; he wouldn't bloody dare.'

'And what did they argue about?'

Barnes glanced at his wife. 'It was money, wasn't it?' She nodded, still seemingly incapable of speech. 'I don't think either of them made much money in their jobs and they struggled to live in London. Andrea wanted them to move up to Leeds and live in our Caroline's flat, but he wouldn't have it. I think he wanted her to sell it.' He sighed. 'I wish they bloody well had come up here. We could have watched them more closely.'

Which is probably why they didn't, thought Granger.

'To your knowledge, did either of them have any enemies?'

'Our Andrea?' said Barnes. 'No, everybody liked our Andrea. She was . . .' He didn't finish the sentence and his eyes had a far-away look. The reality of what had happened was still too painful to contemplate. Granger decided it wasn't fair to keep them long. They could speak to them again later if necessary.

'Well, thank you for coming in,' Granger said. 'If you think of anything else about your daughter and Holgate, let me know. It could be important. We'll release your daughter's body to you as soon as we can so you can arrange the funeral.'

At this Mrs Barnes started sobbing again.

'Yes, we'll get her away from here all right,' her husband continued in a tone of desperation. 'I've always hated this place. Your damn brother doesn't make it any better.'

Mrs Barnes looked up. 'There's no point blaming Ian for anything, Fred. He's got nothing to do with it.'

'Who are you talking about?' enquired Granger gently.

'My brother-in-law, Ian Withington. He has a jeweller's shop down on Church Street. He used to have one in Leeds but he had to leave because he was on the fiddle. He's a rogue; always on the make. He got my mother-in-law to change her will so he got most of the money.'

'Fred, please!'

'What happened?' asked Granger. She felt the need to ask about this even though it was unlikely to have any bearing on the case.

'She was losing it, poor woman, and he went round to her house telling her this and that, and before long she'd signed documents leaving the house to him and some of her cash. He told her his business was in trouble and that Joyce and I were okay financially, that kind of stuff. He's a sneaky bugger.'

'I see.'

'You didn't like the fact that our Andrea liked visiting here and she always went to see her uncle,' said Mrs Barnes in a weak and faltering voice.

'No, I didn't. When she wasn't in London she was always over here or in her flat in Headingley. We hardly saw her.'

'Was it your sister that left her the flat?'

'Yes, Caroline. She was arty like Andrea; never married. Those two got on really well. She did well for Andrea in the end. It compensated a bit for Ian's rotten tricks.'

'Yes.' Granger felt she couldn't take much more of this tragic couple. They seemed to have lost their daughter long before she actually died.

Granger was about to bring the interview to an end when Mrs Barnes said, 'You see, Andrea always liked that Whitby jet that Ian dealt in. She had a few pieces of that.' The memory triggered yet more tears.

'I see,' replied Granger, finding it difficult to think of what to say. It was quite a relief when they finally left.

~

Later that evening back at home, Granger was trying to relax. It was Friday evening, but a serious case like this went on continuously until it was solved. She would have to go into work at some point during the weekend.

She was watching television with Ian when Lesley came into the room. She was dressed in all her goth gear with purple lipstick and heavy black mascara. She wore a short black skirt, laddered fishnet tights, a tattered black coat and black boots.

'God, you look disgusting!' said Ian.

'That's the general idea,' replied Lesley, adding some finishing touches as she looked in a mirror.

'Before you go,' said Granger. 'I want to ask you something.'

'What? I've got to go soon.'

'What do you know about escape rooms?'

'Escape rooms? Oh, I forgot; you're investigating that murder, aren't you? Bloody creepy, that is. Bloke kills his girlfriend in Dracula's Lair in Goth Week. Was it a publicity stunt?'

'Unfortunately not. Have you been in one of those rooms?'

'Just one; a lot of them are over-eighteen and they ID. They're cool. It's a laugh. You need a good team to win against the clock though. We didn't.'

'Do you know anything about this one? Dracula's Lair?'

'I know someone who did it. Said it was good. He said there was a funny woman running it who sounded as if she actually was from Transylvania and they have this actor playing Dracula who pursues you through the rooms. It sounds amazing. I'll bet they were doing a good trade at this time of year until that happened. Anyway, have to be off.'

'Back at half eleven,' said Granger. She didn't even bother to comment on her daughter's appearance.

'Okay,' replied Lesley wearily, before leaving the house.

Granger turned to Ian. 'Are you interested in goth stuff?'

Ian laughed. 'Me? No way. It's for losers: dressing up like something from a horror film.'

'You'd rather be in football kit, wouldn't you?'

'Yeah, 'course, any day.'

Granger smiled. Ian was far more predictable and easier to handle, but he was only fifteen. There was still time for things to change.

⁓

The next morning, Oldroyd, Steph and Louise stood outside the grand three-storey mid-Victorian stone-built house in a quiet area off the busy Headingley Lane in Leeds. The pavements were thick with leaves shed by the huge sycamores and beeches that lined the avenue. At the top of the street large trees could be seen on Woodhouse Ridge.

'It's that one on the first floor.' Louise pointed up to a window where the curtains were closed. Louise had visited Andrea there a few times.

Using the key from Andrea's bag, Oldroyd opened the external door and they entered a tiled hallway. He collected the post for Flat 2 and they went up a wide staircase. Louise felt dreadful. This was the second time she'd had to go into Andrea's private living spaces and experience the terrible quiet left by the missing person. Her legs felt weak and she stumbled on the stair. Steph helped her up.

Oldroyd unlocked the door. The interior of the flat was impressive, if a little dusty and untidy in places. There was a high-ceilinged corridor with a polished parquet floor. The walls were lined with sketches and paintings, including some by the local nineteenth-century artist Atkinson Grimshaw. The large living room had chintzy sofas, a thick-pile carpet and ornamental mirrors over an elaborate fireplace. There were more pictures on the walls. There was also an uncanny silence everywhere, which unsettled Louise. She kept expecting Andrea to walk into the room at any moment.

'Was your friend's aunt an artist or a collector?' asked Oldroyd as they gazed at the opulent surroundings. 'It's a very impressive display.'

'She did some of her own work. That's one of hers over the fireplace.' Louise pointed to a dales landscape in watercolour. 'She wasn't an expert or anything, according to Andrea. She never studied art; she was a civil servant in the tax office, I think. She acquired everything gradually throughout her life; just bought what took her fancy. She lived here for over forty years and then she passed it all on to Andrea. I don't think Andrea knew what to do with it. She didn't know much about fine art either, but she liked the flat. It had a lot of memories for her. I think she felt bad about changing anything, although the decorations and the furniture are not her style. She said she felt her aunt wouldn't like it.'

'I see. Well, let's have a good look round, though I don't know what we're looking for. Are you okay to do this?'

'Yes. With Steph's help.' She smiled at the detective sergeant.

'Okay, Let's get going then.' They all put on plastic gloves. Oldroyd and Steph began a painstaking examination of each room while Louise watched and answered questions. In the living room she noticed a framed photograph of Andrea and Dominic; they were laughing and seemed to be having a great time at some party or other. It caused grief to well up inside Louise again. How could everything have changed so quickly and so dramatically?

Unfortunately, the flat, like the bedroom in the Airbnb, yielded little of interest. There was nothing in Andrea's possessions or in any letter or document that gave any hint of what had been going to happen in Whitby. There was some more jewellery made with Whitby jet: a pair of earrings and a gothic-looking piece with a black spider on a silvery web.

'She certainly liked this Whitby jet stuff, didn't she?' asked Steph.

'Yes. I think the blackness of the gemstone appealed to her. She'd been a bit of a goth when she was a teenager, and I guess she never quite grew out of the love of black.'

'I see. Did she go to Whitby quite a bit then?'

'I think she might have. She once mentioned an uncle who lives there but you don't need to travel to places to buy local stuff anymore, do you?'

'True.'

Having searched everything as thoroughly as he could, Oldroyd glanced around the flat in frustration. It seemed as if the visit was fruitless. Then, as they were about to leave and he walked into the hallway, he finally noticed something and stopped.

'It looks as if there was something hanging there until quite recently,' he said, pointing to a gap at the end of a row of pictures.

He examined the walls. 'There're still some remnants of the dust that would have collected behind it. You said she was reluctant to change things in here. Did she ever say anything about taking a picture down? Or maybe even selling one?'

'No, she didn't. I can't see why she would do that; her aunt's legacy was very important to her.'

Oldroyd looked again at the space. He could see no obvious significance in the absence of whatever it was that had hung there. But, like any little detail which had no immediate explanation, it made him think.

~

Oldroyd dropped Steph off in the centre of Leeds near the flat she shared with Andy overlooking the river. Then he drove out to Chapel Allerton to take Louise to her mother's house. As they drew up outside the house in the terraced row, Julia, seeing the car, came quickly out of the door and embraced Louise as soon as she got out of the car.

'Oh, come here! How are you?' she said anxiously.

'I'm okay, Mum. I'm coping. Don't worry.'

'But it's such a terrible thing to happen. Poor Andrea; I remember her well. She used to come here quite a bit when you were at the sixth-form college, didn't she? Dark-haired girl. Oh, I just hate to think about it! What about her poor parents?' Julia was starting to cry herself. 'Come on inside and I'll make a cup of tea.' She put her arm round Louise's shoulders and then seemed to notice Oldroyd for the first time. 'Oh, Jim! Hello. Won't you come in, too?'

Reluctantly, Oldroyd followed them through the door and down the narrow hallway to the dining area at the back of the house. A one-storey kitchen extension led from this out across the yard to the back alleyway. Julia had lived alone here since the family house had been sold when she and Oldroyd had split up. It was immaculate and very artfully decorated and furnished. She had made a big effort to make it into her space.

Oldroyd sat down on a bouncy bentwood chair from IKEA. It would be better if he stayed out of things as much as possible. He was never sure whether Julia's attitude towards him would be friendly or hostile. Louise and her mother sat at the table.

'I can't imagine what you've been through,' Julia went on as she brought the mugs of tea over.

She seems more upset than Louise at the moment, thought Oldroyd, as he wondered what effect staying here would have on his daughter. He hoped her mother's presence would be helpful and would not amplify Louise's feelings. 'You must stay here for a while until you feel better.'

'Well, I . . .' began Louise and looked across at her father.

'She can't stay for long,' he said. 'She'll need to come back to Whitby. The inspector in charge has not given permission for those involved to leave the town yet. Louise is only over here because we needed to look at Andrea's flat in Headingley.'

'What?! Jim, she can't go back there. It's too traumatic for her. And it's not safe; you haven't caught the killer yet.'

'Mum, it's okay. I can manage. I'm not on my own.'

'No, but the others will be in the same state as you.'

'That's why we're supporting each other. I have to go back and help the police if they need me. Dominic might send another text message.'

Julia shuddered. 'Oh, it must have been so creepy to get that.'

'It was, but the next time it might lead the police to him.'

Oldroyd sat back and said nothing until Julia spoke to him.

'Will you be going back over there, Jim?' she asked.

'Yes, but I'm not sure for how much longer. It depends on whether they need me and if Tom Walker agrees to it. I really don't

72

think she's in danger, Julia, and I don't think she'll need to be there for long.'

'Would it help if I came over? I'm sure I could get some compassionate time off if necessary.'

This was what Oldroyd wanted to avoid. Luckily Louise felt the same way.

'No, Mum. Really. You'd only get worried and, anyway, what would you do?'

Julia shook her head. 'I suppose I'd only get in the way. I just don't like to think of you there with a murderer on the loose.'

It took a while, but Julia eventually accepted that Louise would return to Whitby after the weekend but would ring every night to reassure her mother that she was all right. As Oldroyd had expected, Julia made it clear that she held him responsible for their daughter's welfare. Leaving Louise with her mother for the weekend, he was quite relieved to make his escape and drive over to Harrogate. It was not without some sadness on that journey that he reflected on how he now wanted to avoid the company of the woman he'd once loved. For many years after their separation he'd been keen to see her and remained hopeful of a reconciliation. But those feelings had now faded.

～

It was mid-afternoon by the time Oldroyd reached Harrogate and his flat overlooking the Stray. Deborah was waiting for him. She was lying on the sofa reading a book and looking very relaxed. She shut the book when Oldroyd came into the room. He sat down heavily in an armchair.

'Jim! I'm glad you're back. How was it? I've been thinking about poor Louise. Is she okay?'

'Not bad, considering the circumstances. I've just dropped her off at her mother's. We've been to the flat of the girl who was murdered; see if there were any clues.'

'How gruesome! And were there any?'

'Not really, just something that made me think.' He told her about the missing picture. 'The problem is: there's no one who can tell me what was there. Her boyfriend might have known, but he's apparently the murderer and has disappeared. Louise can't remember and I don't know anyone else who's actually been into that flat.'

'Surely some of her friends must have visited her.'

'Yes, I'll have to ask them when I get back.'

'And her parents? Where are they?'

'They've come over from Leeds. Alice Granger's dealing with all that. It's the nastiest job in policing: dealing with parents whose child has been murdered.'

Deborah winced at the idea. 'Absolutely terrible. So what's the plan now? I take it you're not just going to leave the police over there to sort it out as you mentioned going back. And I notice you said "apparently" in relation to the murderer. Are you sceptical?'

'You know me: I'm always sceptical. I don't like open-and-shut cases. I'm always looking for something more complicated. There are some things that puzzle me about this case.'

'Not everything is complicated though, is it? Sometimes the most obvious solution is the right one.'

'Oh yes, in fact most of the time. I don't really see the routine cases anymore, which are actually the vast majority. When I'm called in it usually means there's a mystery to solve. The difference here is that I've only got involved in this case because of Louise.'

'So maybe you're making more of it than you need to.'

'Perhaps. Interestingly, Louise is not happy with the obvious answer either, despite being a witness.'

'Like father, like daughter, then?'

'Yes. Though at the beginning I thought her attitude could be due to shock. Imagine what it's like to see one of your friends murder another. Now I'm not so sure.'

'Horrendous! And I see what you mean. It would be hard to accept that it had really happened.'

'There's also some weird stuff going on.' He told her about the texts from Dominic and the aborted meeting at the church. As a psychotherapist, Deborah took an interest in this.

'That is strange. It sounds as if the stress and shock of what he did could have caused some kind of psychosis around the Dracula theme. Also, he may want to talk to his friends so he contacts them but is overcome with guilt and can't face meeting them when it comes to it. Have the police over there really no idea where he is? He sounds as if he's in a desperate state.'

'No, and that's another strange aspect. We all thought that he'd have turned up by now, especially as he's not a local and doesn't know the area well. It's all very puzzling and worrying. It's one of those situations where you feel a bit paralysed. All we can do is wait for something to happen.'

Deborah got up from the sofa and put down her book. 'I can see frustration and constant rumination about to set in. You missed parkrun this morning, so I prescribe some exercise. We've just time to drive over to Bilton and have a walk in the Nidd Gorge before the light goes. That'll do you good.'

Despite his weariness, Oldroyd agreed: he rarely refused a walk in the countryside.

~

Back in Whitby, Ben was lying on his bed. It had been such an exhausting few days and he felt very tired even though it was only mid-afternoon. He wanted to get away and back to London but knew that was impossible until things had settled down. He couldn't leave the others to deal with the aftermath of the terrible things that had happened and the police were still around and asking questions. Maybe in another few days things might be different, but of course they could never be the same again. When things like this happened it often broke up friendship groups because some people didn't want to be reminded of what they'd been through. There was a gentle tap on the door.

'Ben?'

'Yeah?'

'Can I come in?' It was Jack.

'Okay.'

Jack came in. 'Sorry. Were you asleep?' He sat on a chair by the bed.

'No, just dozing.'

'I feel a bit in the way down there with those two.' He smiled.

'Well, they should go to their room if they want to get it on,' said Ben.

'I suppose so. I just came to check on you. You must have had the most traumatic time of all attending to Andrea after she'd been stabbed.'

'It was pretty bad. Actually, I'd rather not talk about it. I'm trying not to dwell on the memories.' Ben passed a hand over his face.

'I don't blame you. I had a lucky escape.' Jack shifted in his chair. 'What do you think about Louise's dad getting involved? It's a bit sort of weird, isn't it?'

Ben yawned. 'Dunno. I can see why she'd want him to come over. He's a top detective or something, isn't he?'

'I suppose.'

'If he helps to find Dom and get everything sorted out, it'll be good.'

'Yeah. Maybe. It just feels like he's on top of us all the time.'

'Chill out. What have you got to be scared of anyway?' laughed Ben.

Jack looked uneasy for a moment. 'No, nothing. It's just, I'd rather the police were at the police station and not here.'

'Well, it won't be for long. Something has to happen soon. Dom will give himself up or they'll find him. Then we can all get away from here. Anyway, I'm going to have a kip for a while if you don't mind. I'm absolutely knackered.'

'Fine. See you later.'

Jack went back downstairs still feeling very uneasy about the police and their investigation.

∾

Downstairs, Maggie and Mark were sprawled on the sofa together. Mark was nervous. There was something he needed to tell her.

'God, I'm so lethargic,' groaned Maggie. 'It's an effort just to get up from here.'

'It's the shock; it's exhausted you.'

'Yeah, seeing what happened. I still can't believe it. Dominic's just not like that.'

Mark paused before replying and looked down at Maggie's face. She had her eyes shut. 'No, but there are things about him that you don't know about.'

Maggie opened her eyes and looked up sharply. 'What things?'

'Well, he got into serious trouble at uni for plagiarism.'

'What! I never knew that.'

'No. I didn't want to say anything because you're all friends with him, but he's not a paragon of virtue. He copied someone's essay and passed it off as his. It got the other person into trouble too before Dom admitted that he was the one who'd copied.'

'Bloody hell! That's a rotten trick.'

'Yes, and the thing is, that person was me.'

Maggie recoiled. 'No! I didn't even know you were on the same course as him.'

'Yeah, Business Studies at St Thomas's. The thing is, he never did any work; spent all his time messing around in student plays. He was on the wrong course really. Anyway, he was always behind and looking for short cuts. I didn't know him that well, but I was always ready to help someone out. I sent him an essay to look at and he copied the whole thing and submitted it. It didn't take them long to realise they had two identical essays. The worst thing was, I had to establish that he'd copied from me and not the other way round, though to be fair he owned up fairly quickly.'

'Why've you never told me about this before?'

'Because it's all in the past. When our paths crossed again through you and Andrea, I spoke to him and we decided to let it lie for the sake of the group. It's several years ago now since it happened, but I still don't think he's a person you can trust.'

'Wow. That doesn't mean that he's violent though, does it?'

'No, but I wonder what situation he might have got himself into which might have made him desperate?'

'What do you mean?'

'Say he's in financial trouble and Andrea refused to help him. He could have got very angry with her.'

'But that's all speculation! We don't know anything for sure. Maybe you should tell this to the police.'

'They'll find out soon enough and they can come to their own conclusions. It doesn't really change anything; maybe it just begins to explain how he might have been capable of doing what he did.'

'I think that's making a lot of—' She stopped because two things happened abruptly. Jack came back into the room and her phone pinged.

'How is he?' asked Mark.

'Fine, I think . . .'

'Oh my God it's him again, Dom!' blurted Maggie, sounding nearly hysterical. 'No! I can't bear it!' She threw the phone on the floor and herself onto the sofa, sobbing.

Mark picked up the phone and read:

I cant go on. Goodbye. Dom

~

Deborah and Oldroyd were picking their way down the muddy paths into the Nidd Gorge beyond Bilton. The light was fading and creating shadows among the trees while leaves fell noiselessly to the ground.

'I must say dusk in the woods is spooky at this time of year,' said Deborah.

'Well, I don't mind about that. Give me a straightforward shimmering white ghost any day after all this gory Dracula and goth stuff I've seen over in Whitby. By the way, what's that over there?' He pointed to a black shape, which looked like a figure with its arms spread wide leaning over the river. 'It looks as if the vampire Count may have followed me here.'

Deborah grasped his arm. 'Jim, stop it! You know I get nervous about things like that.'

Oldroyd laughed. 'Don't worry it's only a gnarled old tree stump.' He went over, grasped a bare bough and shook it. 'And you such a rationalist and analyser of the human mind!'

'That may be,' replied Deborah, walking warily round the stump and mounting one of the boardwalks which had been erected over the wettest parts of the paths, 'but we all have our weaknesses and things we're afraid of. It's part of being human and living in a universe we don't understand and where terrible things can happen.'

'How do you mean?'

'I think one of the functions of these werewolves, ghoulies, vampires and stuff is to give concrete form to our insecurities. They embody our fears of being attacked, bitten, eaten, but it's all at a distance because we know they don't really exist and we either read about them or watch them on film from the safety of a chair.'

They were walking through the gorge by the side of the river Nidd with the steep wooded valley to their right. A dog walker passed them with an enthusiastic Labrador enjoying itself getting wet and filthy in the mud. It threatened to jump up, put its muddy paws on Deborah and give her a big lick until the owner called out, 'Judy! Get down.'

'Don't worry,' called Deborah, laughing as she stroked the dog. They continued on the path, now passing the beautifully restored Scotton Mill by a weir on the river.

'How would you like to live there?' asked Oldroyd.

'Beautiful spot, but maybe the water going down the weir would be noisy and it would be scary out here in the woods at night.'

'You're right though, at some level we like being frightened, don't we?' said Oldroyd. 'That's why there are so many horror stories and films and why people like dressing up as vampires and monsters.'

'Yes, it's all in a controlled and safe way.'

The path started to climb up through the trees away from the river, which continued on to Knaresborough.

Oldroyd made a suggestion. 'I've been thinking. Why don't you come over to Whitby for a few days while I'm involved in this case? We could do a bit of walking and maybe go out on a sea trip.'

Deborah turned to him. 'Jim, that's a lovely idea, but won't you be busy?'

'No more than I am here and we still manage to do plenty. What about your clients?' Deborah had a private therapy practice.

'I can always rearrange things.'

'Good. I just hope you don't get scared with all the goth stuff.' Oldroyd had a twinkle in his eye.

'I promise I won't. And I hope you don't become obsessed with the case. Getting away from the office will be a good time to relax a bit . . . and maybe write some of your poetry?'

'Yes, I will, don't worry. By the way, have you ever been to the Whitby Museum?'

'No, I don't think so.'

Oldroyd rubbed his hands together. 'Good, well, treat in store then. That place is really spooky.'

'Is it? Why?'

'No more information. And we'd better get a move on; it's really getting dark now and all the goblins and sprites will be out practising for Halloween in a few days' time. Come on, let's jog and we'll have a drink at the Gardener's Arms.' Without another word he started to jog down the bridleway back towards Bilton, followed by a laughing Deborah who soon caught him up and passed him even though she'd already run 5 km that day.

~

It was late on Saturday night at the climax of the Goth Weekend. The streets of the old east side of the town were packed with revellers in various macabre costumes. A number of drinkers were standing outside the popular Old Ship Inn in Church Street. As they drank, joked and laughed they thought nothing of the solitary black-caped figure coming slowly down the street, wandering from side to side until it reached them. The figure's face was difficult to see under a black hood and there was the white glimmer of a mask. It pulled out a gun. Assuming it was a joke, people laughed and one of them put up her hands in mock surrender. But then the figure raised the gun and fired two shots: one hitting a plant pot and the other smashing a light above the door. The woman screamed, someone shouted, 'What the hell!?' and some people dived for cover underneath wooden tables.

The Dracula figure shouted something indecipherable and was seen to be sobbing and shaking. Then it ran down one of the narrow ginnels which led to the sea and disappeared into the darkness. There was chaos at the pub. Random shouts were heard: 'He's got a gun!' 'Stay inside!' 'There's some bloody lunatic out here!' Then another gun shot was heard. 'What the hell was that?' 'Call the police; there's someone firing a gun off.'

After this there was quiet. Tentatively, people started to come out of the pub, edge their way down the street, glance down the dark alley, and then run down the street away from the scene. With the siren blaring and flashing blue lights, a police car came down the street and stopped at the pub. After being briefed about what happened, officers went down the ginnel with flashlights but could find no trace of the strange goth figure with the gun. The festivities had been ruined in that part of the town; the mood had changed and everyone quickly dispersed. Dressing up in ghoulish ways was one thing, but a brush with real danger was something else.

Outside the Old Ship a group of frightened young people emerged tentatively from underneath a wooden table where they'd been hiding ever since the first shot had been fired. One of them was Lesley Granger.

'Shit! What the hell was that lunatic doing?' said a young man, looking at the smashed plant pot, which was quite near to them. One girl was crying.

'It's okay, Mandy, they've gone,' said Lesley.

Mandy crawled out, her costume smeared with dirt and her make-up running. 'They ran off down there!' She pointed to the ginnel. 'They could come back.'

'I doubt it,' replied Lesley. 'Look, we have to get out of here quick. If the police stop me, I'm going to be in big trouble with my mum. Come on. I'm going to call her, and we need to dodge the police.'

The little group walked gingerly down the street, keeping to the side and hiding in doorways.

Lesley took out her mobile and called her mum.

'What's going on? Do you know what time it is?' Granger was not pleased and had clearly been waiting for this call.

'We were on our way back, Mum, but something's happened.' She described the incident at the Old Ship while Granger's alarm grew.

'Okay. I'm on my way now. Stay away from the police officers.'

'We are.'

'I'll never live it down if you get involved with the police.'

'Mum, we haven't done anything; we were just at the pub and—'

'That's enough, isn't it? You're not eighteen, Lesley. It's against the law for you to drink in a pub.'

'We were outside.'

'So how did you get the drinks? Someone went in to get them. Here I am, a detective inspector at the local police station and my daughter risks getting arrested for underage drinking. How is that going to look?' Lesley was silent. 'Get across the harbour bridge and wait at the other side.' Granger brought the conversation to an abrupt end.

As she drove down to the old town, she reflected on the trials of parenthood and concluded that things could be much worse. She picked up the little group of downcast goths, looking rather forlorn and whisked them away from any compromising circumstances.

As yet she didn't know the real significance of the incident at the Old Ship.

∿

Early next morning a fisherman returning from the open sea, spotted something floating near the harbour wall. He pulled his boat up close and saw a human head face down in the water and a black cloak swirling around in the current.

Police sirens were heard again in Church Street and a small crowd gathered to see the body pulled out of the water. At this year's Whitby Goth Weekend, death was real and not just a fantasy.

∿

DC Hampton had to knock on the door of the Airbnb for some time before anyone answered. Eventually a sleepy-looking Maggie opened the door.

'Oh God, what's going on? It's only eight o'clock. It's Sunday.'

'I need to come in,' said Hampton with a sombre expression on his face. 'Can you call everyone together? I have some important news.'

'What?' cried Maggie. 'What has he done? Is he dead?'

'Just call the others please. It will be better if I tell you all together.'

Maggie rushed around the house rousing everyone. She had to bang loudly on the door of Ben's room and also the room that had been Dom and Andrea's and where Jack was now sleeping, before she got a response from both men. They'd been out late the previous night. Soon the whole group of surviving friends were assembled in the lounge, except Louise, who was still in Leeds. DC Hampton went straight to the point.

'This morning we recovered a dead person from the water down in the harbour. We believe this to be the body of Dominic Holgate.'

'Oh no!' Maggie burst into tears. Mark held her, and she put her head on his shoulder.

'Bloody hell!' Ben groaned. 'How can you be sure?'

'We can't until the body is identified, which we will need one of you to do.'

They glanced at one another. 'I'll do it,' said Ben. 'I was one of the last to see him alive.' He shook his head, put his hand up to his forehead and looked away. He started to weep. Jack went over to console him.

'I'm sorry to be the bearer of this news,' continued Hampton. 'The cause of death was most probably a gunshot wound to the head. An unidentified person who resembled Mr Holgate was seen behaving very strangely last night outside a pub on Church Street. Two shots were fired; then the figure ran towards the harbour. Another gun shot was heard so it seems likely that the wound was self-inflicted. Given that a gun holster was found in Mr Holgate's possessions, it seems likely that he was using a gun he brought with him to Whitby.'

There was silence as they tried to absorb the horror of it.

Hampton turned to Ben. 'If you could come with me then. It won't take long. It's just a short drive to the hospital.' He turned back to the others. 'Again, I'm really sorry for your loss. I don't suppose it's come as too much of a surprise after that last text. You did the right thing to report it to us.'

'Is this the end of it, then?' asked Jack.

'It appears that way. I know it's a great shock to you all, but maybe you can now start to move on. We'll let you know when it's okay to leave,' replied Hampton, and he and Ben left the house.

The remaining three were left in stunned silence. They all sat down heavily on the sofas and Mark put his arm around Maggie's shoulders.

'It's all right him saying that,' she said in a weak voice as if she could hardly get the words out. 'How can you ever recover properly from something like this? Two of your friends gone and . . .' She started to cry again. Mark hugged her closer.

'Bloody hell,' said Jack, shaking his head. 'I never thought he'd kill himself.'

Maggie gave him a hostile look. 'You didn't like him though, did you? He took Andrea from you, didn't he? I'll bet you're glad he's dead.'

'Hey, steady on.' Jack rushed to defend himself. 'That's not true. What's the matter with you?'

'That wasn't fair, Mags,' said Mark. Maggie looked at him sulkily, shook her head and cried again.

'Oh, I'm sorry,' she sobbed. 'I don't know what to think about anything or anybody. I'm all confused. Why has it all gone wrong like this? We were such a great group of friends and now. It's just . . .' She trailed off, unable to make sense of the inexplicable things they were going through. They all sat down, stunned by this latest news.

'I'll have to call Louise,' Maggie said after a while. 'Can someone please tell me when all this is going to end?'

Louise was still in bed at her mum's house when her phone rang. Grimacing, she clutched at it on the bedside table, looked at the screen and saw it was Maggie.

'Maggie?' There was a pause and she heard the sound of crying.

'Louise, it's . . . it's Dom. They've found him . . . dead. He was in the harbour. They're saying he shot himself and then fell in . . .'

'Who?'

'An officer came round. Ben's gone with him to identify the body. It was that detective constable again. He was very nice but . . . It's, it's just awful . . . First Andrea, and now Dom. I can't deal with it. I keep wanting to wake up from this nightmare.'

Louise could scarcely speak. Although they'd always known this was a possibility, it was no less shocking now that it had happened. 'Oh my God, that's bloody terrible,' she said eventually.

'I know. Are you coming back over? I really need to talk to you about it. Mark's here but you and I knew them both for so long. I can't . . .' She broke down in tears.

'Yes, I'm coming back tomorrow,' said Louise, though she knew her mother would oppose it. 'I need to be with you too. I can't believe we'll never see them again. Bye, see you soon.' She hung up, sat down and put her face in her hands.

There was the sound of footsteps on the stairs and then a knock on the door and her mother's anxious voice: 'Louise? Are you okay? What's happened?'

'Come in,' said Louise. Julia entered the room and sat on the bed next to her daughter. 'Dom's dead; they found his body in the harbour.'

'Oh no. I'm so sorry.' Julia put her arms round her daughter.

'Mum, that's two friends I've lost in a few days. What's going on?' Louise lay back on the pillow.

'It's terrible. You must stay here for a few days until you feel a bit better.'

'No, Mum, I can't. I've got to go back. Maggie needs me; she's in a bad state and the police will want to ask more questions.'

'Surely all that can wait?'

'No. I can't run away from it, Mum, and leave Maggie and the others to deal with it without me. I'm going back with Dad as we planned.'

Julia sighed. She knew too much about her daughter's determined character to argue anymore. She didn't say this to Louise but at least the fact that the murderer was now dead himself meant that there was no further threat to anyone else.

'Okay. I'll go down and get you some breakfast. What would you like?'

'Just some coffee and toast, thanks.'

Julia left and Louise closed her eyes. How long would this horror go on for? It took her a while to summon up the energy to call her dad.

'Dad? I suppose you've heard?'

'Yes, love, Dominic's body was found in the harbour. Inspector Granger called me not long ago. How are you feeling?'

'Devastated, even though I suppose I knew this could happen.'

'Yes, well, take it easy.'

'I've got to go back over there with you, Dad. I was explaining to Mum; I can't just leave the others to cope. Maggie sounded in a bad way. Her boyfriend's there, but she needs me too. We knew Andrea and Dom for a long time.'

'Okay, I understand. I can still pick you up tomorrow morning if that's how you feel. What does Mum think?'

'She can't stop me.'

'That's true, but be careful and don't overstretch yourself.'

'I won't. I actually think it will be better to be with the others at this point. It feels weird to be here. We can help each other to process it.'

Oldroyd smiled. 'You're probably right. You sounded just like Deborah, then. It's a very mature and healthy attitude.'

'Thanks.'

~

'Come on, let's go, we need to get out of this place for a while.'

The despondent group of friends had been planning to go out for Sunday brunch until the shocking news of Dominic's death. Jack, however, had got to his feet to urge them to go ahead with the plan.

'Someone text Ben; that detective said he wouldn't be long. He can meet us at the café.'

Mark looked at Maggie, who sighed but got up from the sofa. 'Okay then, I think you're right.'

It was a fine day but cold; the first day in the late autumn in which there was a hint of winter. They walked slowly down past Pannett Park, shuffling through the thick autumn leaves. No one said much. They reached a café near the harbour and managed to get a table for four.

They'd not been there long when Ben arrived, looking very sombre.

'Hi,' said Jack. 'How was it?'

'Pretty grim,' replied Ben as he sat down. 'I've never seen a dead body before apart from . . . you know. It was Dom all right but he looked different; very still, like a waxwork.' He shook his head. 'It was awful.'

'Oh, poor you!' said Maggie, sitting next to him. She put her hand on his shoulder. 'That was a brave thing to do and thanks. I'm glad I didn't have to do it.'

'That's okay. Have you ordered?'

'No. Here's a menu.' They all consulted the menus in silence.

The waitress took their orders and brought their coffees over. The warm drinks and the bustling atmosphere lifted their gloom a little.

Jack took in a deep breath. 'Do we have to stay round here for much longer? To be honest, it's giving me the creeps. It's a shame because it's such a nice little place but I don't think I'll be coming back to Whitby in a hurry.'

'I assume the police will give us the go-ahead to leave soon,' said Ben.

'Yeah,' said Mark, turning to Maggie, 'I think we should get back to London. You need to get a bit of distance from all this now. There's nothing more you can do. The terrible truth is they're both dead and you can't change it.'

Maggie winced. 'It sounds so brutal when you say it like that.'

'What's the alternative? Stick around here getting more and more depressed? It's all over and you have to move on.'

Maggie turned on her partner. 'It's easy for you to say; you weren't really close to them.' She was close to tears again. 'It's bloody hard losing two people like that who you knew for a long time.' She put her head in her hands. Mark put his arm over her shoulder.

'I'm sorry; I shouldn't have said it like that. I was being insensitive.'

'Mark's right, though, Maggie,' said Ben. 'We need to go and we've no choice anyway. The booking on the apartment expires the day after tomorrow, so we have to leave on Tuesday morning. Out by eleven.'

Maggie nodded and wiped her eyes with a tissue. 'So we all head back to London then?'

'It's for the best,' said Jack.

'What about Louise? I'm not leaving before she comes back. I need to talk to her. We both knew Dom and Andrea for years.'

'Isn't she coming back tomorrow? That's Monday. We'll still be here.'

Maggie closed her eyes and shook her head. 'Yes of course. Oh, I'm so bloody shook up and confused! I don't even know what day it is.'

'Don't worry,' said Mark reassuringly. 'It's only to be expected.'

'You two look completely knackered as well,' said Maggie, looking at Ben and Jack, who had gone silent and appeared to be nearly falling asleep.

'I stayed out too late last night,' replied Ben, yawning. 'I found a pub with live music and they had an extension until one o'clock; must be because of the Goth Weekend. Where did you get to?' Jack and Ben had gone out the previous night and left Mark and Maggie together in the apartment.

'Oh, that place wasn't my scene,' said Jack. 'I found a club in some cellar behind a pub in that old street – Church Street, isn't it? It's all a bit hazy.'

'Church Street?' said Maggie. 'Did you hear or see anything of what happened with Dom? The police said he went to a pub down there and fired some shots.'

'Naw. I was inside and the music was pretty loud. They were blasting out the goth stuff: Dark Wave, Banshees. I don't think I would have heard anything.'

'No.'

'Hey, I'll tell you who I did see though,' said Ben. 'I almost forgot. That bloke who was playing Dracula at the escape room. He was walking towards the swing bridge. I recognised him out of his vampire stuff and I think he recognised me, but he looked away and just went on.'

'You go over that bridge to get to Church Street,' said Maggie thoughtfully. 'Maybe he had something to do with it.'

'With what?' said Jack.

'Dom's death.'

'How?'

'I dunno. He was in the escape room when it all happened.'

'So what? Look, stop trying to make something out of nothing. Dom killed Andrea and then he killed himself. It's absolutely terrible but it's all finished with. I'm not surprised that bloke didn't want to talk to Ben after what happened; he must be as traumatised as the rest of us.' Jack was sounding very exasperated.

Maggie didn't reply.

The waitress brought their food, and for a few minutes they made a lacklustre attempt to eat.

'I think I'm going to head back,' said Ben when he'd finished eating. He got some money out of his wallet. 'Here's my share of the bill. I need to lie down for a while.'

'Me too,' added Jack, who similarly produced some cash.

'What do you want to do?' said Mark to Maggie. 'Do you fancy a walk up through the park? It's still fine. I think the fresh air will do you good.'

Maggie agreed. They paid the bill and left.

As she and Mark walked slowly back up the hill and turned into Pannett Park up some steep steps, Maggie reflected sadly on how such an exciting weekend had turned so horrible and tragic. When they reached the centre of the park they saw a children's playground and she couldn't prevent herself from being overwhelmed by sadness again. She and Andrea had talked a number of times about whether they would have a family one day and Andrea was keen. She'd said she liked children. Now it would never happen.

'It's strange how so much can be wiped out so quickly,' she said. 'Andrea had so much living to do. And so did Dom.'

'Yes. Now we know how people feel after car accidents and stuff when someone dies suddenly and nobody was expecting it.'

'I suppose so.'

A woman with two kids went past them. The kids were dressed in mini goth costumes and had skeleton masks. Maggie found it chilling.

'Oh, look at that! It's awful; they're only children,' she said.

Mark laughed. 'They're only having fun. You know what kids are like; they want to get in on the act with the goth thing. Or maybe they're rehearsing for next week. It's Halloween on Friday.'

Maggie shuddered. 'So it is. I used to enjoy that when I was a kid. Not anymore.'

'Someday you will, especially if you have kids of your own.'

Maggie tried to look ahead and imagine how she might feel about everything years into the future, but she found it impossible.

Three

It was early on Monday morning when Alice Granger knocked on Lesley's bedroom door.

'Lesley, can I come in?'

'Yeah.'

Granger went inside to find her daughter still in bed.

'Aren't you going to school today?'

Lesley turned over and yawned. 'Yeah, later. I don't have a class till History at ten o'clock and I'm not going to registration. It's a complete waste of time. It's just like when we had form period when we were younger. We never do anything.'

Granger would normally have challenged her daughter, but in the circumstances decided to pass it over. Lesley had gone straight to bed on the Saturday evening after the trauma down at the Old Ship, spending most of Sunday in her room, no doubt frantically texting her friends about what had happened.

'We need to talk about Saturday,' said Granger, sitting on a chair by the side of the bed.

'Do we have to? I'm okay about it, really.'

'I'm glad to hear that, but I was thinking with my police officer's hat on. I told you yesterday that a body has been found in the water near where the last shot was heard.'

'Yeah, well, I wasn't surprised. They were obviously mad.'

'That's why I need to talk to you: you're a witness, you see, so I need to ask you some questions.'

'God, I never thought about it like that.'

'If you don't like it I can get one of my detective constables to come out and interview you instead.'

'Are any of them fit?'

Granger laughed. 'Yes, I suppose one or two are, but I don't think they'll show any interest in you, especially knowing that you're my daughter. Can't you just tell me what you saw?'

'Okay.' Lesley sat up in bed and closed her eyes as she summoned up her memories of Saturday night. 'We were outside sitting at one of the tables. I was facing down Church Street and there were lots of people in goth stuff, you know. The street was packed with them. I saw this person coming down the street staggering from side to side. I thought they were drunk until they got close and I saw they were dressed like Dracula. They stopped near the pub and just looked towards it for a while, then pulled out a gun. I don't know what it was, but something made me think this was serious. I mean guns aren't really a part of goth costumes so what were they doing? Some people thought it was a joke and were laughing, but I called to my friends to get down. We were just getting under the table when they fired the first shot; then there was another. Then there was chaos: screaming, people running all over the place, chairs turned over. There was a third shot in the distance. We stayed underneath the table until everything went quiet and then crept out slowly. Mandy was in a right state, but I felt okay.'

'Why was that?'

'Because I don't think we were ever in danger. I don't think they meant to shoot anybody. They deliberately aimed at things rather than people. That's why I'm not surprised they killed themselves; they were obviously deranged. Anyway, after that I called you and we walked back to the bridge.'

'Right. I think you were very sharp to notice what was happening and very brave.'

Lesley shrugged. 'Maybe.'

'I just want to ask you a bit more about this figure. You keep referring to them as "they" even though they were dressed as Dracula. He's usually a man, isn't he?'

'Not necessarily. Women dress as vampires too. It was a fairly tall figure but there was a mask over the face, so it was impossible to tell whether it was a man or a woman.'

'They didn't say anything then?'

'No.'

'And nothing to give away whether it was male or female?'

'No, but as they found the body, don't you know that it was a man?'

'Probably, but we have to be very careful not to make assumptions: in this case that the figure you saw was the person whose body was found. Anyway, thank you for that. You'll have to write it up as a statement but that won't take long. You could do it now.' Granger got up from the chair. 'I've got to get off for work. So get out of bed now and tomorrow you'll have to make it to registration. I'm sure it can't be that bad.'

Lesley sighed and pulled the duvet back over her head.

'It's getting worse over there, Jim.' Back in Harrogate, Oldroyd was in Tom Walker's office. 'I saw it on the news last night; a body found in the harbour.'

'Yes, Tom, not entirely unexpected. He's the suspect, and he's been on the run and behaving strangely since the murder. He threatened to kill himself and it seems like he has. So this could be the end of it.'

Walker looked at him closely. 'You don't think so, though, do you?'

Oldroyd smiled. 'To be honest, no. It's an instinct thing again. You know how you sometimes feel after many years in this game. There are some things that don't ring true for me. I won't bore you with the details.'

'So you want to carry on over there for a while?'

'Yes, if that's okay. I have a plan of what I'd like to do and it may involve swapping DS Johnson for DS Carter at some point if that's okay?'

Walker grunted. 'Well, I've had such a glowing report from Inspector Granger over there about how helpful you've been and asking if the secondment can continue. It'll be a big feather in our cap if there is a twist to this case and you can crack it. So you'd better get over there. I'll be able to tell Watkins what an excellent force he's got here in Harrogate. He should be proud, but he's not interested in real police work, just bureaucracy and image. Do you know what the latest thing is? He's . . .'

Oldroyd usually found a way of subtly curtailing Walker's rants against his superior, but as Walker was allowing him to continue over in Whitby, he felt it judicious to hear his boss out on this occasion.

It was a little while before he could escape to the old Saab, where Louise and Steph were waiting for him. Louise was still insisting that she go back over to Whitby with him, despite her mother's pleas.

The drive over to the coast was even more subdued than the one on Thursday had been in response to Louise's urgent call. There was very little conversation throughout the journey except for Louise asking a few questions. She was still sceptical about the conclusions being reached in the official investigation.

'How do they know he killed himself anyway? Someone could have shot him and pushed him into the water.'

'Not impossible,' replied her dad. 'I can't say more at this point until I've spoken to Inspector Granger. It ties in with that text he sent to your friend though, doesn't it? It certainly sounds as if he was saying goodbye.'

'I know, but . . .' She shook her head, still refusing to accept what appeared to be what had happened.

As Oldroyd had told Walker, he'd expected Holgate's body to be found at some point, although he'd not said this to Louise. When Holgate had not been found alive or turned himself in after three days, the signs were not good. He was keen to find out more about the circumstances of his death and whether this development did finally solve his problems with the case or only added to them.

The weather had broken again. The sky was dark over Fylingdales Moor and when they descended into Eskdale at Sleights, they could see heavy clouds over the sea. Spots of rain appeared on the windscreen and by the time the Saab drew up at the flat, the rain was quite heavy and the wipers were on.

'Right then,' said Oldroyd. 'I'll be in contact later. Are you sure you're okay?'

'Stop sounding like Mum,' replied Louise as she got out of the car. 'I really want to see Maggie. I know she'll be feeling terrible. Bye and thanks for everything.'

She walked quickly through the rain to the door and waved as Oldroyd drove off.

'I don't think you need to worry about her, sir,' said Steph. 'She's pretty tough and determined. I wonder who she takes after?' She grinned at Oldroyd in the rear-view mirror.

'I haven't the faintest idea,' he said.

~

As she entered the house, Louise was met by Maggie in the hall. They embraced and started to cry.

'Oh God, I'm so pleased to see you. It's just dreadful,' sobbed Maggie. 'I can't bear to think about it anymore. I don't see how I'm ever going to get over it. Mark says I will but I don't see how.'

'Come on.' Louise led the way into the lounge and they sat down. 'You will get over it and so will I. Life goes on; we've got a lot of time ahead of us to recover and start afresh. We can't give up on life.'

'Yes, but how can we ever forget what's happened? Two of our friends are dead.'

'It's still raw and painful. We'll need help, and not just from our friends, but professional help.'

'You mean, counselling? Therapy?'

'Yes. We've been through awful things and we can't just ignore them.'

Maggie looked wary. 'Do you think so? I'm not sure. I've never had anything to do with stuff like that.'

'There's nothing to be ashamed of. I'm going to arrange something as soon as I get back to London.'

'Right. Talking of which, we have to leave here by tomorrow at eleven o'clock; the booking expires.'

'I know. I assume everyone's going back to London.'

'Yeah, I think so. They're all up there packing. The police say it's all right to leave. Me and Mark are going today, and I think the others are too; I can't see any point in waiting any longer. Aren't you going back, too?'

Louise hesitated. 'I don't know. I want to see how my dad and the others get on with the investigation.'

'Oh, I can't be bothered with that anymore. They're dead; it's all over. I don't understand it, I don't think I ever will and it makes me feel worse just to try. As you said, we've got to somehow try to put it all behind us, so don't hang around picking over it for too long. Where will you stay?'

'Not here; I'm going to go back to Leeds and I'll stay with my mum for a while. Then I'm in striking distance if I'm needed or something happens.'

'Well, rather you than me. I want to get away from here. Jack was saying it's a shame, but he doesn't think he'll be coming back here any time soon. I feel the same.'

At that moment, Jack came into the room. 'Did I hear someone taking my name in vain?' He laughed.

'You're in a good mood,' observed Louise, looking at him suspiciously.

Jack looked sheepish and raised his hands. 'Yeah, sorry. It's awful that Dom's dead, but I can't say I was surprised. I suppose I feel like this because I'm leaving here soon, if you want me to be honest. I can't wait to put some distance between myself and this town. It's sad because it's a lovely little place, but that's how I feel. Anyway . . . Hi . . . How are you?' He came over and gave Louise a hug.

'Okay,' said Louise, whose hug back was half-hearted. 'Some of us are obviously more upset about Dom's death than others.'

Jack pulled back. 'Hey, don't you start! She was having a go at me yesterday.' He pointed at Maggie. 'Just because I was with Andrea for a while before she got together with Dom. Okay, he wasn't my favourite person in the world, but I didn't want to see him dead. If I hated him that much, why would I stay part of this group?'

He'd worked himself up into an angry state. The calm he'd previously shown was clearly only on the surface.

Mark came in. 'What's going on? I heard shouting.'

'Oh, nothing, forget it,' said Jack with a wave of his hand. 'Sorry, I lost my temper. We're all on edge. I just can't wait to get away from this damned place,' he repeated and then stalked out of the room. His footsteps could be heard on the stairs.

'Hi, Louise,' said Mark, looking at the door as though to make sure Jack had gone. 'Wow! What was all that about?'

'Nothing,' said Maggie wearily. 'Have you packed your stuff?'

'Just about.'

'Where's Ben?' asked Louise.

'In his room as well. Packing, I think.'

'I'm worried about him.'

'Are you?'

'Yeah. He's had the worst time of any of us: he tried to save Andrea and he was holding her when she died. Then he volunteered to identify Dom's body. Sights and experiences like that can make a big impression. He seems to be by himself a lot. I hope he's not dwelling on those images and getting depressed.'

'He seemed okay earlier. I'll call him.' Maggie went across to Ben's room and knocked on the door. 'Ben, are you okay in there? Louise is back.'

'Okay,' came a voice from within, before Ben finally appeared, looking bleary-eyed.

'Hi, Louise.' He gave her a hug. 'I was asleep. I can't stay awake at the moment. I suppose it's the stress and I'm not sleeping well at night.' He yawned.

'Me neither,' said Maggie also yawning.

'Are you leaving now as well?' Louise asked Ben.

'Yeah, I don't think there's any point in hanging around. I'm needed at work too. I've got some teaching lined up starting in a couple of days and I need to prepare for it.'

'Right.' Louise sounded a little sad.

At that moment Jack came back into the room still looking shamefaced. 'Look, why don't we all go down to that café and get a bite to eat before we leave. It's brightening up outside. It would be a nice way to end all this instead of us arguing and then just sloping off by ourselves.'

They all agreed and soon they were walking down the hill past the park together for the last time.

~

'Well, sir, it's all kicked off here over the weekend and no mistake. I've got lots to report . . . and now my daughter's involved in this, too.'

It was lunchtime, and Oldroyd and Steph were in Inspector Granger's office at the Whitby station. She had called them straight in following the dramatic events of Saturday evening and the discovery on Sunday morning. She explained to a puzzled Oldroyd how her daughter had been at the pub where the incident had happened.

'Oh dear,' said Oldroyd smiling. 'I know the feeling. As a police officer you're always hyper-vigilant about your own kids doing anything wrong and coming into contact with the police. It's not fair, though. Why should we be held to higher standards of parenting?'

'You're right, sir, but that's the way it is. She's been very quiet since Saturday so I'm hoping this quells her desire for going out on the town. We'll see.'

'Don't count on it.'

Granger laughed. 'I won't. Anyway, I'll just run through the details and confirm everything that's happened.' She referred to a summary on her screen. 'First off, the body of Dominic Holgate, wanted in connection with the murder of Andrea Barnes, was found in the harbour area yesterday by a fisherman. Holgate had a bullet wound to the temple and was also submerged in the water. It appears that he shot himself at the harbour edge at the end of a wooden jetty and then fell into the water. His body was identified by Ben Morton.'

A belt and braces suicide, thought Oldroyd.

'We've got divers looking for the gun, and I'm waiting for the report from forensics,' continued Granger. 'We assume death was from the bullet wound and not drowning. The police were called out to an incident on Saturday evening at a pub in Church Street. A person answering the description of the dead person walked up to the Old Ship Inn, fired two shots towards the inn and then ran down an alley towards the sea. Witnesses said the person seemed to be very upset: shouting things out and crying. Then another shot was heard. Police were called but found nothing.'

'Did the onlookers get a good look at the face?' asked Oldroyd.

'No. It was dark. The figure was wearing a hood and maybe a mask, which he presumably removed before he shot himself. None of the witnesses said they would be able to confirm that the dead person was the figure they saw, but the circumstantial evidence is very strong, don't you think, sir? Especially as we have evidence from another text message sent to Maggie Hinton.'

Oldroyd sat back, frowning. 'Yes, my daughter told me about that. Maggie did the right thing this time, informing you. Was anything else found on the body?'

'Just the usual in his pockets: money, wallet with cards and so on. No phone though.'

Oldroyd raised his eyebrows. 'Really? That was the phone from which he sent the text messages. I'm surprised he didn't have it with him. It's unusual for a person of that age not to be carrying their phone.'

'We assume it must have dropped into the water. We're searching for it, though if it has been in the water it won't be able to tell us very much.'

Oldroyd thought for a moment. 'Well. It seems that Holgate couldn't live with what he'd done and was losing his rationality. He turned up in an agitated state, fired the gun he'd brought to Whitby at random, shot himself and his body was found next day. And so ends this unhappy story: a terrible murder committed in a fit of rage or something and then the tormented, unstable perpetrator commits suicide. At least that's what we're expected to think.'

'I see you're still sceptical, sir.' Granger smiled, remembering how Oldroyd doggedly pursued every loose end in a case until he was satisfied he had the right solution. 'You'll be interested to know that the substance found in that sarcophagus was human blood. We're checking it against Holgate's and if it proves to be a match that will be interesting.'

'Indeed: it would strongly suggest that his attack was planned and he hid inside that thing, but how his blood got there is still a mystery unless we stay with the theory that he cut himself when he attacked the victim. Have you managed to contact the owner of that escape room yet? We need to ask him about that trick sarcophagus.'

'No, but the search is ongoing.' Granger clicked the mouse, closing one file and opening another. 'Next item: I have some reports from the Met. First, from the detectives who searched the Tower Hamlets apartment rented by Holgate and Barnes.' Granger was looking at her screen. 'They found nothing that could be connected to the case. Nothing that might suggest a motive for Holgate to murder his partner. No diaries, letters, notes and nothing on the computer. They also spoke to people living in adjoining apartments, but none reported hearing any serious rows and nobody saw any evidence of violence.

'Another team spoke to work colleagues of the couple. Holgate worked in a media production company in Hackney. Everyone he worked with had nothing but good words for him and some had met Barnes on social outings. These latter confirmed that the couple argued sometimes but it never got really serious. Barnes was part of a female theatre group based in Tower Hamlets. According to the person who ran the group, she was, I quote: "A very special person and a crucial member of the team who will be badly missed." Apparently quite a number of the women there were in tears when the detectives spoke to them. So there's nothing here either except . . .' She scrolled down the page while Oldroyd and Steph waited with anticipation.

'One of the women Barnes worked with reported seeing her in a café near the theatre group's office with a man she didn't recognise. They were easy and friendly with each other and the woman says he may have given her a packet of something, but she was too far away to be sure.' Granger stopped reading from the report and turned to Oldroyd and Steph. 'It's very thin stuff, but I suppose she could have been having an affair and Holgate found out. Maybe they rowed about it, but kept the details from their friends.'

'That would be understandable, sir,' added Steph. 'They'd want to try to resolve it without anybody else knowing what had happened, but maybe they failed. Barnes wouldn't stop seeing this other man and eventually Holgate lost it with her.'

'Yes, you're right,' said Oldroyd, sounding reluctant and fidgeting in his chair. 'It all fits together nicely. Too nicely for me. I've got so many warning bells in my head, the jangling's driving me mad.'

'What worries you in particular, sir?' asked Granger.

Oldroyd raised his arms and dropped them in a gesture of dissatisfaction. 'A lot of things. Judging from the despairing and remorseful texts his friends received, the murder appears to have been committed by Holgate in a fit of anger, or maybe jealousy now we've heard about this other man. He regretted the attack immediately afterwards. But then how come he had a knife with him and hid in the sarcophagus? That clearly suggests planning. Then what's all this about meeting his friends at the church late at night and then ducking out at the last minute without a word? Very strange. Then we find out he had a gun, which was probably the one he got from his uncle, but why did he bring it with him to Whitby? Did that mean he felt threatened by someone? Or was it part of some plan? Finally, on the night he killed himself, presumably with this same gun, he created a rumpus first, outside a pub, by firing off the gun. Why? And then we can't find the phone; wouldn't it be in his pocket?'

'Some of that behaviour would be consistent with someone who had become irrational. Maybe through guilt and despair?' suggested Granger.

'Maybe.' Oldroyd sighed. 'I'm always suspicious when we try to explain difficulties away by ascribing them to madness; it's too easy. But anyway, I defer to you, Alice, as it's your case. If you think you have sufficient evidence to wrap things up, then fine. But I have my doubts. What about you, Steph?'

'I agree there are some odd things in the case, sir, but surely the evidence is unavoidable that Holgate stabbed Barnes whether he planned it or not. He did it in front of reliable witnesses and then left the building. Whether he hid in the sarcophagus first, I don't know. Maybe he'd been mentally unbalanced for some time; his later behaviour certainly suggests that. We found the gun holster and ammunition, and if the gun is retrieved it is likely to be the gun he brought to Whitby and which he killed himself with. If he was paranoid about some non-existent threat, then that would be consistent with his failing mental health.'

'Very good. So you also think the strange elements can be accounted for by the murderer's mental state?'

'I think it's likely, sir. It's hard to get away from the evidence we have regarding the murder and suicide. Sometimes people success-fully conceal their failing mental health, don't they?'

'They do and I tend to agree with Steph, sir,' said Granger, 'but I'm happy to carry on with the investigation until you're satisfied. What do you think we should do?'

'I'd like to find out a lot more about the past lives of all the people involved and see if we can turn up something interesting. The past is so often the key to unlocking these mysteries.'

'If there is a mystery, sir,' added Steph with a smile.

'Yes, well, I'm not infallible and I don't mind being proved wrong . . . but I want to know a lot more about who they all are, what they've done, where they've been. And by the way' – he paused and raised a hand – 'I don't want either of you to think I'm doing this just because my daughter has doubts. I definitely believe we need to keep the investigation going.'

'Of course, sir,' replied Granger, though there was the hint of a smile on her face too as she didn't entirely believe her former boss and mentor. As a parent herself she knew that there was always a powerful tendency to humour your children's ideas.

'By the way, how did you get on with the parents?' asked Oldroyd as the meeting came to an end.

Granger frowned. 'Not pleasant. The mother was almost speechless with grief and kept bursting into tears. The father was angry and he seemed to be taking his grief out on Whitby; claimed he hated the place. Apparently Andrea had an uncle here who her father described as a rogue; said he had to close his business in Leeds because he was on the fiddle.'

'Louise told us that Andrea had mentioned an uncle in Whitby.'

'Ian Withington. He has a jeweller's shop in Church Street – Whitby jet and all that.'

Steph looked up. 'We found a necklace containing Whitby jet amongst Barnes's things in the flat,' she said.

'Nothing unusual in that,' said Granger. 'Mr Barnes said his daughter often visited her uncle here.'

'Did she?' said Oldroyd thoughtfully. 'I think we should pay him a visit. Does he actually have a record of criminal activity?'

'Not as far as we know, sir,' said Granger. 'But as you know, that doesn't mean he hasn't been up to no good.'

~

Oldroyd and Steph walked down the length of Church Street to Withington's Whitby Jeweller's shop, which was housed in an old building near the steps up to the abbey. The rain had completely cleared and the sky was now bright. The sun glinted on the puddles in the street.

The Goth Weekend was over, and though the streets were no longer full of people in elaborate costumes there were still a few goths around. Gothic was now part of Whitby's identity throughout the year, and it tied in well with the Dracula tradition.

On the way to Withington's they passed a number of other jeweller's shops, all of which were at least partly trading in the eponymous black gemstone for which the town was famous.

'Do you know,' observed Oldroyd, 'Whitby jet is actually a form of coal? It's made from wood that has been under extreme pressure. It's been used in Britain to make ornaments since the Neolithic period.'

'Really, sir?' replied Steph with a very slight edge of sarcasm and a smile on her face. She had a deep admiration for her boss in many ways, even if his enthusiasm for all things Yorkshire at times descended a little into mansplaining. She had learned to subtly undermine this.

Oldroyd looked at her and frowned. 'Sorry, I'm at it again, aren't I? Giving you an unwanted, probably boring lecture about something.'

Steph laughed. She approved of the way a man of Oldroyd's generation was prepared to learn and change. And that he was prepared to take it from a woman who was his subordinate in rank. 'It's never boring, sir, but it's great that you're more aware you're doing it.'

'Good! Who knows? Someday I might be certified as fully "woke"!'

Steph laughed again just as they arrived at the shop. Their attention was immediately caught by the window display, which combined craftsmanship in silver and jet with a gothic emphasis on spiders of all sizes fashioned into earrings, brooches and ornaments. Some were on silver webs and all had heads and abdomens made of the black jet. The centre piece was a magnificent and terrifying creature of impressive size attached to a necklace. In addition to an enormous heart-shaped black abdomen and diamond-shaped head, sections of its wonderfully long, curved and delicate legs were also made of jet.

Steph shuddered. 'God, that's creepy, sir. I wouldn't fancy wearing any of that stuff. It might appeal to my sister, though. She went through a goth phase when she was a teenager, and she still sometimes dresses in black and even kept the light-purple hair. She used to hang around outside the Corn Exchange in Leeds on a Saturday afternoon. Drove my mum mad, said she looked like a witch.'

'It has a terrible beauty about it, though, don't you think?' said Oldroyd, admiring the huge spider necklace. 'I'll bet that one costs a bob or two. Anyway, let's go in – if we dare!' He pretended to tremble as he opened the door.

Inside they found the goth and black-jet theme elaborated in greater variety in the jewellery cabinets. There were black bats with silvery wings and skulls with jet eyeballs; a bracelet was laced with silver skulls and black jet roses. The first assistant they saw was wearing black jet spider earrings. The detectives showed their ID.

'We'd like to speak to Mr Withington, please.'

'I'll get him for you.'

Oldroyd looked around the shop. 'Never has the goth who is serious about ornamentation been so well catered for,' he observed with his usual wit.

'At a cost, though, sir. Have you seen the price tags?' replied Steph.

The assistant returned. 'He says to come into his office.' Oldroyd and Steph followed her into a back room where a sharp-faced man with reddish hair and a moustache turned from his computer. Oldroyd thought he looked like the classic spiv as he introduced himself and Steph.

'Ooh, well, I don't often get a visit from the police,' said Withington in a pretentious and false accent, which Oldroyd had heard before and always described as 'posh Yorkshire'. The clumsy combination of Yorkshire and RP vowels grated on him. 'But I suppose that's a good thing. What can I do for you? Is it to do with Andrea's murder? Absolutely shocking. My sister will be devastated. I've been trying to summon up the courage to call her; not an easy thing to do.'

'No,' replied Oldroyd, thinking that Withington didn't seem very devastated himself. 'We've spoken to your sister and her husband.'

'How was she?'

'As well as to be expected in the circumstances.'

'Good. Well, her husband's always hated me. I don't know what he's been saying but I can imagine the type of thing.'

'We know about the dispute concerning your mother's will, but I'm more interested in your relationship with Andrea. I understand you saw quite a bit of her?'

Withington shrugged his shoulders. 'Well, I don't know about that. She always came to see me when she was in town and we got on well. She didn't share her father's attitude towards me.'

'And how often did she come to Whitby?'

'Every few months; she liked it here, being by the sea.'

'Did you know her partner, Dominic Holgate?'

'He's the suspect, isn't he?'

'He was, but he was found dead in the harbour on Sunday.'

'Good God, I hadn't heard that! I didn't know him well. He came into the shop with her a few times. They were based in London, weren't they? I know she had this flat in Leeds she inherited from her aunt – that's her father's sister – but I don't think the boyfriend came up with her much.'

'Apparently they rowed a lot. Did she ever talk about that?'

'No.'

'Did she talk about any enemies she had? Were you aware of anyone who'd wish her any harm?'

'No. Andrea was a nice person. I can't see who would want to attack her. I can't imagine why her partner would do this.'

Oldroyd took up a piece of jet jewellery from Withington's desk: a small spider with a jet body in a delicate silver web.

'She was fond of this Whitby jet jewellery, wasn't she?' Oldroyd looked at Withington directly when he said this and detected a slight flicker of alarm in his eyes.

'Yes. She got a few pieces from me; one for a birthday present, I think, and the others at cost price. It's a beautiful gemstone, jet, don't you think?'

'Yes. I notice you've got plenty of the goth stuff in for the festival.'

Withington was warming up as he moved onto a sales pitch. 'Oh yes, Chief Inspector. You have to give the public what they want. But it's not just for the festival. We sell that stuff all year round now, just as you'll find the goth outfitters are open all the time. We've got a number of really talented jewellery workers making our stuff; it's the best there is. Have a good look before you go.' He looked at Steph. 'I'm sure you'll find something you like. There's a long tradition of making it here in Whitby. It's unique.'

Steph gave him a rather icy smile. 'I don't think it's my style actually.'

'Well, we've got lots of other stuff in different styles, not just goth.'

'I may come back when I'm off duty,' said Steph, bringing an end to his patter.

'I understand you used to have a shop in Leeds,' asked Oldroyd, and his keen eyes searched Withington's face from which the smile vanished.

'Yes I did.' Suddenly his speech became terse.

'And what happened to it?'

112

'I saw the opportunities of getting into the Whitby jet market over here.'

'Wasn't that a bit of a come down? This is a little backwater in your line of business compared to Leeds I would have thought. I wonder if there were other reasons why you left.'

For the first time since they'd started questioning him, Withington became angry and defensive. 'This is Fred again, isn't it? I wish he'd stop spreading rumours about me. I suppose he told you I was doing dodgy stuff.'

'Something like that.'

'Well, it's not true, Chief Inspector. My move here was entirely due to what I saw as a business opportunity.'

Oldroyd gave him a long stare. 'I see. Okay, well, that's all for now. If you remember anything you think we ought to know please contact us.' Oldroyd gave Withington a card and prepared to leave. But then he turned back. 'Oh, by the way, when did Andrea last visit you here?'

Withington hesitated. 'She, she came in on Tuesday I think it was. Yes, Tuesday. It's terrible to think I won't see her in here again.'

Oldroyd shook his head. 'It must be. Thank you for your cooperation.'

'Very interesting,' remarked Oldroyd as he and Steph walked back down Church Street. 'You noticed how he hesitated before answering that last question?'

'Yes, sir, it seemed to unnerve him.'

'It did. That's an old trick of mine, you've seen it before: pretend you've finished the interview and they lower their guard. Then you suddenly give them the rapier thrust of another unexpected question and they stumble if they've got something to hide. He had to make a quick decision whether to tell me or not and probably decided we'd find out anyway.'

'What is he trying to conceal do you think, sir?'

'I think there was something going on with this jet jewellery and Andrea. You notice he said she came in on Tuesday, but that was the day before they all gathered here for their long weekend. So why did she come up here a day early? I can't believe it was just to see her uncle.'

'He's also not being straight about his Leeds shop, is he, sir?'

'No, and we must get that investigated.' He sighed. 'I've still no idea how all this might fit together, if it does.'

They'd reached the harbour swing bridge, which had moved across to let a tall yacht through. Traffic stood by the flashing yellow lights high above the water while the tall masts and white sails moved slowly along in a ghostly manner as if by themselves and disconnected from the invisible yacht below as it made its way to the open sea. It gave Oldroyd an idea of what he and Deborah could do when she came over.

~

Withington went to the door of his office and watched Oldroyd and Steph leave the shop with a look of relief mingled with anxiety. He shut the door, sat down at his desk again and picked up a brooch containing a particularly macabre spider design in black jet. He toyed with this, thought for a while and then reached for his phone and called a number. He sat back as he spoke and continued to fondle the spider brooch as if it had a calming effect on him.

'I've just had the police here asking questions about Andrea . . . Yes, I've been expecting it, but let's just stay calm . . . Yes . . . if they track you down then just tell them what we agreed . . . Look, they've got absolutely nothing on us so don't worry . . . Yes, I've no doubt they'll be looking into my past, but I'll handle that . . . Yes, I'm sure. Okay . . . Bye.'

He put his phone back into his pocket and placed the brooch back on his desk. His face was still grim. He didn't like the look of that Chief Inspector; the man seemed far too sharp. He would make a formidable opponent.

~

When Oldroyd and Steph arrived back at the flat, there were cases in the hallway. It seemed that everyone was ready to leave. Jack was loading his stuff into a nippy-looking sports car parked outside the apartment. When he saw Oldroyd and Steph, he stopped what he was doing and came over to them.

'Hi. I'm off soon, and so's everybody else . . . I think.' He turned to Oldroyd and Steph. 'I just wanted to say thank you to you both for coming over and, you know, helping with things. I know you're involved because of Louise, but I'm sure you've been a great help to the police here.'

Oldroyd nodded.

'Thanks,' said Steph.

'It's a pity,' continued Jack, 'that there wasn't more for you to do. It's pretty clear-cut really, isn't it? Dom had some kind of blow up or breakdown or whatever you want to call it, lost it with Andrea and then killed himself.'

Steph nodded.

'It certainly looks that way,' said Oldroyd.

'I was lucky that I wasn't here so I didn't have to go through it all.' He shook his head. 'To think that I was annoyed that I couldn't get here in time for the escape room. It's going to take the others a long time to recover, especially Ben. He's really not been himself since it happened, but neither have any of us really.'

'I'm sure you're right. Anyway, we'll just go in and see the others. Are you going straight back to London?'

'Yes.'

In the lounge, Louise was talking to Maggie and Mark. They all looked up at the detectives as they came in.

'Hello, Mr Oldroyd,' said Maggie. 'Have a seat. Mark's got something to tell you before we leave.'

Mark looked uncomfortable. 'I'm not sure how relevant this is, but Louise said you should know. The fact is, Dom cheated when he was a student. He plagiarised essays including some of mine. We were on the same course.'

'I see,' said Oldroyd as he sat down. 'You've done the right thing. Any information in a case like this is useful and maybe more important than you think. Do you know of any other victims other than you?'

'No, but I think there must have been some because he was suspended for a while and I think he was threatened with expulsion so he must have offended more than once. It's such a big deal in the academic world, any kind of cheating like that.'

'Yes, and it must have been a bad experience for you. The fact that he involved you in something like that must have made you angry,' said Oldroyd, looking at Mark very directly.

Mark could see where this was going. 'Yes, but I had no desire to hurt him. I just let the authorities deal with it. He apologised in the end. It was quite a while ago now and we decided to forget about it when I met him again through Maggie.'

'Okay. I will report this back to Inspector Granger who's in charge of the investigation, but you're still free to go.'

At this, everyone stood up and made to leave. It was an emotional moment after all they'd been through. As they departed, singly and in pairs, Louise and Maggie hugged each other and shed some tears. Jack zoomed off in his sports car, and Mark and Maggie in Mark's old Citroen. Ben was the last to leave. He was walking to the station and going on the train to visit his parents in Manchester.

'Don't stay around too long,' he said to Louise. 'We need to keep checking on each other.'

Louise smiled at him. She liked the fact that he was so sensitive.

As she gave Ben a hug, Oldroyd glanced at her, wondering what exactly her feelings for Ben were, but he didn't say anything. He offered to give Ben a lift to the station but he refused, saying he wanted the exercise.

'God, it feels really weird in here now everyone's gone,' said Louise as she, Steph and Oldroyd sat back in the lounge.

'Why don't you pack your stuff, love? It's time we were getting back. Are you sure you want to stick around like this and stay with your mother in Leeds?'

'Yes, Dad, at least for a while. I want to see this through. There's more to find out yet, I'm convinced of it.' She went off to her room.

'I think she's right,' said Oldroyd as soon as she'd left. 'But I don't think we're going to find the answer here. My plan is to pursue them all down to London and see what emerges from a thorough investigation into each one of them.'

'You think one or more of them is involved, sir?' replied Steph. 'I must say, it seems unlikely to me. They all seem such nice young people.'

Oldroyd smiled. 'Yes, I know how you feel and Inspector Granger probably agrees with you, but there's something too easy about it all to me. Now, when I said that we'll pursue them, I actually meant that Andy will, though he doesn't know it yet. I'm going to swap you and him to keep DCS Walker happy. I don't think he'll want to lend out two of his detective sergeants to a Whitby police investigation. This is where Andy's London experience will come in handy. I'll be coming back here to help Inspector Granger.' He saw a brief look of disappointment on Steph's face, but she was too professional to express it. He knew she enjoyed working with him.

'Good plan, sir. I'm sure he'll be keen to help.'

'Don't worry, I've also got some jobs for you too: looking into that jeweller's past and keeping an eye on Louise. She's going to be in Leeds for a while so you could call in on your way home sometimes and see how she's doing.'

Steph smiled. That was much better.

~

Jack smiled to himself as he sped round the Malton bypass on his way to York, before heading south on the A1. The car was handling very well. He loved it; it so fitted in with his image: the debonair man about town conducting a high-octane social life.

It had been a difficult few days in Whitby, not at all what he was used to. But he had acquitted himself effectively and managed to conceal certain things which he wished to remain secret. Now that Dom's body had been found he didn't expect any more trouble from the police. Once he got back to London he would be able to resume his normal life.

He was glad that he'd not been there to witness the murder; that would have been very traumatic. And then Dom's suicide. To lose friends was always a bad thing, but, hey, let's move on, he thought to himself. He was sure the group would carry on without Dom and Andrea. There were lots of things to look forward to. He pressed his foot down and the car surged forward. The further he travelled south and away from Whitby, the better he felt.

~

Mark and Maggie were proceeding at a more sedate pace in the Citroen and had reached the market town of Pickering.

'This is a lovely little place,' said Maggie. 'I sometimes think I'd like to live in a little country town like this someday, where you could walk to things like shops and stuff and get to know a lot of people.'

'Who then get to find out about everything you're doing,' replied Mark. 'I think I might find it a bit claustrophobic. Anyway, forget it in the south – houses in places like this would be right out of our range.'

'I suppose so.'

'You're sounding a bit middle-aged today.' He laughed. 'Is it time to settle down? Am I the lucky man?'

Maggie kept looking at the pretty old streets, the shoppers and the little parks. 'You might be.' She turned to him. 'I feel different about things, you know, life and stuff after all this.'

'How?'

'Well, you never know what's going to happen, do you? You've got to get on with life and do the things you want to do. I've drifted a bit since Oxford and my travels. I think I'm going to look at doing an MA. In London somewhere. Louise has inspired me. I've got the money saved up and I can carry on part time in the café.'

'What will you do it in?'

'Maybe something to do with social work. I enjoyed working in the refuge. Don't worry, I'll stay in London.'

They'd left Pickering and were now crossing the vale named after the town towards Malton. Cows and sheep grazed in the flat fields divided by hedgerows.

'It's been nice to see the countryside as well as the sea,' said Maggie, enjoying the views.

Mark looked around without enthusiasm. 'Yeah, but you can't have everything. You'd get bored out here after a while and where would you practise your social work?'

'You'd be surprised. Don't think that all the social problems are in the inner cities. There's a lot of rural poverty too.'

'You wouldn't think so around here judging by the gorgeous-looking villages we've passed through and the number of Range Rovers on the road.'

She looked at him and realised he was teasing her. 'Get lost,' she said, and leaned her head against his shoulder. 'Louise's dad was right, by the way,' she said after a while. 'You did the right thing to tell him about Dom's plagiarism.'

Mark shifted in his seat. 'Yeah, maybe. It's probably made me a suspect though.'

She raised her head and looked at him. 'A suspect? You weren't even there when it happened.'

'No, but I could have orchestrated it from a distance,' he said in a mockingly sinister voice.

'Rubbish,' replied Maggie, putting her head back against his shoulder. 'Anyway, you explained to him that it didn't bother you that much. You're hardly going to murder someone about a stolen essay from years ago, are you?'

'No,' replied Mark tersely; there was an angry glint in his eye. 'I think Louise's dad isn't happy with what seem to be the facts of the case.'

'Oh, I suppose he's just humouring her. She still won't give up the idea that somehow it didn't happen the way we saw it. I think she's in denial. I told her as much before we left. I expect her dad'll go along with it for a while until she realises it's nonsense.'

'Maybe,' said Mark. 'But I don't think we've heard the last of it or of him.'

~

It was a circuitous route to Manchester by rail from Whitby, involving a slow train to Middlesbrough, a change for York and then another change at Yorkshire's old capital to the slightly faster Trans

Pennine service across the hills to Lancashire. But Ben was glad he wasn't driving. He was still feeling utterly exhausted after all that had happened. He hoped he would never have to go through anything like that again.

A couple of days with his parents would be very refreshing, he thought, as he relaxed in his seat and watched the countryside of Eskdale pass by. Then he would have to get back to London, try to forget what had happened in Whitby and focus on his affairs in the capital. There were some important things he needed to do. He'd been struggling to get by on his part-time teaching contract for some time. The pay rate was poor and his art sales had been disappointing recently. It was so competitive in London to get any gallery space and what you had to pay often cancelled out any earnings from sales. Now he had thought of a way to do things differently. His phone rang. He looked at the caller ID and frowned.

He answered the phone. 'Hi . . . Is everything okay? Yes, don't worry, it's all fine . . . I'm on the train – I'll call you when I get to Manchester . . . It'll be several hours . . . Yes, okay – speak to you later.'

He ended the call, shook his head and returned to looking out at the countryside. After a while he nodded off and only woke when the train arrived in Middlesbrough.

~

It was late at the end of another long day when Oldroyd, Steph and Louise arrived back in Harrogate. Leaving Louise in the car where she was dozing, Oldroyd and Steph went into HQ and found Andy in the office.

'Okay, Andy, make a cup of tea, will you? It's been a long drive. Perhaps we might even be allowed a biscuit.' He turned to Steph with a questioning look. Steph had the key to the cupboard where the biscuits were kept, and she doled them out sparingly.

'Just one,' she said with a smile.

'How have things been over here?' asked Oldroyd as Andy put on the electric kettle.

'Fine, sir. Fairly quiet, luckily. I've checked in on DCS Walker a couple of times and he's happy.'

'Good.' As they drank their tea, Oldroyd explained his plan to Andy. 'Steph thinks the case is over,' he said, nodding towards her. 'Holgate's dead, apparently suicide. All the evidence points to him being the murderer. But I'm not sure we have the full story about what happened and the people most likely to lead us to further insights are the other members of that group, including the ones who weren't actually in the escape room that day. They're not the only suspects, but they are the people who knew Holgate and Barnes and may have had motives to commit murder. I know it's a long shot, but I want you to go down to London and investigate them. There have only been very cursory enquiries into them so far and I'm sure your old mates at the Met will give you a hand. Find out anything you can about their pasts and their lives in London going back to their student days and even before. We've all seen many times how often the answer to a mystery lies in the past. Sometimes the distant past.'

Andy had sat quietly listening. Now he looked at Steph and took in a deep breath. 'Sir, I'm sorry to have to say this, but your daughter Louise is part of that group. Have you got good grounds for eliminating her from any suspicion?'

Steph flinched as she saw how this hit Oldroyd hard. It was very bold of Andy to ask the question. Oldroyd also took a deep breath before replying.

'The honest answer is no. I haven't got any information that completely exonerates her so she's not eliminated. If there was some

122

plot going on I'm unable to say for sure that she wasn't part of it.' He was speaking very slowly as if it was a real effort to get the words out. 'On the other hand, I don't regard her as a likely suspect, mainly because if she was involved, I don't think she would have been keen for me to help to solve the case.' He sounded as if he was carefully reassuring himself. There was silence for a moment and then he turned to Andy. 'That was brave of you. Well done. It had to be said.'

'Sorry if it came out a bit abrupt, sir. It wasn't easy.'

'Don't apologise.' He smiled. 'That's the way I've taught you: don't defer to authority in matters like that. You're actually doing me a favour in case anybody ever accuses me of protecting her. It'll be on record that I'm not and she will be on the list of people who need to be looked into, though she's staying in Leeds at the moment and won't be in London. So I'll be asking Steph to keep an eye on her.'

'Okay, sir,' Andy said.

Oldroyd sighed and looked relieved. 'Where are those biscuits? I think I deserve another in the circumstances.'

'Very well, sir,' said Steph, laughing.

Oldroyd continued as he munched a ginger biscuit. 'You've still got some work to do,' he said to Steph. 'Though be careful it doesn't take up too much of your time. You're back here now and working for this station, so any work on cases here must come first, but try to get to Leeds and investigate Withington's past. What kind of a jeweller's shop did he have? And find out what happened to make him scarper over to Whitby. Make sure you report your findings to Inspector Granger as well as to me. And the same goes for you, Andy.'

'That's fine, sir,' said Steph. 'If I get here early in the morning I can leave early and do some investigating on my way home.'

'Good. Well, it might turn out to be a wild goose chase, but at least we'll know we were thorough.'

Oldroyd had a final word with Steph before he left. 'As I said, I also want you to watch over Louise. Check that she's okay, and also ask her some more about her activities and relationships with the group.' He paused. The next thing was hard to say. 'If at any time you have any grounds for suspecting she may have been involved in anything untoward, then you must report it immediately to Inspector Granger. Understood?' He sighed. 'That's it; I've said it.'

'Yes, sir, and don't worry. You're doing the right thing by covering yourself like this but I'm sure that nothing of that nature will come up. I'd stake anything on the fact that Louise is completely innocent.'

'Yes, I'm sure you're right,' replied Oldroyd, unable to contemplate any other outcome.

~

That evening, Oldroyd and Deborah were relaxing with a bottle of wine in Oldroyd's flat. Dusk had seemed to fall rapidly and Oldroyd got a sense of approaching winter as he looked out at the twilight early evening sky. A crow flapped past, a black outline against the darkening sky. It made him shiver.

'The clocks will be going back next week,' he observed in a rather glum tone of voice. 'It's going to get dark really early in the evening.'

'Well, no need to be melancholy about it. It's nice and cosy in here. Winter has its own charms.'

'Yes.' He drank some wine.

'Are you okay?'

'Not really.' He told her about the conversation with Andy and Steph about Louise. 'Of course I don't suspect her, but I can't leave her out, and I can't really tell her she's being investigated. It makes me feel awful, supervising an investigation into my own daughter.'

'You must have known something like this would happen when you agreed to help that inspector over there. It must be very unusual for any police officer to be associated with a case in which a close relative is involved.'

'Of course it is. It's only happened because of my senior position. Also that I know Granger and she wanted me to help, plus Walker was understanding. I'm beginning to wish it hadn't happened this way. Maybe I would have been better staying out of it.'

'In the end, you didn't have a choice, though. No parent is going to ignore a call from their daughter like that.'

Oldroyd looked thoughtfully into his glass. 'I suppose not. It just feels such a betrayal that I'm having to get Steph to investigate her surreptitiously while also checking if she's okay.'

'She's not stupid, though. She must realise that she's part of that group of friends which is being looked into.'

'Maybe. I don't know and I can't talk to her about it. At this point that would be really compromising. All she knows is that, like her, I'm not satisfied with aspects of this case and I'm continuing to work with Inspector Granger.'

'Is that why she's staying up here and not going back to London?'

'Yes. She wants to be on hand if anything happens. She'll be fine at Julia's for a while. I think she's going to look up some of her Leeds friends.'

'Well, never mind. I'll be there to keep up your morale.'

'Yes, it will make a big difference. I've planned some interesting activities, but I'm not telling you about them.'

'Good! I like surprises. It's great to be having a little holiday late in the year like this. I've managed to rearrange my sessions with clients for a few days.'

Deborah was travelling back to Whitby with Oldroyd the following day and staying with him. A hotel had been booked.

'Good. I've still got to work with Granger, but I'll manage some time in between.'

'That's fine. But just remember, Jim, you can't be right every time. If nothing crops up soon you'll have to accept that the case is simpler than you imagined. Don't make it into an ego thing.'

'No, I won't,' replied Oldroyd, but he still felt in his bones that there was more to discover.

～

Andy and Steph lived in an apartment in a converted warehouse overlooking the River Aire in Leeds. They liked living in the vibrant centre of the city and were enjoying a drink in a hipster bar near the Corn Exchange.

'That was very brave of you this afternoon to confront the boss with the possibility of his daughter being a suspect,' said Steph.

'Well, I thought we needed to get it into the open and it would come better from me as I haven't really been involved up to now,' replied Andy.

'You did the right thing. I know it's hard, but he appreciates being challenged when there's a good reason. I did it during that Redmire Hall case, and he thanked me afterwards. He doesn't want "yes" men and women. He wants people who think for themselves and speak out.'

'Good,' said Andy laughing. 'I'll have scored a few points today then.'

'You will.'

Andy took a swig from his bottle of lager. 'So the boss doesn't think that you've got to the bottom of the case then?' he continued.

'No, and normally I'd follow him, given how amazing we know he can be.' Steph sipped her glass of white wine.

'What's different this time?'

Steph frowned and twirled her wine glass. 'I think he's been influenced too much by his daughter. She was the one that got him involved and she won't accept what seems to me the clear evidence that this bloke Holgate stabbed his girlfriend, ran off, lay low for a while and then killed himself. I know he behaved very strangely when he was in hiding, but the guilt and trauma of what he'd done must have affected his mind.'

'Do you think I'll be wasting my time, then? Investigating these people in London?'

'I'd probably say yes, but at the end of the day you wouldn't bet against the boss, would you?'

Andy shook his head. 'You'd have to be very brave to do that. But nobody's infallible and sometimes your judgement can be clouded by personal connections.'

'Exactly. But all we can do is what we're told and see what happens. At some point that inspector at Whitby will call a halt to things. She seems very sharp. She's worked with the boss before. I think she's humouring him because she admires him. Like us. But there will come a time when she realises the investigation is going nowhere.'

'It gives me a chance to go down to see Mum. I'll stay with her. I'll also see what Jason's up to.'

Steph looked at him sharply. 'You know what he'll be up to . . . so be careful!'

Jason Harris was an old friend of Andy's. He worked in the city, made huge amounts of money and spent it on a wild lifestyle. He seemed unable to progress beyond the hedonism of adolescence. He was a colourful and entertaining person to be with. Steph liked him but considered him a bad influence on Andy. 'Wasn't he supposed to be getting engaged at some point?'

Andy laughed. 'That fell through. As predicted. Jason's not one to make commitments.'

'No, I can imagine.'

'Fancy another?' asked Andy, finishing his drink and getting up to go to the bar. 'Then later on we can have a pizza at that Italian by Leeds Bridge.'

'Sounds good,' replied Steph. 'But one more drink will be enough. I don't want you putting in training for a boozy time with Jason.'

'Don't worry, you know me.'

'I do,' she replied, narrowing her eyes at him as she handed him her glass. 'And that's why I don't trust you.'

～

Over in Whitby, there were fewer people around in the town's old pubs in the harbour area now that the Goth Weekend was over, but there was still a lively scene for the locals in certain venues. Inside the Green Dragon, tucked away in a side street, there was a warm atmosphere, which was welcoming now that the nights were drawing in.

Philip Owen, the Dracula actor, was standing at the bar with some of his friends, describing what had happened at the escape room on that fateful day.

'And there she was, on the floor . . . dead. You could see the knife sticking out of her chest, and the blood.'

'Bloody hell,' said one of the group, a tall man dressed in jeans and a leather jacket.

'And the bloke who stabbed her was her boyfriend?'

'So they say.'

'Shit, that's messed up big time.'

'Yeah, well, I get sick of her sometimes,' said another man with curly black hair, nodding towards the woman standing by him, 'but I haven't thought of stabbing her yet.'

'Get lost!' she said with a laugh and kicked him in the leg.

'Then this bloke ran off?' said the first man.

'Yeah, then shot himself and ended up in the harbour. Haven't you seen it all on the telly?'

'Yeah, but it's not the same as hearing it from someone who was there.'

The curly-headed man winked at his girlfriend. 'From someone who knows all about it.'

Owen took a drink of his beer before replying. 'What're you getting at?'

'Well, when the police find out about your past, Phil, they might start to wonder how much you really knew about what happened. They might think it was a bit of a coincidence that a man like you turned up at a murder scene.'

'Bugger off. What do you mean, "a man like me"? That was years ago.'

The first man joined in the baiting. 'It's on your record though, Phil, the police will always be suspicious of your type. A leopard can't change its spots.'

'What do you mean, "my type"?'

'A danger to the public,' said the curly-haired man in a sanctimonious voice imitating a pompous judge. His girlfriend laughed.

Owen gave his friend two fingers. 'As if,' he said. 'I'm not as much of a danger to the public as you when you get behind the wheel of that car.' He looked at the woman. 'I don't know how you dare drive with him.'

The curly-haired man was a car mechanic and he ran a souped-up car that he'd driven in rallies. Most of the time he drove as if he was actually in a rally.

'He goes slower when I'm with him,' she said. 'I make him.'

Owen laughed again and he took another drink of his beer. He tried to conceal the fact that their teasing had rattled him. He hoped the police wouldn't look too closely at his past.

Four

It was brilliant moonlight and the soft effect of the light over sea and sky . . . was beautiful beyond words. Between me and the moonlight flitted a great bat, coming and going in great whirling circles.

From Mina Murray's Journal in Dracula

'I've got two very interesting bits of information for you, sir,' said Inspector Granger.

'Go on,' replied Oldroyd. He was back in Whitby reviewing the case in Granger's office. He and Deborah had checked into their hotel, which was near the Royal Hotel high up on the west side on the splendid white mid-Victorian east terrace. Deborah was having a leisurely stroll around the town while Oldroyd had come straight to Granger's office.

'We've discovered that the actor who played Dracula at the escape room, Philip Owen, has a conviction for assault. He attacked someone with a knife. So we'll need to talk to him again.'

'And?'

'More important, I think: the tests have shown that the blood on the sarcophagus was Holgate's.'

'Have they? Well, that confirms what I suspected. Together with the fact that he was carrying the knife it supports the view that the attack was planned. He must have got a cut from the knife before he hid in the sarcophagus.'

'But I still can't see why he would do that instead of running out of the building? And did he know it was a trick sarcophagus with two compartments that turned round? And if he did, how did he know?' asked Granger.

Oldroyd smiled. 'I can see you're also starting to question the orthodoxy. I think this confirms that we're looking at something more complicated than what appears on the surface. Have you tracked down the owner of the escape room?'

'No. Which is concerning. He would be able to tell us who else knew about the sarcophagus and so he could be in danger if there are other people involved in this. He supposedly has an office in Sheffield but the police there can't trace it. Or him.'

Oldroyd shook his head. 'I don't like the sound of that. Did you manage to find the gun?'

'Negative. The divers have searched around where Holgate's body was found. Apparently they expected to find it and were disappointed not to, given that it was a small area and close to the edge of the water. I suppose it could have sunk in the mud or been carried away by a current. No sign of his phone either.'

'Mmm. The more I hear, the more I'm sure we need to press on with this. I've got my other detective sergeant to go to London and investigate this group and Steph is going to look into Withington's activities in Leeds. She's also going to speak to Louise and see if anything emerges.'

Granger nodded. 'Understood, sir. Sounds like there's going to be more going on elsewhere than here.'

'Maybe, but we can have another look at all the evidence we have and . . .' A thought suddenly struck Oldroyd. 'By the way, who gave the information about the escape room owner and his office in Sheffield?'

'It was in DC Hampton's report; hold on, I'll call him.' Granger took up her phone and spoke to Hampton. Then she turned to Oldroyd. 'He said it was the escape room assistant Elaine Pesku who gave him that information.'

'Sounds like she was mistaken or lying. It seems we're starting to uncover some promising leads. I'll leave you to question those two again.' He stood up and smiled. 'I've got something else on this afternoon.'

~

Steph arranged to see a detective at the Leeds HQ about Ian Withington's business activities in the city. They met in an office in the new premises on Elland Road near the famous Leeds United football ground. He brought a file with him, which he consulted as he spoke to Steph.

'Yes, Withington, I remember him. There were numerous complaints of dubious activities and he was interviewed a number of times but we could never pin anything on him. He was a crafty sod, but we made it uncomfortable for him. Eventually he cleared off. And you say he's now in Whitby?'

'Yes, he has a jewellery business specialising in Whitby jet.'

The detective smiled. 'Does he now? Well, I'd keep a watch on him if I were you.'

'What kind of allegations were made against him?'

'Oh, the usual: lying about the amount of precious metals like gold that were in second-hand items of jewellery; selling stuff that was fake. Whenever we confronted him, he was very apologetic, repaid the customer and said the items had been sold to him and he'd bought them in good faith. Of course he could never remember exactly who he'd bought things from. It was difficult to prove but it was starting to happen too often, which is when he did a runner. He's a slippery customer and his son is the same.'

'His son?'

'Yes. Alan Withington. They work together – father and son; the son travels a lot. We think he gets hold of the dodgy stuff, and his dad then sells it. What's your interest in the Withingtons, anyway?'

'I've been working with the police in Whitby on a murder enquiry.'

'You mean the one where the bloke killed his girlfriend in the escape room and then committed suicide?'

'Yep.'

'Where does Withington fit in?'

'It was his niece who was killed. At the moment we don't suspect him of being directly involved, but it seems as if his niece might have been helping him with his business somehow. It's a loose end we want to follow up.'

'Right. Well, it might be worth talking to one or two dealers in that street near Kirkgate Market where he had his shop. I'll give you some names and addresses. They might be able to give you a bit more information about how he operated. There was no love lost between them; they were glad to get rid of him.'

～

'Come on then, I have a surprise for you!' Oldroyd had met up with Deborah near the swing bridge. 'Have you got your coat, like I asked?' He was wearing a weatherproof jacket and carried a small rucksack.

'Yes,' replied Deborah. 'But where on earth are we going?'

'Out to sea,' said Oldroyd with some excitement. 'It's a fine day, but it's always cool and breezy out there. I've booked us onto a cruise down to Robin Hood's Bay in one of those boats.' He pointed towards a number of craft moored against the sea wall on Marine Parade.

'Fantastic, how exciting!' said Deborah as they walked towards the *Autumn Queen*, a brightly painted vessel, which was already filling up with customers. People were being helped down the steps by a friendly member of the crew as the boat gently bobbed up and down in the swell.

Oldroyd and Deborah managed to get seats in the bow section against the gunwale from where they had a good view as the launch cruised gently along the smooth water in the lower harbour and through the gap between the East and West Piers, passing a small lighthouse on either side. The boat then reached open sea and turned south. Immediately it became breezy and there was a salty tang in the air. The sky was clear and the sea and the horizon very bright in the sunlight. Deborah put on some dark glasses.

'Jim! This is wonderful!' She gave him a dazzling smile.

'I'm glad you're enjoying it. We should see some interesting birdlife. Look out there: some gannets diving for fish!' He produced a small pair of binoculars and trained them out to sea. Deborah looked in the same direction, and saw the large white birds in the distance; black tips on their pointed wings. They were circling high in the sky but, as she watched, one pulled in its wings and dropped at speed like a pointed missile into the water, its sharp beak hitting the sea first. It was a majestic sight and even more dramatic through the binoculars that Oldroyd passed to her. Herring gulls were following the boat and, as they passed some dark towering cliffs, there were still a few kittiwakes flying around the rocky ledges that had been their breeding ground through the summer. One or two distinctive cries were audible, but nothing to compare with the cacophony during the breeding season.

'Are you feeling peckish?' asked Oldroyd.

'Now you mention it, yes,' replied Deborah. 'But I had no time to think about getting anything for lunch. You just swept me off my feet as it were and here we are.'

'Never mind.' Oldroyd removed the rucksack from his back and started to unload the contents. 'I took the liberty, ma'am, of procuring some savoury comforts from the local purveyors,' he said, imitating the accent and manner of the indefatigable Jeeves from the P.G. Wodehouse stories.

'Oh, Jim! You think of everything!'

As they sat eating the excellent sandwiches, cake and fruit that Oldroyd had acquired and drinking coffee from a flask, the boat passed the picturesque village of Robin Hood's Bay with its beautiful cottages spilling down to the seafront. A little further on they were lucky enough to see some seals basking on the rocks beneath a cliff.

On the way back, after watching some huge tankers pass in the distance, Oldroyd couldn't resist reflecting on the Dracula story.

'Have you ever read the novel?' he asked.

'No, but, like everyone else, I've seen lots of film versions and vampire movies. I didn't know part of the original story was set here.'

'Yes. That part of the story has got a bit lost but Whitby was a favourite place of Bram Stoker's and the count arrives here in a schooner.' He changed his tone to that of dramatic storytelling. 'Of course the weather wasn't like this that day. The count summoned up a storm and thick mists. When the boat arrived at Whitby all the crew were dead, including the captain who had heroically strapped himself to the helm. It was a ghost ship that horrified the people who saw it. When it ran aground on Tate Hill Sands, which are just inside the harbour, a big dog leaped onshore and bounded away. The onlookers thought this odd, but they didn't realise the full significance: that dog was Count Dracula, who had arrived in England. He could shapeshift into animals including, of course, the famous bat. In the horror and chaos of what was happening they didn't realise that . . .'

Oldroyd stopped. After a moment Deborah looked at him. 'Yes, Jim, go on I'm enjoying this and . . . Oh no, he's off on one again.'

'Sorry,' said Oldroyd, shaking his head. 'I am trying to switch off, but there was something there that just made me think.'

'About the case no doubt.'

'Yes.'

'Don't tell me you think Dracula was responsible for that murder.'

Oldroyd laughed. 'No. Although the murder did take place in a Dracula-themed escape room, so maybe he did have some responsibility.'

The boat was cruising slowly into the harbour.

'Did the victim have bite marks on her neck?' continued Deborah, still poking fun at her partner.

'No she didn't. But . . .' Oldroyd stopped and shrugged his shoulders as they got ready to disembark. 'Wonderful! Marvellously bracing,' he said when they were back on shore. 'Stimulates the appetite though. Do you fancy a cup of tea and a scone? I saw into the window of a café on the way down and the scones looked enormous.'

'Do you ever stop thinking about food!?' laughed Deborah. 'Except when you're thinking about a case.'

~

Andy headed down the M1 with mixed feelings. It was always nice to go back to London to see family, friends and his old haunts, although he hardly thought of it as home anymore. He was keen to play his part in this case as he'd felt out of the action while Steph and Oldroyd were in Whitby. But he preferred working with Oldroyd directly. There was nothing so interesting and informative as watching his boss interrogate people and witness at close hand how his thinking on a case developed. He'd learned so much, but maybe it was time to put that knowledge into practice for himself.

He had a dossier of information and he was going to call in at the Met to see if they had anything on anyone he was investigating. His boss had also arranged for the Met to supply a DC to assist him. He passed the time on the motorway by listening to some of his favourite tracks, and stopped for coffee halfway down at Leicester Forest Services.

When he finally arrived at the Met he was pleased to see that DC Jenkins had been assigned to help him. He'd worked with Jenkins before in a case involving violins and gangland killings.

'Nice to see you again, Sarge,' said Jenkins with a grin. 'What's this I hear about a case concerning a murder committed by Dracula in a spooky castle in Whitby?'

Andy laughed. 'Sounds like Chinese whispers have been at work. I'll explain as we go along.'

They headed first to Shoreditch to an address near Spitalfields Market. This was the headquarters of Alpha, a small, but successful publishing company, which employed Jack Ryerson. On the way, Andy noticed displays of lanterns and pumpkins in one or two shops and they passed two people dressed as witches with enormous pointed black hats.

'Look at them, Sarge. Must be doing some kind of promotion for Halloween,' said Jenkins.

'Yeah, it's not long until the thirty-first is it?'

'Only a few days to go. The kids will be wanting me to take them out trick or treating.'

Andy smiled. That seemed like a fun thing to do. He had fond memories of dressing up and going round knocking on doors when he was a boy and his dad was still alive. It would be nice to take a child out and see them getting excited. Maybe he was getting broody in his old age. The idea of family life was starting to have an appeal. What would Steph think?

The offices were in a large ultra-modern tower block. The detectives went through revolving doors into an atrium and showed their identity at reception. Andy asked to see the manager as he was keen to speak to him without Ryerson knowing he was there. He and Jenkins were directed down a corridor and were met at the door of an office by a woman of about forty dressed in a smartly tailored trouser suit and heels. She held out her hand.

'I'm Annette Brown, manager of Alpha UK. Please come in.'

Andy introduced them both, and they followed her into a large modern office and sat on easy chairs. Brown, looking a little puzzled and apprehensive, sat opposite on a similar chair.

'How can I help you?' she asked.

'You have an employee called Jack Ryerson.'

'Yes. He should be in today; I'll just check if you want to speak to him.' She made to get up from her chair.

'No,' said Andy. 'I want to talk to you about him, please.' Brown sat back in her chair looking more concerned. 'Are you aware he's been in Whitby for a few days with a group of his friends?'

'No. I knew he'd taken a few days' leave, but I didn't know he'd gone there.'

'One of his group of friends was murdered and another seems to have committed suicide.'

Brown put her hand to her mouth. 'Oh my God!'

'I'm sorry, I know it's a shock. Can I ask you what he's like as an employee?'

She stumbled a little for words. 'Excellent. No problems. Good team worker.'

'Did he have any enemies? Did he ever get angry or react violently to anything?'

'No. Are you saying that Jack is a suspect for something?'

'Not exactly at this stage. The case seems fairly clear but let's say there are some loose ends we need to tie up. I want to check his movements with you. He didn't actually witness the murder, which was last Wednesday afternoon, because he didn't arrive until the next day. He says this was because he was tied up here at work until fairly late.'

Brown looked puzzled again. 'Wait, that's not right. He didn't come in at all on Wednesday, which was the first day of his leave. I remember because there was a meeting of his team and he wasn't there.'

Andy looked at her gravely. 'I see. In that case we will need to speak to him now and I would be grateful if we can use this office.'

'Of course.' Brown got up looking alarmed and went to get Ryerson. Andy felt a little frisson. Maybe he would have something for Oldroyd.

～

Vicar Lane and the streets near Kirkgate Market were bustling with people as Steph walked through Leeds city centre. A number of shops had window displays with witches, cobwebs, black cats and pumpkins, reflecting the nearness of Halloween. There seems to be no escape from the dark side, thought Steph, who had arrived back from gothic Whitby.

She made her way to a street behind Vicar Lane where there were a number of jewellers' businesses and gold dealers. She reached one shop on the detective's list, which was old and rather darkly lit with a fusty smell that reminded her of an old library. There was a dusty and faded window display, which looked as if it hadn't been changed for some time. Inside, the shop seemed empty until an elderly, portly and bespectacled man appeared through a door that presumably led to a small workshop. His eye was still clutching a lens, but he removed it as he came to the counter. She presented her ID and explained her business.

The man's lip curled when he heard Withington's name. 'Oh, that rogue! We were glad to see the back of him.'

'Why?'

'He gave us a bad name with his carrying on. A lot of the public are suspicious of us as it is; they think we're out to cheat them, especially when it comes to buying and selling second-hand stuff.'

'What did he do?'

'He was devious. He told lies. He sold stuff that wasn't genuine: rubies and emeralds; pretended there was more gold in something than there was. He was always one step ahead of the law. We knew what he was but it was difficult to prove it. If we'd had any hard evidence we would have gone to the police.'

Steph looked at the rings and other jewellery in the cabinet beneath the counter. On top of the counter was an eye glass and some old-fashioned brass jeweller's scales. This was a long-standing and proud profession, which was reliant on trust. Cheating of the kind Withington indulged in was hugely damaging.

'That son of his was no better,' continued the jeweller.

'I understand he was the one who might have procured the things his father sold.'

'Probably. I also saw a woman there once or twice.'

'A woman. Do you know who she was?'

'Someone said it was his niece. She was a student, I think, but she came up here in the holidays. I don't know whether she was involved in the dodgy dealings, but you know students; they're always short of money, aren't they?'

'Yes.'

'Are you after him for something? I'd like to see him get what he deserves.'

'Not exactly. Unfortunately, his niece has been murdered over in Whitby and we're investigating his connection with her.'

The old man's jaw dropped. 'Good Lord! Well, I never thought of him as someone who would be violent, though I wouldn't have been surprised if someone had gone for him.'

'No, but where money's concerned things can turn nasty, can't they?'

'Oh yes. Is that where he is? In Whitby?'

'Yes.'

'He'll be into that Whitby jet, I imagine. Well, anyone who buys any from him wants to make sure it's real.'

'I think you're right.'

Steph thanked the old proprietor and left, feeling that he'd been very helpful in a number of ways.

~

DC Hampton had difficulty finding the narrow back-street house where Elaine Pesku rented a room. He eventually reached the address, which was down a cramped alleyway filled with overflowing grey wheelie bins. He knocked on the door, which was answered by a very pale young woman with grey hair and numerous face piercings. Her eyes looked vacant and her manner was slow as if she were under the influence of some substance or other. Hampton put that to one side; he was here on different business. He showed his identity.

'Detective Constable Hampton, Whitby police. I understand that Elaine Pesku lives here?'

It was some time before the girl responded. 'Yeah, but I think she's out.'

'Can you check please? It's important that I speak to her.'

'Is it about that murder where she works?'

'Yes.'

'That was the darkness at work, mate. What do you expect with all these goths around summoning up evil spirits? When they're

142

here, we go out in white and chant our positive spells to counter them. Have you seen us by the harbour? No point looking for humans; it's the spirit world. If you like we can hold a meeting with the white spirit goddess for you and find out what happened.'

'Thank you,' replied Hampton, with some impatience. 'But can you just see if she's in?'

The young woman looked disappointed but turned back into the house.

'Are you looking for me?' The voice came from behind Hampton. He turned to see the tall figure of Elaine Pesku. She was carrying a bag of shopping. She looked at Hampton. 'You the police officer who came that day? I've already told police everything I know.'

'I have some more questions. Can we go inside?'

'I prefer here. My room is . . . not very tidy.'

'Okay.' Hampton referred to his notes and began the interview. 'You told me on the day of the murder that your employer, Mr Hugh Preston, had an office in Sheffield. We've made extensive enquiries and cannot find any trace of it or him.'

She shrugged. 'That's what he told me.'

'Have you had any contact with him since the day of the murder?'

'No.'

'Isn't that surprising given what happened at his escape room?'

She shrugged again. 'I do not know where he is. Escape room is closed and I am looking for other job.'

'How often did he visit you at the escape room?'

'Not often; now and again.'

Hampton looked at her. Her terse replies and inscrutable demeanour gave nothing away. 'Did you know that there was a trick sarcophagus in that storeroom that was going to be converted to be part of the escape game?'

'What is sarcophagus?'

'It's that large Egyptian coffin thing that is built into the wall.'

'How is it a trick?'

'The thing swivels round and there is another section at the back.'

'No. Mr Preston say nothing about that.'

Hampton had no more prepared questions about the case but he'd started to think about her.

'How long have you been in this country?'

For the first time he saw a worried look pass across her face. 'Three years. I have all my papers, if you want to see. I will fetch them.'

She went inside the house and returned with documents that confirmed she was Romanian, and an EU citizen.

'How long have you been in Whitby?'

'Since May. I come up from London for this job for summer.'

'And where were you before that?'

'In London, student.'

'Did you know anybody in Whitby before you came up here?'

'No, I apply for job advertised online. Mr Preston like the fact I come from Romania. He say it makes everything in the escape room more authentic.'

'I see. Did you see anything suspicious when that party arrived?'

'No, they were just ordinary group of people; they seemed to be having fun.'

Hampton realised he was not going to get any more out of her at the moment.

'Okay, we'll leave it there but don't leave Whitby for the time being. We may want to speak to you again.'

She said nothing and went back into the house.

Hampton left feeling suspicious. He didn't believe she was telling him everything she knew.

In Annette Brown's office, Jack Ryerson faced Andy and Jenkins across a desk. He had a supercilious smile on his face as if in contempt for the whole proceedings. 'It didn't take you lot very long to pursue us to London, Sergeant. I take it I'm not the only one you've come down here to question. Why can't you leave it alone? Dominic stabbed Andrea and then shot himself. Period.'

Andy ignored this. 'We understand that you were once in a relationship with the murdered woman, Andrea Barnes.'

'Yes,' replied Ryerson and continued with mock melodrama. 'But it was a long time ago and, no, I didn't harbour horrendous jealousy of her and Dominic that drove me to plan their gruesome murder.'

'How did you feel about them?'

'God! You're as bad as the others. I was getting some stick from Maggie about this. What can I say? I wished them well. It was all over between me and Andrea.'

Andy regarded him sceptically. He didn't like Ryerson's contemptuous tone, as if he thought this was all very tiresome. 'You told us that the reason you missed the visit to the escape room last Wednesday was because you were held back at work here and couldn't get away until late. Your boss has just confirmed that that wasn't true. You didn't come into work at all that day so where were you?'

Ryerson smiled and shrugged. 'Sorry to disappoint you, Sergeant, but I wasn't orchestrating a murder. I was visiting a female friend, if you must know. It's something I want to keep quiet about because she has a husband. There would be some unpleasantness if he found out.'

'We will need her to verify that you were with her on Wednesday at the crucial times.'

'She'll be happy to cooperate. And I'm sure you'll be discreet about it.' He winked at Andy, who found his nonchalance rather repulsive. 'I'm also sure you'll agree that saying I was at work is a very poor alibi if I was involved in a murder. So easy to disprove. I just said that to cover myself with my friends and, of course, I never expected that any more questions would be asked.'

'I see.' Andy, almost reluctantly, had to agree but he hated the man's attitude.

'I'd be grateful if you didn't mention it to any of the group,' continued Ryerson. 'They may not appreciate that I lied to them and I think some of them would disapprove of my behaviour.'

The women certainly would, thought Andy, whose attitudes had become much less laddish under Steph's influence. Where he might have once smiled and colluded with Ryerson about his behaviour, he now looked upon him with a certain distaste as yet another man who thought women were there for his convenience and pleasure.

'Your little secret will be safe with me,' he said, unable to keep the hostility out of his voice. 'If your story stacks up.'

'Oh, it will, Sergeant.' Ryerson wrote down the address and telephone number of his lover and then got up to go. He turned to Andy as he left the office. 'And if I were you I'd go back to Whitby. Close the case. You won't find anything useful here in London.'

Andy gave him a withering glance. 'We'll see,' he said. He turned to Jenkins as Ryerson left.

'I didn't warm to him, Sarge. Arrogant bugger if you ask me,' said Jenkins.

'I agree, and I'm not sure he was telling us the truth about his feelings for Andrea Barnes. Unfortunately, I have the feeling his story about being with that woman is probably true. That's something for you to check out and make sure you get her to state the precise times he was with her that afternoon.'

'Okay, Sarge.'

Andy frowned. After a hopeful start that was a rather disappointing outcome. However, it was only day one of his campaign in London.

～

Inspector Granger gave herself the task of tracking down Philip Owen, the Dracula actor in the escape room. It turned out he was living with his parents on the outskirts of the town in a small housing estate that had seen better days. The Owens's house, however, was smartly painted and had a neat garden. There were new-looking double-glazed window frames. Aspirational council-house buyers, thought Granger as she parked outside the house. She wondered if their son had been a disappointment to them, with his criminal record.

She knocked on the door, which was answered by a portly red-faced man wearing a cardigan.

'Yes?' he said, looking suspicious.

Granger showed her ID. 'Inspector Granger Whitby police. Can I speak to Philip Owen please? I assume he's your son.'

'Yes, I'm Tom Owen. Is it about that do at that room thing where our Philip works? He hasn't got himself into trouble again, has he? I'm sick o' t'police coming to t'door.'

'I just need to ask him some questions. Is he in?'

'Aye. It's a good job his mother's out, though. This would have upset her. Come in.' Granger followed him into the house, which was adorned with flowery wallpaper and patterned carpets. 'Have a seat.' He directed her to a chair in a small living room crammed with ornaments and remained standing in the doorway.

'We've never had any trouble with our Norman. He's a motor mechanic, married with two little kids; lives up at Redcar, buying his own house. But our Philip; his teachers were always complaining about him. Since he left school he's never had a job that's lasted more than six months and then he started getting drunk and into fights. I'd have kicked him out of here, but his mother won't have it.' He shook his head. 'I don't know where he gets it from.' He turned towards the stairs and called up. 'Philip! There's a policewoman here to see you. You'd better come down.' He turned back to Granger. 'He's idling away in his room; he's had no work since that room thing shut down.'

Granger heard a muffled cry in the room above of 'Shit!' and then the sound of someone coming down the stairs. Philip Owen appeared in the doorway, looking shy and much younger without his Dracula costume and make-up. He was wearing stained jeans and a t-shirt.

'I'll leave you to it,' said his father, giving his son a withering look as he went out.

Owen edged into the room. 'Sit down,' said Granger, but Owen remained standing.

'What do you want? I've told you everything about what happened at the escape room. I wasn't even in the same room when that woman was stabbed and—'

'Okay, take it easy,' said Granger as Owen was starting to raise his voice in anger or fear and probably both. 'And please sit down.' This time he responded to her firm instruction and slunk sullenly onto a chair.

'Why didn't you tell us you had a conviction for attacking someone with a knife? You must have known we'd find out as soon as we made enquiries?'

Owen shrugged his shoulders. 'It freaked me out a bit that she'd been stabbed so I thought I wouldn't say anything as I had this link with knives. I didn't think I was important enough for you to start investigating me.'

'We're more thorough than that, especially when it's a really serious crime like murder; we don't leave anything to chance. Now, tell me what happened when you were arrested.'

Owen winced as if the incident was all an unpleasant memory that he was now ashamed of. 'I was only seventeen, remember that. I was in a . . . a sort of gang. We thought we were tough, defending our territory against other groups. We carried weapons. Sometimes things got nasty. One night we got jumped by this other gang in an alleyway down by the harbour. One of them had a knife, so I pulled mine, too. There was a scuffle and I ended up stabbing him. By accident, really. He had to go to hospital but he was okay. That was it. I took the blame, but I wasn't the only one with a weapon; some of them had knuckledusters and razor blades.' He looked at Granger with defiance. 'And that was it. I've had nothing to do with anything like that since. And I don't carry a knife.'

'Did you know Dominic Holgate before the day of the murder?'

'No.'

'So you didn't supply him with a knife?'

'No way!' Owen denied the accusation vehemently.

'How long have you worked at that escape room?'

'Just this season. It's just a summer job; it was going to shut at the end of this month anyway. There aren't enough visitors in the winter.'

'What do you do then?'

Owen shrugged again. 'Bar work, anything I can find. It's not easy in a place like this off season.'

'Have you ever thought about moving to a bigger place like Leeds or Sheffield?'

'Yeah, but where would I live? You have to earn enough to pay rent.'

And that's why, like so many young people these days, you're stuck with your parents, thought Granger.

'How well did you know Mr Preston, your boss at Dracula's Lair?'

'I only met him once. He owned a few escape rooms in different towns and moved about a lot.'

'Your colleague, Elaine Pesku, told us he had an office in Sheffield. Did he tell you that?'

'No.'

'Did you know that sarcophagus in the spare room with the exit door was a trick and had two containers which could swivel round?'

'What? That big thing on the wall?'

'Yes.'

Owen shook his head. 'No I didn't; it sounds a bit freaky.'

'How long have you known Elaine Pesku?'

'Just since we started working there in May. I'd never seen her before that.'

'And you didn't know anyone in that group involved in the murder?'

'No, never seen them before.'

Granger sighed. 'Well, I think that's all. A word of advice: don't keep information from the police. It only gets you into deeper trouble.'

Owen nodded without replying and seemed to have reverted to sullenness. Granger left the house without any sense of achievement other than to have eliminated a possibility that had always been unlikely anyway.

Andy's second call that day was to St Thomas's, where he began his investigation into Dominic Holgate's background. When he and Jenkins arrived at the 1960s glass-fronted building in Bloomsbury, they initially found resistance to discussing details concerning a former student, claiming that it would be a breach of confidentiality. The junior person from student records who was called to reception to speak to them eventually conceded that they would need to consult someone in a higher authority when they told her they were involved in a murder enquiry. She asked them to wait as she went upstairs to consult her boss.

'Stuff confidentiality, Sarge! They're afraid of something unsavoury about the university getting into the news,' said Jenkins as they waited.

'I know; universities and hospitals are getting like private companies, worried about their image.'

The young woman returned. 'Please come with me,' she said, and led them up to an office where they were met by a severe-looking man in middle age dressed in a sports jacket and tie. He offered them seats, but no smile. Jenkins was right, thought Andy, they were not welcome.

'I'm Brian Timmins, Head of Student Records,' he said without looking at them as he consulted something on his computer screen. 'I understand you want information about one of our ex-students Dominic Holgate.'

'That's right. I don't know whether you're aware that he was involved in a murder last week in Whitby and then his body was found in the harbour there a few days later.'

Timmins shot Andy a look of alarm. 'Good grief! No I wasn't. I saw that incident reported on the news, but I didn't make the connection. We have so many students, you understand.'

'Yes.'

The news seriously disturbed Timmins's composure. He looked at the screen and then down at the table before continuing. He seemed to be calculating his response and exactly what to say next. 'That's terrible, for him and his family, obviously, and not good news for us either,' he said at last. Jenkins smiled. This was Timmins's real concern: how it reflected on the university. 'We're always very reluctant to discuss former students as I'm sure Anne explained to you: for confidentiality reasons and also because it can lead to some very bad publicity if the press get hold of things and twist them as they often do. You know, things like drug taking, sexual misconduct, students getting drunk and involved in fights.'

'Yes, I appreciate all that,' said Andy, 'but this is a murder enquiry, and we need to ask you about the fact that Holgate was involved in cheating: copying someone else's work and passing it off as his own.'

'Plagiarism,' replied Timmins in a weak voice, and then he coughed. He'd turned pale. Just the kind of thing he doesn't want all over the papers, thought Jenkins.

'Yes, well, you're right. He was involved in malpractice.' He paused as he read from the screen. 'Twice, in fact. It was several years ago now. The first was a minor offence: he failed to acknowledge a source and we accepted that that could have been an oversight. The second occasion was more serious. He presented a coursework assignment which was over eighty per cent similar to that presented by another student on the same course. We have software to calculate these things.'

'That other student was Mark Garner,' said Andy, consulting the brief he'd been given by Oldroyd.

This fact appeared to surprise Timmins again. 'You already know that?'

'Yes, because Garner is another member of the group of friends involved in the events at Whitby.'

'I see.' He looked paler still.

Jenkins smiled. This was even worse: two students from the university!

'What was the outcome of this incident?'

Timmins consulted the screen again. 'His assignment had to be re-submitted and he could only be awarded the lowest available pass mark. He was given a final warning: any further transgression would have meant expulsion from the course. He was lucky, especially after he tried to blame Garner. He claimed that Garner had copied from him.'

Andy looked up. 'Really? When we spoke to Garner about this, he said that Holgate had admitted to what he'd done, even apologised.' He checked what his boss had written in the brief.

'Not according to these records. Garner had to prove by using computer records to date his files that he'd written the material first. Holgate eventually backed down and admitted his guilt but it became very acrimonious.'

'Did Garner ever threaten him?'

'There's no record of that, but he may have done so outside the official meetings. Look, Sergeant, will it be necessary to make all this public? We would appreciate your discretion if at all possible.'

Andy disliked the pleading tone and the bureaucratic mindset of the man, whose first thought was for the institution. Nevertheless, Andy tried to sound as reassuring as possible. 'It depends on the way the investigation develops. If Garner proves to be more directly involved than we realised, then I'm afraid the evidence you've given me might prove important, but if we're able to eliminate him, then I think things can remain private.'

Timmins sighed and was clearly relieved.

Andy had not finished. 'Is there anything else in Holgate's records which might be of interest?'

Timmins went back to the screen. 'No, I don't think so. There are no more incidents recorded. He graduated with a poor degree: a third class. There's no record of what he went on to do afterwards.'

'Okay. We'll need you to send a copy of that file to Inspector Granger of the Whitby police.' Andy gave Timmins the email address. 'As I said, the material will be treated as confidential unless it is needed as part of a prosecution and a trial. Let's hope not.'

Another look of alarm had crossed Timmins's face at the prospect. 'Indeed, Sergeant,' was all he managed to say.

∼

That evening Oldroyd and Deborah were having an early evening meal at the Seagull Café, a famous local eatery which served top-class fish and chips. They'd been for a walk along the east side and up to the abbey, so they felt justified in tackling the huge platefuls of battered haddock, chips and mushy peas that were now in front of them, not to mention the slices of bread and butter and the large pot of tea.

'Good Lord! I'll never manage all this!' exclaimed Deborah as she looked at her plate. 'But you're not helping me out, you've got enough there.' Deborah shared with Steph a concern about her partner's weight and a desire to monitor their intake of food and alcohol.

'Don't worry, I think I'm going to struggle,' replied Oldroyd, whose comment was belied by the way he was crunching into the crispy batter with great gusto. 'By the way, I'll probably get some calls from my sergeants reporting back to me, but I'll keep them brief.'

'Never mind, it's been a fantastic day. That boat was wonderful.' She took a drink of tea just as Oldroyd's phone went.

'Oops! Here goes,' he said. 'It's Steph. Hello?'

'Hello, sir. I've followed up on Withington as you asked. I spoke to a detective at the Leeds station and then I visited a jeweller who has a business near to where Withington had his shop near the market.'

'Well done. Anything to report?' He ate a couple of chips as he listened to her answer.

'Yes,' Steph said, 'I think it's worth pursuing. The view from both sources was that he was a rogue, but the police couldn't pin anything on him. They both mentioned his son as probably being the supplier of fake and dodgy stuff and the jeweller mentioned a young woman who visited the shop and was thought to be his niece. So that was most probably Andrea.'

'Interesting. That's the connection we're looking for. Did Andrea know too much? Did she want to pull out of whatever her involvement was and threaten to expose them? It's not very likely, but there could at last be a motive there for someone else to want her out of the way.'

'Yes, sir, and I wonder if that man Andrea was seen with in London was not someone she was having a relationship with, but her cousin, Alan Withington, arranging something with her.'

'You could be right. Well done. I'll report to Inspector Granger tomorrow and then I'll get back to you. I've got some fish and chips to eat now.'

Steph laughed. 'Okay, then, sir. And *bon appétit*. By the way, I'm going to call in on Louise tomorrow.'

'Thanks.' The call ended. 'She's such a good person to have on my team: absolutely dedicated and reliable. Walker and I knew she was going to be good when she first joined us from school. She's a fast learner. I think she'll rise through the ranks.'

'You'd better watch your back then, Jim,' replied Deborah, who was nearly full although she still seemed to have a mountain of chips in front of her. 'You need to have a good group to work with in your job, don't you? You can't operate alone like I can.'

'No, it's a team effort. You need more than one mind on the job. That's why I've trained her and Andy to think and—' His phone rang again. 'Talk of the devil, here he is.'

'Hello, sir . . . just to report back. I've been to Alpha Publishing, where Jack Ryerson works. I thought I was onto something to begin with because his boss destroyed his alibi. He wasn't at work last Wednesday, which is what he said kept him from doing the escape room, but when I confronted him he said he was visiting a married woman he's having an affair with. I got the details, and we'll have to verify it, but I imagine it's genuine. Other than that his boss gave him a good report so we've nothing on him at the moment, but he was an arrogant piece of work and I don't know whether he told us the truth about his feelings for Andrea Barnes. There's still a possible motive there, I think.'

'Fine. Well done and keep going. We've very little on any of these people; it's a question of probing away to see if anything turns up.'

'Right, sir. I also managed to get to St Thomas's University to follow up on Holgate and the business of him cheating.'

'Good. You have been busy.'

'Thanks. Something interesting turned up there too. It seems that Garner wasn't telling the full truth to you about what happened. Apparently Holgate initially tried to blame Garner, before Garner proved he was in the clear and it all got a bit unpleasant, though there's no record of any physical threat. I've got the bloke we spoke with to email a copy of Holgate's file to Inspector Granger.'

'Good work again!' said Oldroyd. 'I wonder why he kept that from us? I suppose he thought it gave him a motive to harm Holgate.'

'And it does, sir, though it was a while ago. It's a bit of a stretch to think of him spending years plotting his violent revenge over a thing like that. It didn't do him much damage, did it?'

'No, I suppose not,' said Oldroyd, 'but you'll need to follow it up with him as soon as you can.'

'I'll be onto it tomorrow, sir.'

'Also, Inspector Granger has arranged for you to meet with Holgate's father. He and his wife didn't come up to Whitby; apparently the mother is too distraught and under sedation – not surprising. He wants to meet you at the flat his son and Andrea Barnes shared. He doesn't want you to come to the house. That would be too distressing to his wife. Granger will text you the details and while you're in the flat give it the once over. Officers from the Met have already been in but it won't do any harm to have another look.'

'Okay, sir.'

'Good man! Bye, then.' The call ended.

'Jim, for your own good, you need to turn that phone off now,' insisted Deborah firmly.

'Yes I will.' Oldroyd put his phone away but couldn't resist a further comment. 'Andy's another one: absolutely great. Been so good since he came to us from the Met. You're right, I'm lucky to have such a good team.'

'Yes, there they are working away, while you enjoy yourself here,' replied Deborah.

'Oh, they need me to supervise them,' said Oldroyd with a mischievous wink. 'Anyway, talking of enjoyment, do you fancy a dessert?'

'Jim! You're not serious . . . After all that?'

'Well, no, of course not,' he replied in a tone that suggested he might well be.

~

That evening Andy called Steph from his mum's house in Croydon.

'How is everyone down there, then?' asked Steph.

'Fine. Mum's in good spirits though she seems to get a bit slower every time I see her.'

'Well, she's not getting any younger.'

'No. It's good that Clare and the kids are close. She sees a lot of them and she's dropped some hints again about us. Can she expect any more grandkids soon? And before that will she have to buy a hat for a wedding?'

Steph laughed. 'Oh, bless! She only wants what she thinks will be good for us.'

'Yeah. That was the way of life for her generation. Family was everything.'

'So what did you say?' asked Steph mischievously.

'I just stayed non-committal as usual. It leaves her with a bit of hope without an expectation that anything's going to happen soon.'

'Good, well done. How's the investigation going?'

'Got a few leads, not that brilliant though. I got down here early afternoon and picked up the DC. It's that bloke Jenkins again. He's good to work with; got a good sense of humour. We went to where Jack Ryerson works and busted his account of his whereabouts on the afternoon of the murder, but it turns out he was shagging a married woman.'

'Is that how you described it to the boss?'

Andy laughed. 'Not in so many words. Anyway, we've got to check his story out, but it's probably true. Didn't like the bloke. Bit of an arrogant sod. Still think he could have been involved somehow. Anyway, after that we went on to St Thomas's University and that business with the copying essays was a bit more serious than that bloke Garner was letting on, so I have to follow up on him tomorrow. How about you?'

'We might be onto something with this jeweller, who's obviously a crook, and his niece, that's the woman who was murdered, was working for him in some way. So we'll have to see where that goes.'

'Good. Anyway, I'd better go. What're you doing tonight?'

'Oh, not much – might watch a film and get an early night. How about you?'

'You'll be pleased to know that I'm staying in with Mummy . . . and we're going to watch *EastEnders*.'

'And tomorrow?'

'Painting the town red with Jason.'

'I see. Do the police know this is happening?'

'No, and anyway, they've got far more important things to deal with.'

'Well, take care. You know what he's like.'

'You don't need to worry. I think he's calmed down a bit; much more serious and sober.'

Steph laughed. 'Serious, maybe. Sober, never.'

Andy laughed too. 'Well, we'll see.'

The next day, Louise spent a listless morning at her mother's house in Chapel Allerton, beginning to wonder if staying in Leeds was a good idea after all. Her mother was at work, and so she was alone in the house.

She found the quiet strangely unnerving. She tried to read but couldn't concentrate. She sent and received texts from her friends but missed being with them. The charity had been very understanding in allowing her time off, but maybe she needed to go back to London and to work after all. What could she achieve here?

She was considering all these questions when the doorbell rang. It was Steph.

'Oh, come in, it's great to see you,' said Louise as they went into the living room. 'I was just about to make coffee.'

'That would be great,' said Steph with a smile. She sat on a sofa and looked at the tall and well-stacked bookshelves on either side of the fireplace while Louise made the coffee. Louise returned with a cafetière of coffee, mugs, a jug of hot milk and a plate of chocolate brownies.

'I'm glad you've come around,' said Louise. 'Dad said you would be calling.' She sat down and poured the coffee. 'I'm not feeling that good.'

Steph raised her eyebrows. 'Oh? Why is that?'

Louise sighed. 'Not sure I've done the right thing. I'm not sure why I'm here in Leeds.'

Steph noted Louise's worried expression and pale face. She was definitely not in a good place.

'Isn't it because you're not ready to go back to London and normal life yet?' she said. 'I think you still feel that there's unfinished business with what happened, so staying up here in the north not too far from Whitby is a way of staying involved. Am I right?'

'Yes, I suppose so. But I can't really do anything, can I? I thought I could just stay here and somehow help you, Dad and the inspector to solve it all but that could take a long time and . . .' She shook her head. 'Oh, I don't know. I've really not been thinking clearly at all.'

'That's not surprising considering what you've been through.' Steph drank some of her coffee.

'I ought to go back soon because there is something else. I'm really worried about Ben. He went through some really traumatic stuff, especially trying to save Andrea that day. He looked exhausted and shaky when he left Whitby.'

Steph looked at Louise with her head on one side. 'Is there any reason why you're especially concerned about him?'

Louise laughed. 'You're very sharp. Yes, I haven't said anything yet to Mum or Dad, so please keep it to yourself, but I really like Ben and I think he's fond of me. That's as far as it's gone at the moment.'

'But you're hoping it will go further?'

'Yes, and I think it will, which is another reason for going back.' Louise drank some coffee and nibbled at a brownie. 'How about one of these?' She offered the plate to Steph, who, in the absence of Oldroyd and Andy, took one eagerly. She was a bit fed up of setting a good example to those two, by policing their consumption of sugary treats. It was about time they developed some self-discipline.

She enjoyed the brownie and finished her coffee. 'Look, take a day or two and then decide. I think you'll benefit from the rest and I don't think Ben will run off with someone else before you get back.'

Louise laughed. 'No, you're right. I could do a bit of shopping in Leeds and see a few old school friends. It will take my mind off things.'

'Good,' said Steph, getting up. 'I'd better be off, much as I'd like to spend the morning chatting to you. I'll pop in again before you go back. You've got my number, haven't you, if you want to call me?'

'Yes, Dad gave it to me.'

'Great. Bye for now, then. Thanks for the coffee.'

'Bye.'

Louise felt much better after Steph's visit. She texted some of her old Leeds friends and made arrangements to see them, then she made a sandwich for lunch. She was about to go into Leeds when she heard the key turning and the front door opening. She thought her mother had come home but it turned out to be Mrs Adams, her mother's cleaner, a cheerful, talkative and bustling woman in her fifties who lived in Hunslet.

She reacted with surprise when she saw Louise. 'Oh! You gave me a shock there, love. I wasn't expecting anyone to be in.'

'I'm sorry. I'm just spending a few days here with Mum.'

'Well, it's nice to see you again. I've heard about what happened over in Whitby. It must have been terrible for you, losing your friends like that. I don't know what the world's coming to. My Terry thinks there's too many of these computer games; all violence and people shooting each other and stuff. Anyway, it's nice to see you. I can't believe I won't be seeing Andrea again.'

'Andrea? Do you mean Andrea Barnes? My friend?'

Mrs Adams was moving around as she was talking, getting cloths and buckets out of cupboards while Louise followed her around. 'That's right. I used to clean for her too. I worked for her aunt for donkey's years and when she died Andrea kept me on, though I only went once a month. There was no one living there most of the time so it didn't get dirty. It was just dust. It's a lovely flat, isn't it?'

'Yes it is. I'd no idea you knew Andrea.'

'Well, I can't say I knew her well because, as I say, she was in London most of the time. I don't think she knew what to do with the flat; whether to move back up here, rent it or sell it. I don't think she could bear to sell it really, but I imagine the money would have come in handy.'

'You're right. I visited her there a few times. She kept it just like it was when her aunt lived there with all that beautiful artwork.'

Mrs Adams had started to clean the kitchen sink. 'Yes, and I'll tell you a funny story about that. I was due to go to the house the other day. I have my own key like I do here. Well, it was after what had happened and I thought, well, should I go or not? I decided I would. I didn't want to see the place get really dusty. So I went and I have to say it felt really odd to be there knowing she was dead. I didn't like it at all. And then I noticed something. When you go round a place, you get to know where everything is and if something's been moved. A painting in the hall had been taken down.'

'Yes, I went in there with my dad and we saw the shape on the wall where it had been hanging. Do you remember what it was?' asked Louise.

'Oh yes. I didn't like it much. It was a funny picture of a man and woman. You know hugging, but when you looked closely, as I had to when I was dusting, it looked like the woman was biting the man on the neck.' She shuddered. 'It wasn't nice somehow. I don't know where Miss Barnes, that's Andrea's aunt, got it from.'

'And you don't know what happened to it?'

'I don't. And how are you, love? Andrea was a good friend of yours, wasn't she?'

'Yes she was. It's . . . difficult.' She gave Mrs Adams a wan smile, and the cleaner continued with her good-hearted chatter. Louise, however, found it hard to concentrate on what she was saying, because a disturbing idea had begun to form in her mind.

∿

Back in Whitby, Oldroyd and Granger met to report back to each other. Oldroyd began. Despite the lack of real progress, he was feeling upbeat after his sea trip the previous day and a pleasant breakfast at his hotel. Deborah was doing a video session on Zoom with a client who found it difficult to leave the house due to social anxiety.

'We need to pursue this Withington character. I think his niece Andrea Barnes was involved in some underhand dealings with him. Sergeant Johnson reported that Barnes visited Withington's shop in Leeds. Also, Withington's son was involved. The Leeds police seem to think he was the one who travelled round and procured stuff. Sergeant Johnson thinks that the son could be the person Barnes was seen with in London.'

'Her cousin?'

'Yes. If they had some long-established arrangement and Barnes wanted to pull out, Withington may not have liked it. Perhaps she knew too much about his operation.'

'Okay, we'll speak to Withington again and the son.' Granger frowned at Oldroyd. 'Withington may have had a motive, sir, but are you saying that he got her own boyfriend to kill her and then himself?'

'I admit it sounds ridiculous, but we have to pursue all the possibilities. We don't know what other connections there were between these characters yet. I think we're going to find more and this is where Sergeant Carter comes in. He's discovered that Ryerson's reason for arriving late in Whitby and missing the escape room was bogus. Apparently he was with a woman, but the story will have to be checked out. Andy thinks we shouldn't discount Ryerson yet because of his past relationship with Barnes. He will be investigating more of them today and we'll see what he comes up with.'

'Our interviews with Elaine Pesku and Philip Owen didn't yield much. DC Hampton said Pesku was very cagey. She claimed not to know anything about the whereabouts of Hugh Preston, the owner of the escape room, or about the trick sarcophagus. Hampton felt she was keeping things back.

'I spoke to Philip Owen, the escape-room actor, and his account of himself and his conviction for assault was plausible. It was a teenage gang thing when he was only seventeen. There's no motive with him so I don't feel there's much point in pursuing him further.' Granger paused and shook her head. 'So it's all pretty thin, isn't it? Unless something crops up soon, we may have to accept the obvious solution, although I agree there are some odd things about it.'

'We're in what I call the grind stage,' replied Oldroyd. 'We need to carry on until the breakthrough comes.'

At that moment, Granger's phone rang. She listened intently, asking a few brief questions before putting the phone down. 'Well, talking of breakthroughs, there's some worrying news but it might prove significant. Hull police have been in touch. Hugh Preston's wife contacted them to say her husband has gone missing. He's not answering his phone and she's tried everywhere she can think of where he might be. Apparently he travels a lot to places where he has these escape rooms and he's not good at keeping in touch, but it's unlike him to go so long without letting her know where he is.'

Oldroyd whistled. 'He knew about the sarcophagus trick and we don't know who else he told about it. He could be in great danger and we may be too late.'

'I suppose it's possible that he heard about what happened in the escape room here and then ran off because he thought he might be blamed in some way.'

'Unlikely,' replied Oldroyd. 'So Pesku's story about him having an office in Sheffield was false?'

'Yes, but it may have been a genuine mistake. He lived in Driffield, you know, just north of Hull. He had an office there, so it's possible she misunderstood what he said, particularly because English is not her first language.'

'Hmm, well, maybe, or is that what we're meant to think? It caused us to waste our efforts contacting Sheffield police.'

'Buying time for what?'

Oldroyd shrugged. 'To complete whatever the plan is, and we don't know what that is yet. But Preston's disappearance suggests to me again that we don't yet understand what's really going on in this case.'

'What do you think our next move should be then, sir?'

'Help Hull police to find Hugh Preston. Other than that, I'm not sure there's much more we can do at this end. We need to see what Andy will come up with in the next few days.'

Five

From Whinny-muir whence thou may'st pass,
Every nighte and alle,
To Brig o' Dread thou com'st at last,
And Christe receive thy saule.

From the Lyke Wake Dirge

On the same Wednesday morning, Maggie Hinton looked out of the window of Café Nico onto the autumnal London street where large orange and yellow leaves were falling from the plane trees onto the pavement. The café was busy and she was glad to be back in London and at work. She was beginning to feel some sense of normality returning, but it was still on the surface. If she thought about the events in Whitby, she immediately felt anxiety welling up inside her, but at least they'd done what they could. She was glad she and Mark were out of it. The worst was now over.

The whole affair had given her the chance to reassess her life. She could think about this while she performed the tasks in the café on auto pilot, she was so familiar with them. She didn't intend to stay in the café for the rest of her life, but graduate employment opportunities were poor. Like many of her generation, she found it difficult to see how she would ever be able to do the things her parents had done and taken for granted: buy a house, raise a family, have a secure, well-paid job, retire on a good pension. Not that she necessarily wanted to follow this pattern, which seemed stifling and conformist, but as an Oxbridge graduate, she hoped to achieve something reasonably substantial in the world.

Maybe it was her fault. She'd done her work in the refuge with Louise and then gone round the Far East and Australia for a year. Was it time to commit to something more long term? Doing a Masters was the first step. It was time to do some research. She would have to fund it somehow, but it would be possible.

The café was quite near where Mark worked and he often came in at lunchtime to have a sandwich with her and a chat. At twelve fifteen he walked in wearing his smart work clothes. She served him his coffee and a toasted sandwich. 'Sit over in that corner.' She nodded to the place. 'I'm due a break.'

Soon they were sitting together at a table eating their lunch.

'How's it going?' asked Mark.

'Pretty good, though I feel wobbly if I think about what happened. I could do without that.' She pointed to a small Halloween display around the counter: spiders' webs and a black bat. 'I'm sick of all that black-witches-and-spiders stuff. But apart from that . . . I've never enjoyed work so much. I'm just glad to be away from that spooky town. It'll be a long time before I go back if ever.

'More important,' she continued, sounding excited, 'I've been thinking; I'm definitely going to do the Masters.'

'That's great to hear,' said Mark, eating a piece of his mozzarella and cherry tomato panini. 'What in?'

'I'm going to do the Psychology Conversion. You can do it at St Catherine's. I did quite a bit of counselling at the refuge and enjoyed it. I think I'd enjoy being a therapist.'

'You'd be brilliant,' said Mark, leaning over and grasping her hand. 'I'm so pleased. When everything's settled down life's going to be great again.'

A sad thought came over Maggie. 'It won't be the same without Dom and Andrea though, will it?'

Mark frowned at her. 'Won't it? I know it's tragic and terrible and so on, but they were a bit of a pain, weren't they?'

'Mark!'

'They were though, weren't they? Be honest. Always bickering, holding things up, spoiling the atmosphere. Our friendship group's going to be much more harmonious without them.'

Maggie was shocked. She put down her tuna sandwich. 'That's really unfeeling. How can you talk about them like that?'

Mark looked a little sheepish as he ate some more panini. 'Sorry, but whenever I was with them they never seemed happy. I suppose I haven't known them as long as you, so I don't have the attachment you have.'

Maggie took a bite of her sandwich and glared at him. 'The fact is you didn't like Dom because you never forgave him for copying your essay.'

'Oh God! Don't bring that up again.' He seemed really angry.

'It's true though, but I don't know what you had against Andrea.'

'Look, I didn't have anything against her, okay? It was just the two of them together; it was bad chemistry and . . . Oh, let's just forget it.'

After this they were silent for a while and then spoke briefly to discuss what they were doing that evening. Mark left shortly afterwards.

Maggie returned to work. As she operated the espresso machine, she reflected on Mark's uncharacteristic attitude and behaviour. It was true that Dom and Andrea had never really been his friends and that there was history between him and Dom. She could see how from his point of view their group would seem better without them and their prickly relationship. But still . . .

~

Andy and Jenkins arrived at the address in Tower Hamlets where Barnes and Holgate had shared a flat during their student days. It was in the gentrified part of the East End borough and appeared to be in a converted warehouse.

As the two policemen approached the door, a man got out of a car and walked up to them. It was a cold day, and he was wearing a coat with the collar up. His face seemed empty of expression and only his eyes gave a hint of the deep pain he was experiencing.

'Are you Sergeant Carter?' He had an East London accent. He held out his hand. 'David Holgate, Dominic's father.' His voice faltered a moment but he quickly regained control. 'Let's go in.' He produced a key and opened the door. The three went into a lift in silence up to the second floor, where Holgate opened another door.

'Come in; this is where they lived. The police have been over it all once, but you're from up there, aren't you? Where it all happened,' he said, addressing Andy. 'You don't sound like it.' Andy explained that he'd been brought up in Croydon and had moved up to Yorkshire for promotion. Holgate perched on a wooden chair, looking exhausted and extremely uncomfortable to be in the flat.

'I told the officers that came round: I don't believe it, any of it. He wouldn't have harmed anyone, especially Andrea. They were a close couple. And as far as killing himself, well . . .' He stopped and shook his head as if the idea was beyond expression.

Andy and Jenkins had sat down tentatively on armchairs. 'We have reports that they argued a lot.'

'What couples don't? It's par for the course, isn't it? I know he wouldn't have harmed her.' He looked away and seemed to be on the verge of tears. 'I feel sorry for her parents; they must think our Dominic was a monster.'

Andy glanced at Jenkins, who looked sombre. Talking to shocked and bereaved people like this, especially when their loved one appeared to be the guilty party in some terrible crime, was one of the hardest jobs in policing.

'Did your son have any enemies? Anyone who threatened him?'

'No.'

'What about Mark Garner, his fellow student he copied his work from?'

Holgate seemed surprised, as if he'd forgotten about the matter. 'Oh, that. Our Dominic was definitely in the wrong there. We gave him hell about it. He nearly got himself expelled, but he admitted it in the end. That other young bloke, I know he was angry about it, but that wouldn't be reason to kill someone surely.'

Andy tended to agree.

'The problem with Dominic's time as a student,' continued Holgate, 'was that he was on the wrong course. I don't know why he was doing that Business Studies or whatever it was. I blame that school; they talked him into it. I think he was bored. He spent his time being in plays and stuff. He should have trained as an actor like Andrea.'

'What about his job? Did he get on okay at work?'

'I think so. He worked at a media company, not far from here.'

'"Heart Productions",' said Andy consulting his notes again.

'That's right. He had to earn most of the money because Andrea didn't get much working for that little drama group. I think they argued about money a bit.'

'What about this flat Andrea inherited in Leeds?'

'That caused some disagreements. I think Andrea would have moved up there. She didn't really want to sell that place. It belonged to her aunt, didn't it?'

'Yes.'

'Dominic wouldn't move. He would have had to find another job and he's not a northerner.'

Me neither, thought Andy, though I'm really happy up there.

'She would have rented it out or sold it eventually. That would have helped their money worries.'

'So their finances were actually improving when they . . . died?' asked Andy as gently as he could.

'Yes,' said Holgate with a deep sigh as he was reminded of the shocking reality of what had happened.

'To your knowledge, did your son ever possess a gun or a knife?'

Holgate scoffed at this. 'I never saw him with a knife, unless he was sitting at the dining table. And as for a gun, he wouldn't have had any idea what to do with one.'

'Apparently he told his friends that he had a gun which his uncle had given him.'

Holgate looked momentarily surprised but then nodded his head.

'Our Mick? Well, I knew nothing about it, but actually it would make sense. Mick and Dominic got on well together. Mick was a bit of a wreck when he came out of the army after what he'd seen in Afghanistan, I wouldn't be surprised if he'd hung onto some guns. He got a bit paranoid. I didn't know he'd given one to Dominic. And you're saying that he took one with him up to Whitby and shot himself with it after he'd stabbed Andrea to death with a knife. That's bloody ridiculous!' He was starting to get angry and agitated. He got up from his chair and angrily stabbed his finger at Andy, who stepped in to calm him down.

'Look, Mr Holgate. That appears to be what happened, but we're not entirely convinced. That's why we're continuing with the investigation, so if there's anything you can think of that might help, it's important to tell us. Please sit down.'

Holgate seemed to collapse back into his chair and his head drooped forward. 'I'm sorry. I can't think of anything. He was never violent, and I think he loved Andrea. If someone killed him I've no idea who or why. The only thing I do know is that this is destroying

171

my wife. She'll never be the same again.' He sighed and seemed to pull himself together again. 'Anyway, the police down here said you wanted to have a look round the flat. You may as well get on with it.'

'Okay,' said Andy. 'We appreciate this, Mr Holgate. We know how difficult it is for you.'

Holgate nodded and remained still and silent in his chair while the detectives searched the flat. The couple's computer and laptop had already been taken away for analysis. There was nothing of interest apart from a collection of unusual clothes and masks in a large chest. Andy asked about this.

'Oh, they used to call that the dressing-up box. They were fond of fancy dress and playing odd characters. It was part of their love of acting. They liked any excuse for putting on a strange outfit.'

Just as they did for the escape room on that fateful day, thought Andy.

~

Oldroyd and DC Hampton walked down Church Street to pay another visit to Withington's jeweller's. Oldroyd noticed the subtle changes in the ghoulish shop displays from the Dracula and steampunk of the goths to the witches and pumpkin lanterns of Halloween. In commercial terms it was a very effective segue, which kept the horror theme going.

'Have we established that this bloke's a rogue, then, sir?' asked Hampton.

'Pretty much. He and his son have been involved in dodgy stuff for years over in Leeds and now here. There's never been enough evidence to pin anything on them, but from our point of view, the crucial thing is that Andrea Barnes, the murder victim, was Withington's niece and she was involved with them in some way. We need to find out if that had any bearing on this case.'

'Right, sir.'

'Okay, here we are. Hey, look! We may have got them both together!'

Hampton looked into the shop window through the gruesome displays of jet spiders and cobwebs to see two men talking behind the counter.

'The older one is Withington and I'll bet the younger one is his son. They've seen us.' As the detectives watched, Withington, who had spotted them through the window turned and said something to the younger man, who looked towards Oldroyd and then bolted into the back room where Oldroyd and Steph had spoken to Withington on their previous visit.

'I think he's making a run for it,' said Oldroyd. 'Quick, get round into the lane at the back; there will be an exit there.'

Hampton ran off behind the shop and into a narrow cobbled lane just in time to see a figure come out of a door and run off.

'Stop!' shouted Hampton. 'Police!' But the man ran on.

Hampton chased him along the lane, and down a sharp turn back onto Church Street where his quarry ran into a group of tourists sauntering up towards the abbey steps. He ran past them, despite their angry cries but the collision enabled Hampton to gain on him. In desperation the man turned into an inn yard. Hampton closed in and pulled him to the ground.

'Not a wise move, sir, running away from the police,' he said as he hauled the man to his feet. 'It always makes you seem guilty. I think we'll make our way back to the shop, shall we? And then to the station.'

The sullen young man said nothing and just stared at the ground. He had no choice but to obey Hampton, who held him firmly by the shoulder with the other hand grasping his arm.

Ben was on the train again, this time travelling from Manchester Piccadilly down to London Euston. The short break with his parents had proved very restorative. He smiled to himself. It was wonderful how he could always expect the same welcome at home even though he was now nearly thirty and his parents were getting on a bit. By this stage, they knew very little about his life, which was probably just as well. Their world was very different from the one he now inhabited.

He got his laptop out and placed it onto the table. There were no people in the seats opposite. He needed to look through his PowerPoint slides for his next lecture. He enjoyed the teaching but felt exploited: temporary, part-time contracts were all he'd ever had in the academic world. In some ways he preferred part-time work because it gave him the chance to do his own artwork, but there too he'd not been as successful as he would have liked. Why were his talents not properly acknowledged? So many of the people with tenured jobs in universities were not as academically capable as he was. As for some of the artists whose artwork was praised, he believed his own work to be much better. It was often the way with gifted artists; they struggled for recognition from the establishment. It had been the same throughout history and he wasn't the only one now in this position but at last he could see his prospects improving.

He gazed out of the window at the fields and hedgerows as the train sped south towards Birmingham. He was looking forward to meeting up with everybody again in London. After what had happened he was determined to make a new start and show them all what he was capable of.

It was a pity Louise was not going to be there. He wasn't sure exactly what he felt about her at the moment, but he'd had clear signals from her that she liked him. Everyone's feelings had been all over the place in Whitby, but there would be time to sort things out when they both got back to London.

'I think it's time for some plain talking,' said Inspector Granger firmly with a grim expression on her face as she confronted the elder Withington across the table in the interview room. A solicitor was present.

When Alan Withington had bolted out of the shop, Oldroyd had gone straight inside to find the father furious with his son, calling him a spineless coward and much worse. Customers were staring at the two men so Withington again took Oldroyd into his office at the back. He'd refused to answer any questions and called his solicitor to meet him at the police station.

Granger continued. 'What exactly has been going on with your jewellery sales and how was your niece involved? We're having samples of all the items you have on sale analysed, so there's no point trying to conceal anything. The game's up. What the police in Leeds never managed to prove, we will, so you might as well tell us everything now.'

Withington paused, looking grim as if he was weighing up the options. 'All right,' he began, 'not everything we sell is genuine Whitby jet. But it looks just as good so I don't really see the problem.'

'The problem is you're selling it as if it's made of a rare local gemstone and charging accordingly when it's actually made of some kind of paste. It's what's called fakery, cheating, being a crook or however you want to describe it,' said Oldroyd, who was angry at the man's unapologetic attitude and had adopted his powerful and hawkish interviewing technique, which cowed the most hardened criminal.

'Okay,' said Withington, backing down. 'We get a supply of stuff from this bloke in London who produces fake jewellery. We give him an original and he produces several copies. Alan negotiated the deal. He's good at that, just no backbone when things get a bit tough.'

'And where did Andrea fit in?'

'She was just a courier. She brought stuff up when she came to visit. She did the same when we were in Leeds. We knew the police were watching me and Alan so it was less chancy for her to carry it and I wouldn't trust the post or any delivery service where things might go missing.'

'Why did she do it?' asked Granger.

'Money. I paid her; she was often short of cash, especially when she was a student, but her job in that theatre company didn't pay much either.'

'So she collected the stuff from your supplier and brought it up to you?'

'Yes, then I gave her the money for the next consignment.'

'But it all changed last Tuesday, didn't it?' said Granger. 'She came up here a day before the others. Was that to tell you she didn't want to be involved anymore?'

Withington sighed. His scam was collapsing around him and there was no way to avoid telling the truth. 'She'd inherited that flat from her aunt and said she was going to rent it out so didn't need to do any work for me anymore. She made it clear she'd never been easy doing it. I always reassured her on that point. She just brought the stuff to me; it was my decision what to do with it.'

'Obviously your moral sophistry didn't satisfy her,' observed Oldroyd acidly, but Withington ignored him if he even understood what Oldroyd was implying. 'So when she wanted out of the arrangement, did she become a liability and a danger to you? She knew all about your operation, didn't she?'

Withington realised what Oldroyd was driving at. 'Hey! Hold on. You can't seriously think I would harm my own niece.'

'Most people who are murdered are killed by a relative. She could have exposed you and maybe sent you to prison.' Oldroyd pinned Withington with his penetrating grey eyes.

'So I arranged for her boyfriend to stab her in an escape room and then persuaded him to kill himself? Sounds like a crap scheme to me.'

'Stranger things have happened. You may have been working with other people who had a motive.'

'Like who?'

'That's what we want you to tell us. And let me inform you we have a significant amount of forensic information concerning these deaths and if any of it leads back to you then you're in real trouble.'

Withington scoffed and shook his head. 'You're wasting your time. I've got nothing to hide and neither has my son. If he had, you'd easily get it out of him.'

The interview ended. Oldroyd and Granger convened in her office. Oldroyd was downbeat.

'You'll be interviewing the son to cross-check a few things, but at the moment it doesn't appear that this is going to take us very far. I was trying to unnerve him by ramping up the extent to which we suspect he might have been involved, but it didn't seem to have any effect. He confessed to his crooked dealings because he has no choice; he knows we're onto him. But I didn't get the feeling he was concealing anything about his niece's death, did you?'

'No, I agree. We'll finally put a stop to his business practices, but I think that's all we're going to get out of it. We need to track down this supplier and I think we'll find that he was the person Barnes was seen with in the café.'

'Most likely.' Oldroyd sighed. 'Okay. We'll just have to wait to see if Andy comes up with anything in London. I'm even more convinced the answer lies within that group of friends. I don't think Whitby is going to yield us anything else.'

Events were shortly to prove Oldroyd wrong.

∾

The next port of call for Andy and DC Jenkins was the Imperial College of Art where Ben Morton worked and had also been a student; it was in Bloomsbury like St Thomas's. This made Andy think about whether Morton and Holgate may have known each other in their student days but there was a bit of an age gap between them and just because the institutions were physically close, didn't mean it was likely that they'd met, given the number of students in the area.

The Imperial College of Art was housed in a much older building than St Thomas's and the entrance hall was bedecked with abstract paintings and pieces of sculpture. After the usual preliminaries they entered the office of Morton's head of department Dr Anna Murphy, a stylishly dressed Irishwoman in her forties with long auburn hair tied back. Andy did the introductions and explained the reason for their visit.

'Ben's still on leave,' said Dr Murphy in a soft southern Irish accent. 'We extended it after what happened. He's not due to return until Friday.'

'That's fine,' said Andy. 'It's you we want to speak to.'

'About what exactly?'

'We're investigating every remaining member of that group of friends who were in Whitby together when two of them were killed. I want to ask you how you find Morton as an employee.'

'Ben? Well, fine. The students like him. He's conscientious and hard-working. We've no complaints and we continue to employ him on a part-time termly basis. He's also an alumnus of the college although I wasn't here when he was a student. Some of the older staff remember him from those times and I've heard them speak highly of him.'

'I assume that contract doesn't pay very well.'

'To be honest no, it's the way higher education is at the moment. Lecturers are poorly paid until they get a tenured job and those are very hard to come by now. But Ben always seems satisfied. It allows him to spend time on his artwork.'

'How do you find him on a personal level?'

She laughed a little nervously. 'Goodness, well, we get on fine up to a point.'

'How do you mean?'

'It's all a bit on the surface. He never gives much away about his feelings or attitudes to things. He always seems like a bit of a dark horse.'

'In what way?'

'I'll give you an example. He organized an exhibition of his artwork in a small gallery in Kensington but he never told anybody here. None of us knew anything about it until somebody read a review of the exhibition.'

'Maybe he doesn't want to mix his work here with his creative stuff,' suggested Jenkins.

'Possibly,' said Dr Murphy. 'It just struck us as odd. But you're right in the sense that I always get the impression that his artwork comes first. His teaching is just to support himself and he didn't want to invest too much of himself in it. I sensed he's very single-minded and determined about his creativity and wants to be successful.'

'You keep using phrases like "the impression" and "sense of" as if you weren't sure about anything,' observed Andy.

'No, like I said, he's a difficult person to get to know.'

'And what is your opinion of his art? Is it good? Does he deserve more recognition?'

Dr Murphy paused to consider. 'That's a difficult one. I have seen some of his work. Ben's style is abstract and experimental. I find it very vibrant and effective, if predominantly dark, but as far as success goes, if you mean prominence, fame, money, then in the performing and creative arts we all know that can never be guaranteed however talented the artist. There's a great deal of fortune involved in attracting the attention of critics, the media, sponsors, publishers, theatre directors and so on.'

'That must be very frustrating to those who want to be successful but feel they're not getting what they deserve.'

'Yes, whether you're an artist, actor, musician or whatever. It can be very hard.'

'Does Morton ever talk about his private life? His relationships?'

'No, and I think that was another way in which he seems a little remote; we know very little about him.'

'Do you think he is capable of being violent towards anyone?'

She thought for a moment and then shook her head. 'I can't see it. He's always very genial and considerate. I've never seen him angry with anything or anybody. It would surprise me, but then again I wouldn't really know.'

~

'You know, I haven't done this for years!'

Oldroyd and Deborah were on the sandy beach at the west side of the town. They'd taken off their shoes and socks, turned up their trousers and were paddling at the edge of the water. Oldroyd was carrying their footwear in a rucksack. The sea was cold to their feet but invigorating. It was a windy afternoon with clouds scudding across a huge blue sky, which stretched out across the choppy North Sea. The wind was whipping the dry sand up into their faces and they had to keep turning their heads away from the more severe gusts. Herring gulls were sailing effortlessly overhead without flapping their wings as they used the eddies in the wind to keep themselves in the air. Oldroyd prodded about in the wet sand with his toes, winkling out shells and coloured stones.

'It's wonderful!' exclaimed Deborah as she allowed the tiny waves at the edge of the water to lap over her feet. 'Look at all these colours. I'm going to make a collection of these to take back.' She spent some time collecting rounded and flat stones of differing hues. She loaded them into the rucksack and took a drink from their water bottle. She handed the bottle to Oldroyd and then suddenly announced: 'I'm going to run.'

'What, in your coat?' asked Oldroyd. They were both wearing weatherproof jackets.

'Yes, why not? Come on!' she called to him, setting off down the beach, slapping through the water in the direction of Sandsend. Deborah had persuaded Oldroyd to start running and they did parkrun in Harrogate on Saturday mornings when they were at home and sometimes a little 'parkrun tourism', as it was called, visiting other parkruns nearby. His fitness levels had improved but he couldn't keep up with Deborah, who was lean and very fit. She had been running regularly for years. He set off after her, mentally making the excuse for his no doubt inferior performance that he was carrying the rucksack. He jogged at a steady pace, watching Deborah disappear into the distance but enjoying the exhilaration that he'd discovered running gave him, which was worth the effort involved.

After they'd gone some distance, Deborah arced away to the left up onto the dry sand and towards some rocks. Oldroyd finally reached her, puffing up the slight gradient from the water's edge. Deborah was sitting on a rock looking as if she'd merely strolled to that point.

'That was great,' she said as Oldroyd sat down. 'Let's have another drink and a snack.'

Oldroyd, out of breath and sweating slightly, took off the rucksack. Deborah opened it and took out the water bottle and two muesli bars. Oldroyd would have preferred a chocolate brownie, but accepted Deborah's supervision of his diet which, together with the running, had enabled him to lose weight and feel much fitter.

'You did well – especially carrying that rucksack. I thought we needed a bit of extra effort to burn off last night's indulgence,' said Deborah, referring to the fish and chip treat at the Seagull Café.

'Yes, you're right. I think we'll go back to the Seagull again tonight, it's such a great place, but I promise not to have fish and chips this time. I'll have fish, but something healthier like scampi.'

'That's still fried,' cut in Deborah, 'and I expect you'd have it with chips. I think a nice fish pie would be better.'

'Okay, you win, I—' His phone went off, and he scrambled to get it from the rucksack. 'Sorry, it's Andy reporting back. I was expecting him about this time.'

'Fine, I'll go for another paddle while you're talking to him.' She strode off down to the water. In the distance another group of gannets was circling in the sky and diving into the sea. Some raucous gulls flew overhead.

'Andy, how's it going?' began Oldroyd.

'Okay, sir, can I hear seagulls in the background?'

'Yes, I'm on the beach. Paddling actually.'

'Wow, isn't the water freezing? It's the end of October.'

'Pretty cold, yes, but it feels great.'

'I think I'll stick to the indoor pool at our gym,' laughed Andy. 'Anyway, sir, I followed up on Holgate. We met his father at the apartment. That wasn't easy; he was gutted as you can imagine. Needless to say, he doesn't believe his son would have killed his girlfriend, nor would he have killed himself. He said that Holgate could have got a gun from his uncle – that's Holgate senior's brother who was in the army. He wasn't aware that his son had any enemies. He dismissed the plagiarism business as a motive for Garner to harm his son. I've still got to follow up on Garner, but unless we find out something new about that incident I tend to agree with him.'

'Did you have a look round the flat?'

'Yes, but there was nothing. The only unusual thing was a kind of adult dressing-up box with all kinds of outfits in it. The father said they enjoyed dressing-up for special occasions. You know, parties and bits of plays they were in. They were both into acting, weren't they?'

'Yes, and ironically they were doing it on their last day in the escape room.'

'That's just what I thought. But altogether not much of any use there. We went on to Imperial College and spoke to Ben Morton's head of department. She gave him a good report, although she did say he kept himself to himself. He's very keen on his own artwork apparently. She made him sound a bit like the classic struggling artist, you know, keeping himself from starvation in the old garret by doing a bit of teaching. So again nothing of real substance, I'm afraid.'

'Good work, don't worry if you think you haven't made the big breakthrough. All these people need to be followed up.'

'Right, sir. Well . . . next up is Garner and Maggie Hinton. After that I'll speak to the people who worked with Holgate and Barnes.'

'Good. Have a nice evening, then.'

'I will, sir. I'm going out with a mate of mine from well back. It's usually a good night with him.'

'Okay . . . well, don't overdo it. Does Steph know about this great carousal?'

Andy laughed. 'She does, sir. I always warn her when I'm going to meet up with Jason. She worries I'll revert to my teenage years and get arrested for being drunk and disorderly.'

Oldroyd laughed too. 'Well, make sure it doesn't happen. Bye for now.'

The call ended, leaving Oldroyd thoughtful. Deborah returned.

'How did it go?' she asked.

'Nothing particularly startling, but he said something which made me think.'

'What's new?' laughed Deborah.

'I tell you, mate, I've absolutely had enough. That place is a mad-house and so are all the other ones like it.'

Jason looked tired. He and Andy were having a few cocktails in a smart bar in Canary Wharf not far from where Jason worked. Andy was quite concerned; he'd never seen his normally ebullient friend so downcast.

'Why's that?' he asked.

'All you do all day is chase money and gamble with it. It's true what they say, it's just a giant casino.'

'I could've told you that years ago.'

'I know, but I wouldn't have listened.' Jason finished his drink. 'Fancy another?'

'Yeah, but we'll have to go steady if we're hitting it later.'

'Yeah, well, maybe we won't. My round.' Jason went to the bar while Andy reflected on his friend's sombre mood.

'So what happened to the old mischief-maker who enjoyed playing the system and sailing close to the wind?' he asked as his friend returned with the drinks.

Jason shrugged. 'After a while it's just boring. It's like getting one over on the teachers at school.' He took a drink and seemed to look into the distance. 'I think I'm finally growing up.'

'Wow.' Andy briefly considered teasing him about this but he saw that Jason was serious. 'So what are you thinking of doing?'

Jason gave him a shy look. 'Don't laugh, but I quite like the idea of being a maths teacher. In a hard school. I think I'd know how to get through to the kids and make a difference.'

'Bloody hell! Talk about poacher and gamekeeper. But it's great. You'd have a big cut in salary, you realise.'

'Yeah, but I might achieve something worthwhile apart from making rich people even richer.'

Andy clapped.

'Oh, don't,' said Jason.

'No, mate, don't get me wrong, I really think it's fantastic, and I think you'd be good at it. You would get through to those kids.'

Jason's face lit up and Andy realised he'd been hoping for his approval.

'I've already made some enquiries and I can do a post graduate certificate in education through this Teaching in London thing. There's actually some kind of golden hello package for maths teachers. They're short of them. Come on, let's drink up and go for a pizza, and I'll tell you more about it.'

Pleased to see the old energy back in his friend, Andy readily agreed. His phone rang. It was Steph.

'Hi, how's it going?' she asked. 'Still sober, I hope.'

'Okay, don't worry. We'll be taking it steady tonight. We're not in the mood for anything wild.' He glanced at Jason, who smiled and called out, 'Hi, Steph!'

'Hi, Jason, how are you?'

'Fine. Don't worry, I'll take care of him. I won't let him do anything rash.'

She laughed. 'Well, that's good to hear, though I'm not sure the carer is that reliable.'

'Oh, he's a changed man. Andy will tell you all about it.'

Andy continued the conversation as Jason went off to the toilet. 'We're having a few cocktails and then we're off for a pizza.'

'Sounds very tame,' replied Steph. 'Anyway, how's work?'

'Not brilliant; we're working our way through the list of people the boss gave me, but nothing much is coming up yet.'

'I can hear you're disappointed.'

'Yeah, well, you know how I always like to impress him.'

'I'm sure he's just as impressed by your hard work as when you discover something important. You know what he says: often it's just a question of slogging away until someone gets the break-through and everyone's contribution is equally important.'

'Yes. The problem with this case as far as I understand it is that the solution may be just what it appeared to be at the beginning so I might be wasting my time. Am I right?'

'Maybe. But the boss is still convinced that things are not what they appear to be. I have to say he hasn't convinced me, but we're carrying on until all the possibilities are excluded. I don't know who will be proved right.'

'Well, given past experience I know where my money will be.'

'Maybe. I called in on Louise. She's staying in Leeds for a while.'

'How is she?'

'Still a bit frail. We get on really well. She told me she's inter-ested in Ben, the one who tried to save Andrea the victim after she'd been stabbed. She's been worried about him, so that will have added to the stress. By the way, don't mention any of that to the boss. She hasn't said anything to him and the relationship hasn't really got going yet.'

'I won't. Anyway, Jason's coming back and we'll be off. Have a good evening. Love you.'

'Love you, too.'

∾

While Andy and Jason were enjoying their rather sedate evening out, Louise was meeting up with some of her old sixth-form college friends in Leeds. Cynthia, Aisha and Claudia had all come back to the Leeds area after university. They were in one of their favourite haunts from the old days: The Fox and Goose pub near the univer-sity and their old sixth-form college.

Although they were glad to be meeting up again, it was a somewhat sombre occasion due to what had happened to their friend Andrea.

'I still can't believe she's gone,' said Claudia. 'And you were there when it happened. My God, Louise, it must have been terrible.'

'It was,' replied Louise. 'It's still difficult to get the images out of my mind.'

'Ugh!' Cynthia turned her head away at the idea. 'How are you coping?'

'Okay up to a point. I'm staying with my mum, and Dad has arranged for this lovely police sergeant to check on me. She's really friendly and understanding.'

'That's nice.'

'She was always such a lively person,' said Aisha, getting back to Andrea. 'Do you remember she was in all the plays? She was so good – no wonder she got into drama school. It's so tragic. She could have had a future in acting. Who knows? She could have been famous. What was she up to down there, did you see much of her?'

'Yes, now and again,' replied Louise. 'She was in this little women's theatre group. They performed in small venues all over the place. She loved it, though it didn't pay much. We had this group of friends, I don't know whether it will survive all this, and she and Dominic were part of it. He was keen on acting too.' A sudden spasm of grief went through her. 'I still don't believe he could have killed her. They seemed made for each other.' Her eyes filled with tears and Aisha passed her a tissue.

'Don't worry,' said Claudia. 'It must be awful. It was bad enough seeing her die, but her boyfriend stabbing her? I can't imagine what it must have been like.'

'It seems unreal, doesn't it?' added Cynthia.

Louise looked up. She thought for a moment with a furrowed brow.

'And she'd just inherited that gorgeous flat from her aunt. That would have helped her financially,' continued Cynthia.

'Oh, I wanted to ask you about that,' said Louise, coming out of her reverie. 'There's a bit of a mystery about a picture that's missing from the hall. It's probably not important . . . but did any of you ever visit her in that flat?'

They all shook their heads except Aisha. 'I went round a few times but I couldn't tell you anything about the paintings except there were a lot of them. It was a brilliant collection, like going round a gallery. One time I bumped into her in the market and she asked me to the flat. She said she was just on a flying visit. It was a lovely flat; her aunt had wonderful taste. There was someone just leaving the flat as I arrived. There wasn't time for her to introduce me but when we got inside she said it was a friend of hers from London and they'd admired the paintings too. I wondered if that person was an art dealer and she was going to sell some of them. I know she needed the money.'

'You see, one of those paintings is missing,' said Louise. 'My dad noticed there was a space on the wall. I've been to the flat plenty of times, but there's no way I could remember that particular painting.'

'Well, maybe she did sell one?'

'I don't know. She was very attached to all her aunt's stuff. I don't think she would. Her cleaner, who's also my mum's cleaner, noticed this picture was missing too, but she seemed to think it only disappeared after Andrea had . . . died.' The last word was a struggle to get out.

'Look,' said Claudia, 'forget it, it's not important. This is what happens when you have a shock or a lot of stress – some trivial thing gets blown out of proportion and you can't deal with it or get it out of your mind. You need to leave it to your dad and the other detectives to sort everything out. It's their job.'

Louise smiled. 'You're right. Let's change the subject, shall we? Who wants another drink? It's my round.' She went to the bar feeling much better for the support of her friends. However, things had been said that had set her thinking again.

～

Early next morning in Whitby a group of kids on their way to school were playing on a stretch of waste ground near a builder's yard on the edge of an industrial park. There was a large, old, rusty skip full of various kinds of rubbish ready to be taken to the landfill site. Their parents had told these children to keep away from things like this as they could be dangerous. That made it more exciting. Their favourite game was climbing up the step overhanging the sides of the skip and walking over the rubbish.

A boy and a girl had made it onto the top and another boy was climbing up when there was a screech of metal tearing and the side of the old skip where he was ascending gave way. The boy fell to the ground, followed by lots of the rubbish from the skip. His friends heard him cry out.

'Are you okay?'

'Yeah.'

The others laughed. Two of them pulled some rotting planks from on top of their friend and helped him up. He was filthy but unhurt. A third went to look at what had fallen out of the skip. Amongst the empty paint containers and broken furniture he saw something alarming.

'Oh God! What's that? It stinks,' he cried.

The others turned to see their friend looking at something rolled up in some kind of old sheet. The smell hit them.

'Oh shit! That's hair!' The girl pointed to the end of the rolled-up thing. 'It's a body!'

They screamed, turned away and sprinted back home, not knowing or caring that the search for Hugh Preston, owner of the Dracula's Lair Escape Room, was over.

∼

'He's been there for some time, over a week according to a cursory examination. The cause of death was a stab wound to the chest.'

Inspector Granger and Oldroyd were at the scene of the children's gruesome discovery. It was a chilly, dark day with a heavy grey sky. Blue-and-white tape cordoned off the skip, and a police constable was on duty. A quantity of rubbish, which had fallen from the skip with the body, lay strewn around.

'He must have been in a nasty state,' Oldroyd said. 'Not a nice experience for those kids.'

'No, I agree,' said Granger with a grim smile. 'That'll teach them to climb onto things like this when they've been told not to. They were sent away with a severe warning not to play on skips like that.'

'Right, I suppose it's called learning the hard way. They'll certainly never forget this. So I assume his killer hid his body in here, believing that the skip would be taken to the tip and the body would end up lost in a massive pile of landfill rubbish.'

'Yes, I think so. But apparently this skip is used for general rubbish that accumulates around the industrial park. So it's not emptied very often. That's why it took some time for the body to be discovered.'

'Lucky for us. We needed a break in our investigation. And I was saying only yesterday that we probably wouldn't get any more leads here in Whitby,' observed Oldroyd. 'I think we can assume his murder is connected with the case though you'll need to check that there are no other people around with a motive to kill him.'

'It would be a great coincidence if there were, wouldn't it?'

'Yes, I'm thinking he was killed because he knew about the trick sarcophagus. We were clearly never meant to find his body or work out how the trick worked.'

'They reckoned without you, sir,' said Granger teasingly. 'That still doesn't necessarily mean that the obvious solution to the case is wrong. Holgate could have murdered him after he was told about the sarcophagus.'

'In theory, yes, but in that scenario Holgate premeditates the killing of two people and then himself; he's a violent, deranged murderer and suicide who carries weapons. No one we've spoken to has seen any sign of him being like that. Also how would he have known Hugh Preston? There's no evidence that Holgate ever came to Whitby before last week.'

'The problem with that is neither did the rest of the group. In fact, only Barnes, who was killed, came regularly to Whitby.'

'Hmm, so who did Preston tell about the trick sarcophagus?' mused Oldroyd.

'Whoever it was clearly holds the key to this mystery.'

They were sauntering back to Granger's car when Oldroyd suddenly stopped. 'Wait. I've got an idea. Let's go back to the escape room. I've got a feeling we didn't look there carefully enough.'

~

Dracula's Lair seemed even creepier when it was dark and deserted than when it had been full of police officers. Granger managed to find a light switch and opened the creaking door into the game's first room, but Oldroyd strode on past the reception desk.

'Let's look in here first.'

To Granger's surprise, he opened the door to the toilets and went in. 'Yes,' she heard him cry. 'I thought so.'

She followed him in. There was a narrow anteroom with doors marked 'Men' and 'Women' for the toilets.

'What is it, sir?'

'There's another emergency exit door in here,' he said, pointing to a third door. 'I think we'll find that this leads out onto the street, not far from the exit door from that room with the sarcophagus.'

'So someone could have moved quickly between the two?'

'Yes, without going through the rooms set up for the game.'

'You're thinking of Elaine Pesku? The receptionist?'

'I am. If I remember rightly, Louise said in her statement that when she got to reception to raise the alarm, Pesku was just coming through the door to the toilet. That's a very effective cover. She could have been returning from that storage room which held the sarcophagus. We've focused too much on the main characters in this drama, looking for motives and we've overlooked others.'

'So you think she was lying when she told Hampton she knew nothing about the sarcophagus?'

'I do. What made me think about her was when you said whoever knew about that trick could hold the key to the mystery and she's the obvious person when you think about it. Preston must have told her. Then I remembered what Louise said. There was no one else in reception so she could easily have used the two emergency doors to go to the room where Holgate was. She's involved in this somehow. We need to get after her.'

'Do you think she murdered Preston?'

'Maybe, but if she was involved we know that she was working with at least one other person because there's no way she could have stabbed Barnes.'

'What about motive, sir? We've nothing to link her to anyone in that group, never mind the actual victims. The only person who had any connection with her was the actor Philip Owen and he had no link with anyone else either.'

'We may have to consider him again too, but the urgent need is to find Pesku before any news of the discovery of Preston's body gets out. Once she hears about it she'll probably disappear.'

Oldroyd's phone went. It was Steph calling from the Harrogate HQ. 'Morning, sir. I hope things are going well.'

'Yes, things are livening up over here.' He told her about the discovery of the body. 'I'm pretty sure this means what we've been presented with is not the real story. We're going to track down Pesku and see what she has to say.'

'Right, sir. Is there anything I can do at this end?'

'Just keep an eye on Louise.'

'That's why I rang, sir. I called in to see her yesterday and she seemed okay. She said she was going to look up some old friends in Leeds and meet up with them last night. And just to reassure you, I'm still absolutely sure that she was not involved in anything bad.'

'Good. Well, keep in contact with her. She's been through a lot and I'm still very concerned about her. She obviously likes you.'

'Yes, we get on well, so don't worry, sir. I'll pop in again soon and she's got my number if she wants to call me.'

'Good. I assume you're also keeping an eye on that partner of yours so he doesn't shame us all by getting arrested for being drunk and disorderly.'

Steph laughed. 'I am, sir, but the good news there is that he had a very sober time with his friend. They had a few cocktails, a pizza and then went home.'

'Good lord! How sensible! You've obviously made a man out of him. You want to be careful, he seems to be really settling down. He'll be wanting a family next.'

She laughed again. 'Maybe, but all in good time for that one, sir.'

One of the reasons why Andy had called a comparatively early end to his evening with Jason was that he wanted to make an early visit to the apartment shared by Mark Garner and Maggie Hinton, before they left for work. He collected DC Jenkins and they arrived at the address in Dalston before 8.00 a.m.

Maggie opened the door and was startled by the sight of the two detectives. Andy made the introductions and they showed their identification.

'Is this to do with the deaths in Whitby?' she asked.

'Yes.'

Maggie's face crumpled in despair. 'Oh God, no! I thought we were done with that.' She turned back into the hallway and shouted, 'Mark! It's the police.'

Mark emerged wearing suit trousers and a white shirt without a tie. He was drinking from a mug. He frowned at Andy and Jenkins.

'If this is about Whitby, we've told you everything we know. Anyway, this is a bit early, isn't it? We've got to be off soon,' he said.

'We won't keep you long. It's you we want to speak to but it would be useful if Ms Hinton was here too.'

Maggie was alarmed. 'Mark, what's this about? Is there something you haven't told me?'

'Let's go inside, shall we?' continued Andy. The four of them walked silently into a long kitchen diner and sat down on sofas.

'I'll come straight to the point,' said Andy, addressing Garner as he consulted his briefing. 'When you told DCI Oldroyd about the incident at university concerning Dominic Holgate plagiarising your work, you said that the authorities sorted it out and you didn't get involved. You also stated that Holgate apologised to you in the end.' He looked at Garner, who was avoiding eye contact.

'But we've spoken to Mr Timmins, the head of student records at St Thomas's, and he says that the incident was in fact very acrimonious. Holgate actually accused you of copying from him.'

'Mark! You didn't tell me that. What's going on?' interjected Maggie.

'So,' continued Andy, 'I think it's time you gave a truer account of what happened and your feelings towards Holgate.'

Garner looked sheepishly at Maggie and took a deep breath. 'I didn't want to worry you. You've been in a very emotional state and I thought you might start worrying that I had a motive for wishing Dominic harm.'

'Well, I bloody well do now, you absolute idiot!'

'So tell us what happened?' Andy interjected.

Garner frowned at the memory. 'We submitted our essays and a few days later we were summoned by the head of department to his office. He presented the two essays to us and they were very similar. I was furious because I knew he'd copied from me. I'd lent him my work to have a look at, not to present huge chunks of it as his own. He'd been in one of his bloody plays and done no work that term.

'I couldn't believe it when he claimed that he'd written the essay and I must have copied from him. I think he was terrified they were going to expel him because he'd done something like it before.'

'He had. So what happened?'

'I had a real go at him in front of the head of department and, yes, I threatened him, said I would beat him to pulp and so on. It was all anger; I would never have done it.'

'How was it resolved?'

'I proved that I'd written the essay by presenting dated drafts. He gave in and admitted it. He had to resubmit for a basic mark, but I thought he was bloody lucky to still be on the course after trying to blame me. That was criminal. I should have threatened to go to the police. That's what the authorities always dread: bad publicity. They made us sign a non-disclosure agreement. I felt it was almost making me part of something criminal when I was entirely innocent.'

Andy pressed on. 'Did you ever threaten Holgate again?'

'No. After we signed the agreement, he said he was sorry and I just left it at that. We'd never really been friends, just members of the same course. It soured the rest of my time at university a bit. I avoided him whenever he was around.'

'And then he turned up a few years later?'

'He did. It was a bit of a shock when Maggie's friend Andrea turned up with her boyfriend and it was him. We had a word. He apologised again and we decided to leave it alone for the sake of the friendship group.'

'Very mature and sensible,' remarked Andy. 'But how do you feel about him now?'

Garner paused and Maggie looked at him. 'I was still really pissed off with him, to be honest. It wasn't great going out in a group when he was there and hearing people praise him: "Oh, Dominic, this and that", when I knew the truth about him; he was a cheat. Sometimes I felt like denouncing him in front of the group but I didn't want to upset everything. In particular, I don't know whether Andrea knew about it and I didn't want to be the one who told her.' He paused. 'So that's it.' He turned to Maggie. 'I'm sorry.' She shook her head and looked away, seemingly not yet ready to forgive him.

Andy was not finished. 'So did you see an opportunity to get revenge when you were all in Whitby?'

'I wasn't there when they were killed. I didn't get there until the next day.'

'How do we know you weren't there? Did you plan things with someone else who had a grievance against Holgate?'

'And what about Andrea?'

'I don't know. Maybe you can tell me?'

At last, Maggie came to Mark's defence. 'I think that's ridiculous, Sergeant! We all saw what happened to Andrea, and Mark wasn't there. What reason would Mark have to kill her? Are you

196

saying he killed Dominic after Dominic had killed Andrea? Why can't the police just accept what happened that day? All of us have had to come to terms with it.'

'It's not quite so straightforward,' replied Andy, but he didn't go into details. 'Where were you on Wednesday, the day of the murder, and Thursday?'

'Here at work. I didn't have any time off. I was going to join them in Whitby for the weekend. They let me have the Friday off in the circumstances and I drove up there.'

'Okay. Give the address of your workplace to DC Jenkins. We'll need to check your alibi.'

'Fine.'

When they left, Andy was pleased to have got to the truth about the plagiarism incident but he wasn't convinced that there was much mileage in pursuing Garner any further. His story was convincing.

Andy felt dispirited and tired after his very early start. He still seemed to have found out very little for his boss to use and was wondering whether his work in London was at all worthwhile. However, it was at this point that he received a call from Oldroyd telling him about the discovery of Hugh Preston's body and urging him to continue his investigations.

~

When DC Hampton returned with his boss, Inspector Granger, to the house where Elaine Pesku rented a room, he hoped that he would not encounter the 'white goddess' woman again. There was to be no such luck, as she again answered his knock on the shabby door. She looked exactly the same as he remembered, with her pale face and vacant eyes, peering at him as though the light was too strong. She looked as if she rarely made it out of some dark room, which he imagined to be heavy with the scent of joss sticks and full of outlandish furnishings and ornaments connected to spells and witchcraft.

'Yes,' she murmured, and didn't seem to remember him, although it had only been two days since he was there before.

'Whitby police. Can we speak to Elaine Pesku, please?' he asked, presenting his ID.

'I think she just went out.'

'How long ago?'

'Not long, I heard the door.' She screwed up her eyes and looked closely at Hampton. Was she short-sighted? he wondered. 'Weren't you here the other day? I said you wouldn't get anywhere alone, didn't I? It's nearly Halloween; the powers of darkness are strong. Only the white goddess can save you. If you—'

'Did she say where she was going?' interrupted Granger. The woman turned her dreamy eyes to Granger as if seeing her for the first time.

'No, we don't speak much, but I sense a troubled aura about her.' Not surprising, thought Hampton as, at the very least, she's lost her job and maybe she's involved in something far worse. You didn't need some kind of special powers to work that out.

'Do you know anything about her? Where she was before she came here and what she did?'

The woman looked pained and screwed up her face as if remembering things was an effort. 'She was a student in London. That's all I know.'

'Well, thank you, anyway,' said Granger, and the detectives turned back up the narrow alleyway to the road at the top. As they reached the road, a car went past.

'Hey, that's her, ma'am, Pesku,' called Hampton, pointing at the car. 'In the passenger seat.'

'Yes,' replied Granger, 'and I got a look at the driver. I think I know who it was. Come on.'

They quickly got into the police car and Granger drove off after the other car at speed. The chase took them back downhill towards the town centre. As they got closer, Granger put on the siren. There was the usual pause before a driver realises the police car is actually following them and wants them to stop. Granger flashed the lights and the car came to a halt just as they reached the harbour. Suddenly, a woman dressed in jeans and a jacket threw open the passenger door and leaped out of the car carrying a bag. She ran up a steep street called Flowergate. It was Elaine Pesku.

'Quick! After her,' said Granger, and Hampton got out of the car and started his second chase of the week. Unfortunately, this time the pursued person was already out of view around a sharp bend to the right, and when he turned the corner she was nowhere to be seen. He ran up the cobbled street past a butcher's shop selling meaty snacks and several goth dens now also adorned with Halloween displays. There were several narrow alleys down which she could have disappeared. He spent some time looking in shops, but there were so many places she could hide amongst the dense clutter that it was fruitless so he returned to the car. Granger was speaking to the driver who was none other than Philip Owen.

'I don't know why she's run off,' he was saying. 'I was giving her a lift into town. She lives on my route in.'

'I see. All very innocent again. You're cropping up too many times in this case for my liking,' said Granger. 'Is this your dad's car?'

'Yes,' replied Owen, looking a bit embarrassed.

'I'll bet he doesn't know you're driving it, does he?' Owen didn't reply. 'You'd better look after it, then. Is he insured for you to drive?' Owen looked alarmed but Granger didn't pursue it. 'Did Pesku say anything to you about anything? Was there any particular reason why she wanted a lift? Had she had any news or anything?'

'No, she never says much. She just texted to ask was I going into town and could I give her a lift.'

Granger let him go and turned to Hampton who told her that Pesku had escaped. 'Well, she obviously knows we're onto her. I wonder if she's somehow got word that Preston's body has been found?'

'It's possible, ma'am. That industrial park where the skip was discovered isn't far from where she lives and rumours travel fast, especially once those kids who found it got back home.'

'I wonder what she's going to do now?'

'Lie low somewhere?'

'Yes, but she can only do that for so long. She had a bag with her. She might have been going to leave the town for a while. Okay, let's go back. I'm putting you in charge of the search; you've got the best knowledge of the town and the most likely places where someone might hide. We also need to find out where she was a student. That won't be straightforward given that London's got thousands of them.'

Hampton was a local man who had lived in Whitby all his life and relished a challenge. 'Yes, ma'am, leave it to me. We'll find her.'

~

'Do you want to hear my latest poem?' Oldroyd had joined Deborah in a small café in one of the steep, narrow streets on the west side of the town. 'I was writing it last night when you were asleep. It took my mind off the case, though it is about Whitby.'

'Go on then,' replied Deborah, taking a bite from her smoked salmon sandwich. She'd encouraged him to write as a counter to his tendency to overwork. Oldroyd read from his notebook:

'Whitby Light and Dark

Scudding clouds,
Flicker light and dark,
Across the sea.

Light came with Hilda,
The abbess on the hill,
A beacon of hope.

Darkness with Dracula,
Bounding from the ship
As a black dog.

All is now tame.
Tourists in the bright sunlight,
Goths dressing up in dark.'

'Oh, I like that,' said Deborah. 'I take it the light is with Hilda the
Abbess of Whitby?'

'Yes, she lived in the seventh century and was apparently a
very virtuous, much-loved woman. Then darkness and evil with
Dracula.'

'And why is everything now "tame"?'

'That might not be the right word. I was just thinking about
the contrast between drama and the seriousness of the past in fact
and fiction with today, when everything has become sort of trivi-
alised into tourism. I suppose I was thinking about this Dracula's
Lair thing in the case and people just coming here to sunbathe or
dress up as goths. It's a leisure and entertainment place now and
it used to be a powerhouse of virtue, ideas, exploration. Think of
Captain Cook going out from here to Australia and the South Seas.
Do you know that Caedmon, the first named English poet, looked
after the sheep at Hilda's monastery?'

'Well, fascinating stuff, but it's not like you to romanticise the
past. It's great that people have the leisure to come and enjoy themselves. Life would have been very hard for ordinary people in all
those times you mentioned.'

'I know. It just amazes me what distinguished people there have been in a small place like this.' He put the book aside and carried on eating a cheese and pickle sandwich. 'Do you fancy a walk up the hill on the east side after this? We can see the abbey ruins and the church where Bram Stoker set scenes in Dracula.'

'Sounds good.'

Oldroyd finished his sandwich and drank his coffee. Then he sat back with a sigh. Mixing work with pleasure as he was doing at the moment certainly had its advantages. There was nothing he liked better than pottering around an interesting place like Whitby, especially with such a pleasant companion.

Six

The time and distance seemed endless, and my knees trembled and my breath came laboured as I toiled up the endless steps to the Abbey . . . I could see the seat and the white figure . . . There was undoubtedly something long and black bending over the half reclining white figure. I called in fright, 'Lucy! Lucy!' and something raised a head, and from where I was I could see a white face and red, gleaming eyes.

From Mina Murray's Journal in Dracula

Oldroyd and Deborah sauntered down Church Street towards the abbey steps. There was further evidence of the preparations for Halloween in the shops: pumpkins, witches, black cats and cobwebs were in even greater profusion. When they reached Withington's shop, Oldroyd glanced through the window and caught a glimpse of Withington himself. For a second the crooked jeweller's eyes met his and then he looked away frowning. Oldroyd smiled. That man would be relieved when they went past his shop and didn't go in. He knew the police were investigating his activities and he would most likely be prosecuted. Not before time, thought Oldroyd.

They turned the corner and saw the steps curving up steeply to the right.

'These steps appear in *Dracula*. Mina Murray sees her friend Lucy on a seat at the top with a strange figure leaning over her,' said Oldroyd.

'Dracula himself, presumably,' replied Deborah, who was breezily walking up the steps as if it was all level. Oldroyd tried and failed to keep up with her and had to sit down for a short rest at the top. Deborah joined him on a bench.

'This is about where Stoker imagined Lucy to be, I think,' said Oldroyd, looking around at the church, the abbey and back down over the panorama of the town and out to sea. 'It must still be spooky up here at night and of course this is where Louise and the others came when they got the text from Dom.'

'You didn't tell me about that.'

Oldroyd explained about the strange late-night encounter in the churchyard.

'Good Lord! That sounds like a scene from *Dracula* itself. I'm not fond of films like that. If I'm watching something like that and it gets too horrific, I have to remind myself that it's all acting and special effects, nothing's real.'

'Indeed,' replied Oldroyd rather vacantly because a thought had struck him. For once Deborah didn't notice.

'Come on then, let's have a look round the abbey ruins, shall we?' she said, getting up from the bench.

'Good idea,' replied Oldroyd and he followed her up the path, still deep in thought.

∽

Andy and DC Jenkins's dogged pursuit of lines of enquiry in London continued with a visit to the Women's Theatre Cooperative where Andrea Barnes was employed as an actor. The group operated from the Viaduct Theatre situated under a railway arch near Charing Cross. They parked in a street nearby.

'I'm not sure I'm going to like this, Sarge,' said Jenkins, grinning as they walked towards the theatre. 'It might be a bit too alternative for me. Look at that.' He pointed to a poster showing a woman in a short skirt standing with her foot on a man who was lying on the floor.

'How old are you? You sound like some grumpy old pensioner who wishes he was back in the 1950s. What's wrong with live theatre taking on some radical issues?'

'Dunno. I prefer watching telly. I haven't been to the theatre since I went to the pantomime when I was a kid. What do you think their plays are about?'

'Women's issues: inequality, domestic abuse, male domination of powerful roles in society – things like that I should think.'

'Heavy stuff; not my idea of a fun night out.'

'Do strong and confident women threaten you?' asked Andy mischievously.

Jenkins laughed. 'Hardly. You haven't met Sheila, my partner. I'd like to see any man dominate her.'

They arrived at the entrance just as a group of young women emerged, laughing and talking. The women were eclectically dressed in jeans, dungarees, multi-coloured tops and woollen jackets or cardigans, with their hair in various tints. They wore trainers or Converse. There was an energy and artiness about them. One or two glanced suspiciously at the two policemen. Andy smiled at them as they passed.

'I think they're part of the company. They must have known Andrea Barnes.' It was curious to think she had probably acted with these women.

They went in through the narrow door into a rather gloomy entrance hall from which double doors led into a large space with a massive curved brick ceiling. They were directly under the railway and a sudden deep rumbling noise indicated that a train was passing overhead. The lighting was subdued. In one corner of the room, two actors were rehearsing a scene with a director who stopped them to make comments. Voices echoed in the empty space.

'Can I help you?'

Andy turned to see a woman dressed entirely in black except for her strikingly oversized red glasses. He introduced himself and Jenkins and explained why they were there.

The woman frowned and shook her head. 'I'm Ann Gifford, director of the Women's Theatre Collective. We've already spoken to the police; a detective came from the Met. Is it necessary to go over all that again? It's very painful. Andrea was a much loved and vital member of our group and we were all her friends.'

'I'm from the police in Yorkshire,' explained Andy. 'The investigation is not complete and we're speaking again to everyone involved in the case or who knew the people who died.'

Gifford sighed. 'Okay. You'd better follow me.' She led them into a small office, very different from the ones they'd seen at St Thomas's and Alpha Publishing. It was extremely untidy with scripts and bits of props lying around. A bookshelf on the wall was crammed with copies of plays. 'I'd ask you to sit, but as you can see that's not possible at the moment.' All the chairs apart from one behind a desk had stuff piled onto them.

'Never mind, we'll stand,' said Andy. Gifford sat behind the desk. 'What can you tell us about Andrea Barnes?'

Gifford shrugged as if it was all too much painful effort. 'Andrea was a founding member of this group. That's her in *Consent*.' She pointed to an action photograph on the wall showing a group of female actors on stage. 'Andrea co-authored that play. We write all our own material. She was a good writer too. She joined straight from drama school and she's been a vital member ever since; hardworking, talented, great sense of humour. I don't know what we're going to do without her.' She stopped and looked away. Andy wondered if she was shedding a tear, but she turned back and carried on. Her tone changed to one of anger. 'She's not the first excellent woman to be murdered by a man she knew and she won't be the last until society takes violence against women seriously.'

Andy looked at her. 'Did you know her partner, Dominic Holgate?'

'Not really; he came to meet her here a few times. He seemed okay, he was involved in theatre, but you never know with men.'

At this point Andy did not want to be drawn into a discussion of male violence against women.

'What makes you so sure that Holgate killed her then?'

Gifford looked surprised. 'Isn't that what happened? It's been all over the press. Holgate stabbed her in that escape room or what-ever it was, ran off and then killed himself a couple of days later. It's Shakespearean, the difference between appearance and reality; brutal killers are often full of charm. We dealt with that issue in our last play. It was very well received by the critics. It's very important that these issues are—'

'I'm sure it is,' said Andy, deliberately cutting her off in full flow. 'The fact is we're not sure that what the evidence suggests is actually what happened. We're looking for other people who might have had a motive to do either of them harm. Did Andrea have any enemies to your knowledge?'

'No. Everyone loved her. I don't know why anyone would want to harm her, but that's often the story with domestic violence: good women, women who have helped others, get badly treated by the very people who should be caring for them. It's a huge problem. Do you know women are more likely to be killed by a man they know than anyone else?'

Andy still refused to be drawn. 'Were you aware that Andrea had any financial problems?' he asked.

Gifford looked suspicious. 'No. It's true that none of us make a great deal of money out of what we do – that's not our motivation – but I think Andrea had some kind of legacy, didn't she, from an aunt?'

'That's right, she inherited a flat in Leeds, but we also have evidence that she was involved in some scam with her uncle concerning false jewellery.'

'Andrea? I find that hard to believe. Are you sure there wasn't any coercion involved?'

'Not that we're aware of.'

'Sounds to me like she was trapped in something to do with a male relative. That's very common too: girls and young women being exploited and abused within the family. If not that then she was probably driven to it by the need to survive here in London where women earn considerably less than men.'

Andy glanced at Jenkins and saw to his amusement that the constable was looking alarmed and intimidated by this woman and her strongly expressed views.

Gifford paused and shook her head. There was sadness and regret in her voice. 'I wish she'd talked to us about it if her money situation was so bad and I know why she didn't. She wouldn't have wanted to worry us and she was very committed to the company. She wouldn't have wanted to leave us for something better paid.'

'Right,' said Andy.

Gifford stood up. 'Look, I've got a rehearsal soon. Is there anything else?'

'No, that's fine, thank you.'

She escorted them back to the exit. Her mood was now sombre. 'The awful irony of it all hasn't escaped us,' she said as the detectives were leaving. 'Here she was, performing plays about the way women are treated in society and then she becomes a victim herself. It's shocking and it hurts us a lot.'

~

Louise was having troubling thoughts. Ever since she'd met her friends in Leeds the previous night, something had been preying on her mind. She sat alone in the house in Chapel Allerton turning the problem over. She got up and looked out of the window at the tiny back garden, which her mother had made into a lovely little sanctuary with flowers in ceramic pots and attractive garden furniture. It was looking rather bedraggled now in late October.

She sighed. There was only one thing to do which was to tackle what was bothering her. She got her phone and sent a photograph to her friend Aisha with the text:

Good to see you last night. Is this the person you saw at Andrea's flat?

The message came back quickly:

Hi! Yes pretty sure. Great to see you too.

She texted back: Thanks, then went into the lounge and sat down. She thought for a moment and then sent another text to a different person:

Need to talk about something bothering me. A picture missing from Andrea's flat. You might be able to help.

She waited a while in silence and then a message came back.

Nice to hear from you, hope you're okay. Going to be in
Leeds on Saturday. Be busy but we could meet up.

She replied: Yes. can pick you up, but the answer she received suggested they meet at a certain time and place. She put down the
phone and thought again. Then she called Steph.

'Hi.'

'Hi, how are you?' Steph was at work at Harrogate HQ, looking through reports.

'I'm okay, thanks, but I need your help. You know when we
went to Andrea's flat with Dad?'

'Yes.'

'Did he leave a key for the flat with you? I need to go over there
to look for one or two things. I've remembered that I lent her some
books and I'd like to get them back.'

'Yes, he did leave a key, but I don't know if I should lend it to
you as the flat is still technically part of the investigation.'

'I promise I'll look after it and I won't stay long. I won't touch
anything; I'll just get my books.'

'Are you just going round there by yourself?'

There was a slight pause before Louise answered. 'Yes.'

Steph thought for a moment. 'Okay then, I'll drop it in to you
on my way home tonight.'

'That's great. See you later.' The conversation ended and Louise
put her phone down on the coffee table. She wasn't going to tell the
truth about what she was intending to do. This was a problem she
wanted to sort out herself.

In the afternoon Andy and DC Jenkins arrived at the offices of Reality Media Productions, where Dominic Holgate had worked.

'Well, this is just about our last chance,' said Andy wearily. 'We've followed up on nearly everybody on the list my boss gave me, but nothing's really turned up. Let's see what they made of Holgate here.'

'Don't give up, Sarge, I'm sure we'll find out something useful,' said Jenkins in his cheery manner.

After going through the usual rituals at reception, they were shown into a large air-conditioned open-plan office full of work-stations and huge indoor plants with their green leaves snaking up the walls. They walked through and into a small private office separated from the general area with glass partitions. A bald-headed man dressed in a black waistcoat and white shirt greeted them. Jenkins's eyes were drawn enviously to his impressive hipster beard and glasses as he reflected on his own inability to grow a decent beard.

'Hi. Paul Matthews, Director of Innovation.' He shook hands briskly with the detectives. 'Please sit down. How can I help?'

Andy explained the purpose of their visit.

'We had someone here from the Met,' Matthews replied, echoing Gifford at the Women's Theatre Cooperative. 'I can only repeat what I said then. We all got on well with Dom and he was an excellent member of the team. He was friendly, creative and a good team worker.'

'Was he ever angry with people or threatened violence? Did you ever see him with knives or guns?'

'No, certainly not. The only problem with Dom was that deep down you felt his heart wasn't in the job. He'd done a business degree and had some problems. We took him on based on his personality and obvious intelligence. He could do the job very well but his real love was the theatre. He would have loved to have become an actor. He was a great mimic and used to have us in stitches.' Matthews smiled. 'He loved his practical jokes too. He'd give you some coffee and there would be a frog moulded into the bottom of the mug, or he'd be slumped at his desk and there would be a realistic-looking knife sticking out of his back. That was the only knife I ever saw him with: a joke one.'

It wasn't a joke one that killed Andrea Barnes, thought Andy. 'Did he have any enemies?' he asked.

'Dom? Not that I know of and, before you ask, I did meet his girlfriend, Andrea, and they seemed to get on fine. It came as a great shock to us when they both died.'

'You say that as if you don't believe the account you must have seen on the news that Holgate killed her and then committed suicide.'

Matthews smiled and shook his head. 'Do you? It strikes me you don't if you're still investigating the case,' he observed perceptively. 'I don't know the details. I can only say that for us who worked with him in this company the whole idea seems too monstrous to accept. We've obviously talked about it, and none of us can see Dom as a murderer and certainly not of his girlfriend.'

'Did he ever seem depressed or moody? Someone who might be suicidal?'

'Again no. He was always upbeat. The idea of him killing himself is also something we can't get our heads round.' He smiled at Andy and shook his head. 'I really don't envy you investigating this case, Sergeant. I'll bet nothing makes sense.'

It seemed that Matthews was right, thought Andy as he and Jenkins left the office in silence after a relatively short interview and walked back to their car. No one, except Gifford, seemed to think it was credible that Holgate would murder Barnes and then kill himself. But, as far as he knew, no other explanation of what happened had yet been offered.

'Still in the dark, Sarge?' Jenkins sensed what he was thinking.

'Pretty much,' he replied. 'Maybe the boss can make something from what we've learned, but I can't.'

～

That evening, three of the remaining friends met after work near Old Spitalfields Market. Here there was a line of vans selling street food so they loaded up with burgers, burritos and pizza and found somewhere to sit. The crowds were not as dense as at lunchtime, when the area was a favourite venue for office workers. Jack, Mark and Maggie huddled together at an outdoor table just inside the market. The plan was to progress on to the cinema after eating.

'It feels funny with just the three of us,' observed Maggie, eating a slice of pizza. After a furious row with Mark after the visit from the police, she had finally forgiven him for not telling her the full truth about the plagiarism affair with Dominic.

'Ben's on his way,' said Jack. 'I had a text from him; he's back in London.'

'Good. It's a pity Louise isn't here.' Maggie smiled. 'I'm sure those two are about to get it on.'

'Why do you think that?'

'She was very concerned about him in Whitby.'

'Weren't we all?' said Jack, eating a burrito.

'Yeah, but there was something about the way she looked at him. Maybe it takes a woman to understand.'

'Well, it wasn't exactly the atmosphere up there for romance to flourish,' said Mark. 'Maybe things will happen when they're both back here together. It'll be nice to have something good to celebrate.'

'Oh look, he's here,' said Maggie. She'd spotted Ben in the distance looking for them and waved at him. 'He's coming over.'

'Hi,' said Ben as he reached their table. The others greeted him. 'I'll just go and get something.' He went off to the row of vans and returned with a burger and salad. He brought over an empty chair and squeezed in at the table. 'It's great to be back here, isn't it? And great to see you all. When's Louise coming down?' He seemed much more upbeat now he was away from Whitby.

Maggie gave Mark a furtive glance and smiled.

'Don't know,' said Jack. 'She left it open. She seems to want to stay up there until her dad and the others have finished with the case. I still don't know what she thinks they're going to find.' Jack didn't mention that Andy and Jenkins had been to see him. It would have involved too much explaining. Mark and Maggie had decided on the same approach. They all wanted to put the business behind them and move on.

'I think at some deep level, she's still in denial about things. She can't believe she's lost two friends, that one killed the other and then committed suicide,' said Ben. 'It's a common reaction to something as traumatic as what we went through.'

'Yes, and I think she expects her dad to perform magic. Like she's reverted to being a child. You know, when your parents seemed all powerful?'

'Wow, this is getting into deep psychology!' said Jack. 'But you might be right. I don't think she would have been like this if her father hadn't been a detective.'

'Well, never mind, she'll get over it,' said Mark. He looked at his watch. 'We'll have to get off soon or we'll miss the start of the film. What's everybody doing this weekend? We could meet up and eat somewhere. I could do Sunday.'

'I'm away this weekend,' said Jack.

'I could do Sunday too, preferably evening,' said Ben.

Mark turned to Maggie, who had been exchanging texts and only half listening. 'Oh yeah, Sunday evening's fine. I'm busy Saturday too.'

~

Oldroyd and Deborah were sitting in the lounge bar in an old pub near the harbour when Andy rang to report back.

'Hi, sir. Hope you've had a good day?'

'Not bad at all, Andy,' replied Oldroyd. 'Things have got exciting up here.' He told Andy about Elaine Pesku's escape. 'I think it all proves that there is indeed more to this case than we initially thought. I've suspected it for a long time. Granger's got a team out searching for Elaine Pesku and added to all that we've been for a bracing walk up to the abbey.'

'Sounds good, sir. I wish I had some good news myself, but I've followed up just about everything concerning this group and I can't say we've come up with anything exciting. We've only got Maggie Hinton's employers left, and I'm not optimistic that will throw anything up. The others seem in the clear. To sum up: Jack Ryerson's alibi for Wednesday was backed up by his lover. Mark Garner admitted that he had a nasty row with Holgate about the plagiarism, but his alibi for the Wednesday, that he was at work, was supported by his employer. Ben Morton seemed a bit of a loner at work, but we couldn't find anything against him. Holgate was well thought of at his company and nobody could identify any enemies. They thought he got on well with his girlfriend, Barnes. They even said what a great member of the team he was, entertaining them with practical jokes and tricks with knives where he pretended to be dead. I thought that was a touch ironic, you know.

The knife he used to stab Barnes was real enough and he was dead all right by the end.'

'True enough,' replied Oldroyd. 'And very dark. Fate has some cruel twists at times.'

'So, I'm afraid that's it, sir.'

'Okay. Well done, and don't worry. This grafting is all part of the job; sometimes you have to sift through a lot of dross, as it were, before you find the diamond. It looks like things are swinging back to this end. Our main hope now is to capture Pesku and see if we can get her to tell us what's been going on. She's definitely involved in some way. You might as well stay there and do your final interview tomorrow. Come back over the weekend.'

'All right, sir.' The conversation ended, and Oldroyd hung up the phone.

'Was that your sergeant again?' asked Deborah.

'It was. He sounded disappointed. He's always so keen to do well and help make progress in a case, but he's finding that it doesn't always go the way you'd like it to.'

'No, that's the same in many professions.' Deborah took a drink from a glass of wine and then she sat back on the sofa and sighed. 'Well, I must say, this is the life. It's so relaxing to get away for a while and be by the sea. What's the plan tomorrow? Will you be busy all day?'

'I'll have to check in with Alice Granger and see how the hunt for Pesku is going. Other than that, I thought we might pay a visit to the museum in Pannett Park as the weather's not going to be brilliant. Have you ever been?'

'No.'

'Oh, it's a wonderfully eccentric collection of all kinds of stuff.'

'Sounds good. I can't wait.'

❧

Louise answered the door when Steph knocked. It was six o'clock. Julia was still at work.

'Hi,' said Steph.

'Hi. So you want to come in for a minute?'

'I won't, if that's okay? I've got to get back home, and I'm pretty knackered. Here's the key.' She handed it over to Louise who thanked her. 'How about meeting up on Saturday for a coffee in town?'

Louise looked uncomfortable and hesitant. 'Sorry, I can't. I've got to go out to the flat and I'm . . . I'm meeting someone.'

Steph looked at her with concern. 'Is everything all right?'

'Yes fine. Well, you know, not really, but I think I'm getting a bit better day by day. Maybe we could meet up next week sometime?'

'Fine. Okay, then I'll be off.'

'Bye for now.'

Steph got back in her car but sat thinking for a moment before she started the engine. There was clearly something Louise was not telling her.

∼

The next day was Friday and Halloween. It dawned quiet and still with heavy, dark clouds settling a gloom over the day.

DC Hampton and his team continued their search for Pesku early in the day. They split up, some searching back alleys and outhouses in the town centre and some going round more suburban areas asking people to be careful about who might be hiding in their garage or shed. A message had gone out on local radio with a description of Pesku and the usual injunction to be wary and not to approach the person, who may be dangerous. So far there were no reports of any sightings. There were also officers watching the bus and train stations.

Hampton was coordinating the search and was in contact with the teams. He was with a small group combing the area around where Pesku had escaped from him and Granger.

'Any luck?' asked another DC as Hampton finished a radio call from the team doing street searches.

'No, and I don't think they're going to find her out there in the residential areas. I think she'll be down here somewhere in the old town. This is the area she knew best as she worked at the escape room and she wasn't that familiar with Whitby as a whole. She could easily get lost if she strayed from here.'

'Yeah, I think you're right. We'll just have to knock on doors and check possible hiding places until something turns up. Somebody must have seen her.'

~

At Whitby Police HQ, an animated Granger had news for Oldroyd. 'I've got some revelations about Elaine Pesku. We contacted the Romanian authorities and they had nothing on anyone of that name, but when we sent her photograph through, which we found amongst her things in her room in that house, they recognised her immediately. Her real name is Irina Albesku and she is wanted big time in Bucharest. She was part of a drugs gang and is suspected of being involved in some pretty nasty murders. She fled the country over a year ago and disappeared. The fact that she could come here and successfully take on a new identity with a passport and probably other documents is testimony to the fact that she knew some high-level and clever people in the underworld.'

'I see,' said Oldroyd. 'So she would be capable of using a gun?'

'Absolutely. But what are you suggesting?'

'I'm not certain, but surely it's no accident that someone like that was working at the escape room.'

'We don't know for sure that she was involved, do we?' replied Granger. 'In fact this discovery could explain why she's run off and disappeared again. It may be nothing to do with the murders and the escape room; she may have just thought that we'd found out who she was and had come to arrest and deport her.'

'I suppose so. We'll have to wait until we find her.'

'I've got Hampton and some other DCs on the job. They're all local and they'll find her if anyone can. In the meantime, I'm going to track down where she was at college in London to see if we can find out some more about her time here in Britain. How about you?'

'Oh, I think I'm going to visit the museum.'

~

'This is one of the most unusual museums I know,' said Oldroyd eagerly as he and Deborah walked across Pannett Park towards the museum building in the half light of the dim afternoon.

'I'm looking forward to it,' replied Deborah as she gazed over the still park with the wet grass covered in leaves. 'It'll be nice to get inside on a day like this. It's certainly good weather for Halloween: suitably gloomy and spooky.'

'The place is an amazing cornucopia of all kinds of things. Wait till you see the Hand of Glory.'

'The what?'

Oldroyd laughed. 'You'll see.'

They reached the museum and art gallery, a simple but handsome neoclassical building erected in the 1920s, went in and bought their tickets from the friendly volunteer on duty. It was such a dark afternoon that the lights were on. Deborah smiled as she looked into the main room, which was packed with glass cases stuffed with exhibits. It was full of the atmosphere of an old museum with all kinds of things bundled together. She could see model ships and a dolls' house; a shoe collection and fossils. There was a complicated and eccentric machine called the Tempest Prognosticator, invented by a nineteenth-century curator of the museum called George Merryweather. This supposedly detected oncoming storms by means of leeches in bottles of water linked to a bell.

'Look at this,' said Oldroyd, leading her to a glass case which contained a withered human hand.

'Ugh, that's revolting. Why is that here?'

'It's called the Hand of Glory. I think it says this one was found in the wall of a cottage somewhere.' He read the information board. 'Yes, that's right, at Castleton up the River Esk. They used to cut off the hand of a felon who'd been hanged and then make a candle of fat from the same corpse. They believed that if you placed this candle in the hand and lit it, this would render people nearby motionless. Thieves could use this to burgle places and render all the inhabitants helpless while the intruders stole everything they wanted.'

'What a bizarre and gruesome idea!'

'Isn't it? Fascinating though! Look, I'm just going over there to look at the model ships. Why don't you have a look at the doll collection? I'll meet you over there. It's worth a look.'

'Okay, sounds a bit gender-stereotypical, though,' said Deborah, laughing as she made her way across the shiny wooden floor past glass cases full of clocks, coins, toys and weapons. She encountered a large totem pole and arrived at a large exhibit case full of dolls. Although she'd had dolls as a child she'd always found displays like this a little disturbing. Like ventriloquists' dummies with their exaggerated features and loose jaws, there was always that uncomfortable feeling that they could somehow come to life. She looked at them individually and shivered. Some had quite evil-looking expressions with broken teeth and missing eyes. She noticed something at the back of the display case; surely that ugly face was moving! She let out a little cry and Oldroyd stepped out from behind the case, laughing. He'd covered himself in a white dust sheet he'd found in the corner of the room so only his head was visible. Then he crouched down behind the exhibits staying absolutely still. To a casual glance it looked as if he was inside the case. When Deborah went past he turned his head slowly and put on a grotesque expression with staring eyes.

'Oh, your face!' he exclaimed.

Despite being shocked, she had to laugh. 'You bugger! You really had me there! Oh, it's a great place for a practical joke, isn't it? But it could have gone wrong. What if I'd fallen into the glass or had a heart attack?'

'I don't think that's likely and—' Suddenly his expression changed. Something had moved in his mind again, but no clear idea emerged. 'Fancy some tea in the café?' he said.

'Lovely.'

Later on they went for another meal at the Seagull Café and Oldroyd was rather distracted throughout the evening. On the way back to the hotel Halloween was in full swing with groups of children dressed in ghoulish costumes wandering around supervised by adults. As they knocked on doors their cries of 'Trick or Treat!' could be heard again and again. For some reason this chant stayed with Oldroyd and kept him awake far into the night. He felt as if he was on the verge of an insight but it stayed tantalisingly out of reach.

∾

Early next morning, Oldroyd was emerging from sleep and his mind was still playing the phrase over: 'Trick or Treat', 'Trick or Treat', then: 'Trick!' 'Trick!' 'Trick!'

The single word resonated louder and louder, and he sprung awake. His subconscious must have been working overnight. Things had suddenly become much clearer. He flung the duvet back and jumped out of bed.

'Of course,' he muttered to himself as he grabbed his phone. 'That's what was going on. Why didn't I realise it sooner? All the evidence was there in front of me if I'd put it all together.'

A very groggy voice answered the phone.

'Sir?' It was Andy.

'Andy! I know it's early but tell me again what Holgate's boss told you about Holgate being a joker.'

Andy was in bed, screwing his eyes up against the light. He scratched his head and then shook it to help get his brain into gear. 'He said Holgate had a good sense of humour and enjoyed practical jokes, like pretending to be stabbed.'

'And he used a false knife?'

'Yes, but, sir, we talked about this yesterday. He wasn't using a trick knife in that escape room; that woman died of stab wounds.'

'She did, but that's not incompatible with his use of a trick knife,' Oldroyd replied enigmatically.

'What, sir? You've completely lost me.'

'Never mind. I just wanted to confirm what you'd said. Time to get up anyway, you lazy so-and-so, I can tell you're still in bed. More information later – I think I'm really on to something now.'

'Okay, sir.' Andy put the phone down and yawned. He couldn't understand where his boss was coming from, but he was glad to hear him so upbeat and back to his bumptious self.

Oldroyd made another call. 'Alice? Yes, it's Jim Oldroyd. Sorry to ring you so early but the answer has come to me. I know what happened and how those two were murdered in the escape room and I'm pretty sure I know who was responsible. Yes, they were both murdered. It was a clever scheme. I just need to confirm one or two things. Can you meet me in an hour at the station? Excellent. See you there.'

Deborah moaned and turned over. 'What's going on, Jim?' she murmured.

'I think we've got a breakthrough in the case. I have to meet Alice Granger at the station. I'll see you later.'

'Okay.' Deborah pulled the duvet back over herself and went back to sleep.

~

'Can you get that video footage up from the CCTV at the escape room? I want to have another look.' Oldroyd sat next to Granger at her desk at Whitby police HQ while she brought the video up on her computer. He was full of energy and eagerness after the recent lull in the investigation. 'It's the bit just after Holgate stabs her.'

Granger fast forwarded through bizarre speeded-up scenes of the group in their goth costumes. She stopped when Holgate ran to the emergency exit which led to the storeroom. Ben Morton was leaning over Andrea at the bottom of the picture. You could see the white dress stained with blood, but their faces were not visible.

'Right,' said Oldroyd. 'You can't see much because Morton's in the way . . . and that's deliberate. I think she was probably whispering something to Morton at this point.'

'But she'd been stabbed,' protested Granger. Oldroyd shook his head.

'No. We found some stomach medicine capsules among Barnes's things. I think she used them for something. You see, Holgate only stabbed her with a false knife, and then' – he paused, and the effect was dramatic – 'Morton used the real thing.'

'Morton! You think he was the murderer?' Granger considered this for a moment. 'Well, that would tie up with what I discovered yesterday about Pesku. She was a student at the Imperial College of Art, where one of her tutors was Ben Morton.'

'Well, well, at last we've got the vital link. What was she doing up here?'

'As far as we can tell, she came up here for a holiday job.'

'And if Morton came to see her, he might have got some ideas. Excellent! It's all fitting together at last.'

'But what was the motive to kill one of his own friends, sir?'

'I'm not certain yet and it wasn't just Barnes. Pesku was the accomplice. I believe she killed Holgate in the storeroom. I have an idea what it was all about, but we urgently need to tell Andy to get some support and go round to arrest Morton. I'm assuming he's back in London. I'm going to ring Andy now.'

Andy answered after a pause. It was still only eight o'clock in the morning. 'Morning again, sir. It seems all go today. Has something happened?'

'Yes, so get yourself moving! I assume you're out of bed now. We think we know who the perpetrator is: it's Ben Morton, and his accomplice was Elaine Pesku. We'll deal with her, but he's down there near you. His London address is in that file I gave you. Get some officers from the Met to help you and get round there and arrest him. And watch it, he could be dangerous.'

'Yes, sir, I'm on to it.'

'Also, look out for an old painting. It might not look much, but it's very valuable and I think he may have it. If you find it take care with it.'

'Right, sir.'

Oldroyd ended the call and thought carefully about his next action. Should he ring Louise to tell her about Ben Morton? It would be a terrible shock after all she'd already been through and Ben was miles away in London. It would probably be better to keep her in the dark until they'd wrapped it all up and then he could break it to her gently.

~

Andy Carter swung into action after he'd spoken to Oldroyd. He collected Jenkins and DC Brook from the Met and they sped to Morton's address in Notting Hill. It was still quite early for a Saturday morning when they arrived. The door was opened by a bleary-eyed housemate of Morton's. He looked like a student and was younger than Morton.

'Police,' announced Andy, holding up his ID. 'We understand Ben Morton lives here.'

'That's right. But what—'

'We need to speak to him.'

'Okay, come in. His room's on the first floor, but I think I heard him go out.'

The detectives piled up the stairs and Andy hammered on the door without response. 'Morton, open up. It's the police,' he shouted, but there was still no response. He turned to the person who'd let them in. 'Is there a spare key?'

'Not that I know of.'

'Okay.' Andy put his shoulder to the door and burst it open. They entered a large bedroom which was crammed with painting materials, half-finished canvases and pieces of frame. In one corner was a small untidy bed and a desk covered with papers. The most striking things were a number of completed paintings on the walls. Black and red swirls of colour surrounded vampires, bats, dripping blood and fangs biting into necks. Intense and diabolical red eyes stared out from beneath black wing-like capes.

'Bloody hell, Sarge!' said Jenkins. 'This bloke must be a bit of a weirdo to paint that stuff. It's like a horror film.'

'Well, he certainly liked his vampires, that's for sure.' He turned to the young man who was peering into the room. 'Did he tell anyone where he was going?'

'I don't know. What's all this about?'

'He's wanted for a very serious crime so you'd better call everyone together and we'll see if anyone knows where he's gone.' The young man disappeared. The detectives put on their gloves.

'Sarge, look at this. You said there was a painting missing.'

DC Brook had unwrapped a package and took out a square picture frame. The painting showed a bare-armed woman with long red hair. She had her arms around a man and seemed to be biting his neck.

'Well, whatever turns you on, I suppose,' said Jenkins, grinning. 'I can think of better things for her to do to me than bite my neck.'

'I'm sure you can,' replied Andy. 'But this looks as if it could be the one we're looking for,' he said, shaking his head at the idea that something like that could be worth a lot of money. They continued to search the flat for anything significant. Covered in bubble wrap and hidden in a drawer, Andy found two knives, one with a retractable blade. He put those in a plastic bag.

'I think this bloke must have had a good opinion of himself, Sarge. Look at this,' said Jenkins, who was sorting through the paintings.

Andy went over and looked at a canvas that was covered with artistically enhanced copies of a photograph of Morton. They were in different colours and all bore a single-word title in a variety of fonts: 'Genius', 'Michelangelo', 'Rembrandt', 'Great Artist', 'Famous', 'World Beater', 'Single-Minded' and so on. Underneath an image in black was the phrase 'Destined for Greatness' and underneath one in red was the word 'Killer'. The effect was chilling.

'He has an ego, all right,' said Andy. 'And he seems to be telling us that he'll stop at nothing to assert himself. We need to go through everything very thoroughly. I'll go and talk to the other housemates.'

He went through into the kitchen area to find three sombre-looking people gathered together, two women and one man.

'What's Ben done?' asked one.

'He's the prime suspect in a murder case,' replied Andy.

'What! You mean that thing in Whitby? He was up there, wasn't he?'

'He was and he's in possession of a valuable stolen painting.'

'I can't believe Ben would do anything like that,' said one of the women. 'He was always so quiet and gentle. He was an artist,' she added at the end as if this precluded him having any criminal tendencies.

'How much did you know about him?' asked Andy.

The group glanced at each other. 'To be honest, not a lot really,' replied one. 'He was very private and didn't join in much with anything that was going on. He never asked anybody into his room.'

Not surprising, thought Andy as he noted that what they were saying correlated with how Morton had been described by his colleagues at the Imperial College. He seemed to be an example of what Andy thought of as the loner criminal syndrome: distorted and insane ideas develop in a person who has little contact with others. Nobody had realised what deadly notions were forming in the mind of this solitary artist.

'Do any of you know where he is?'

'No,' said the man who'd let them into the house. 'And James, who might have seen him earlier, has gone out. I've been trying to contact him.'

'I'll take his number,' said Andy. This was frustrating. He would delay calling the boss until he had some idea of where Morton was. Presumably he wasn't far away. They would be able to apprehend him before the day was out. That would earn him a lot of points with DCI Oldroyd.

~

Back in Whitby, DC Hampton and his team met at police HQ early before setting out on their second full day of searching for Elaine Pesku. Their patient enquiries going from house to house had yielded nothing, but Hampton had an idea. Now that the news had come through that she had a violent criminal record in Romania, they were joined by two officers armed with guns. There had been some reports from people who claimed to have seen her but these had come to nothing.

'She's had to spend the nights somewhere, and I don't think it was outside like a homeless person; far too risky. She doesn't know Whitby well, but she will have seen all the boats and yachts down in the harbour. At this time of year most of them are sealed up for winter and covered in tarpaulin. If she managed to get inside one of those it would give her some good shelter.' He looked at his watch. 'It's still early, we might catch her before she moves on but we must be careful. According to Inspector Granger, she's probably armed.'

The four detectives walked down to the harbour where they split up and began to carefully examine the craft there. It was a difficult task involving striding between boats tied together as they bobbed around in the water. It was early on another dull and cold day and there was nobody about. A few herring gulls sat on wooden posts and in the rigging of some of the tall yachts.

Hampton had brought a torch and was shining it under the tarpaulin of a large yacht when he saw one of the team on another boat gesticulating at him and pointing at the tarpaulin covering the deck. Hampton gestured to the detective to return to the harbour side. The others followed, and they met together speaking quietly.

'The tarpaulin's loose on that yacht. I went underneath it and the cabin door's been prised open. Unless there's been a thief at work, she could be in there.'

'Okay, let's have a look at it. We'll group around the boat and I'll call and tell her to come out.' They made their way back to the yacht in question and took up positions. Hampton nodded at the others and then called out in a loud voice.

'Elaine Pesku. We're here to arrest you. The boat is surrounded by armed police officers. You cannot escape. Come out now with your hands in the air.'

The reply was the crack of a pistol firing and a bullet zinging past his head. He dived for cover into a neighbouring boat and saw that the others had done the same. Clearly she was not going to surrender without a fight. It looked like this would turn into a long siege.

<hr/>

At the house in Chapel Allerton, Louise didn't wake up until 10.00 a.m., but for once she'd slept soundly. She picked up her phone but the battery was dead. She put it on charge and made some breakfast. Her mother had left a note to say she'd gone into Leeds. That was good. There would be nobody around to ask questions when she left to meet Ben at the flat.

<hr/>

Back in the office Oldroyd's phone went again. It was Andy, whose tone was urgent.

'Hello, sir. No joy here I'm afraid. We've been to Morton's address, but there's no sign of him. We did find a painting, which

I think is the one that's gone missing. There was some weird stuff here. He's obviously some kind of vampire freak. There were a couple of knives, one fake, which I've secured. His housemates say he went out early this morning, but he didn't say where he was going. One's just called me back now to say he remembers overhearing Morton arranging to meet up with someone in Leeds today. We should alert Steph and the Leeds police. Sir?'

'Right, Andy,' Oldroyd managed to say before ending the call abruptly and frantically trying to contact Louise. There was no answer. After several failed attempts he called Steph instead. To his relief she answered straight away.

'Steph, can you contact Louise immediately? It's very urgent and there's no answer on her phone. There's been a big breakthrough in the case and we're pretty sure Ben Morton is the murderer. I sent Andy round to arrest him, but he wasn't at his flat and we have reason to think that he's on his way to Leeds. If so, Louise could be in danger.'

Steph had rarely heard her boss so agitated. 'Don't worry, sir, I'm on to it now.'

She ended the call. Good job she'd made some preliminary arrangements.

~

'Hi,' said Ben, and he gave Louise a big smile. They were outside the flat in Headingley and he appeared out of the bushes at the side as if he'd been hiding in there. Ben had suggested that they meet here. He said there was something important he needed to show to her about the paintings. She'd texted to offer to give him a lift from the station but he'd refused, saying it was fine, he would make his own way there.

'Hi,' she replied. 'Look, I'm sorry about this but something's come up and I want to talk to you about it and I couldn't do it on the phone.'

'That's fine. Let's go inside, shall we?' Ben was looking around as he spoke, appearing anxious to get inside. Louise unlocked the door and they went into the dark hallway and up the stairs. Ben looked around cautiously as if checking that anyone else was in the building. It was quiet with no sign of activity in the other apartments.

'It's fine,' said Louise, smiling. 'We're not breaking in. We've got the key.'

Ben just smiled back. The apartment felt cold and a bit damp. Louise went into the sitting room and pulled back the curtains. They sat down on armchairs opposite each other.

'I hate coming here,' said Louise, looking around the room with an expression of distaste. 'It's a gorgeous apartment, but it's spooky coming in without Andrea. It's as if she's haunting the place. It was awful when I came here with Dad.'

'I'm sure it was.' Ben smiled sympathetically. He sat with his hands in his pockets. 'What's all this about then?'

Louise frowned and looked embarrassed as if she didn't know where to begin. 'Ben, I think you know I've got some feelings for you,' she said falteringly. He didn't reply and looked away as if he was also embarrassed. 'I also think you might be in a bit of trouble and I want to help.'

Ben raised his eyebrows. 'What kind of trouble?'

Louise looked him in the eyes. 'Did you take that picture that was on the wall in the entrance hall?' She pointed in the direction of the hall.

'Why do you think I did that?'

'Because I know you came to visit Andrea here and you would have seen it then. I think you recognised it as something valuable.

I know you're short of money and want to spend more time on your art. I've been thinking that you could have taken the keys from Andrea's stuff at the flat in Whitby and come over here and taken it.'

'What, in the middle of the night?'

'Look, I know it's a wild thing to accuse you of, but it's been bugging me. Please just tell me if I'm wrong.'

Ben looked down and sighed. After a pause, he said: 'No, you're right, I did take it. It's a lost painting by Edvard Munch, and it's worth a lot of money. I thought nobody would miss it. Have you told anyone else you think I took it?'

Louise was relieved. 'No, and I'm glad you've admitted it. Munch. Didn't he paint that picture called "The Scream"?'

'Yes.'

She looked at him sternly. 'I want you to return it, Ben. You know you shouldn't have taken it. There's a chance you'll get caught and even if you don't it will be on your conscience. I can understand why you did it, but just bring it back and I won't say anything. I don't think you're really a thief; the temptation was just too great. Am I right?'

Ben looked sheepish and then he smiled at her. 'You're right, again. I'll bring it back as soon as I can. Will you let me in here?'

'Of course. And then it's over. No one will know.'

'No, they won't.' He looked at her and then stood up and came close. He took in a deep breath as if he was finding it difficult to know what to say next. 'You know you said that you had, you know, feelings for me?' He tentatively put an arm on her shoulder. 'I'm fond of you, too.'

'Oh, Ben!' Louise smiled up at him. As they entered an embrace, he whipped his other hand out of his pocket. It was holding a ligature which he got round her neck as he moved swiftly behind her. Louise's eyes widened in surprise and shock and she gave out a muffled cry.

Suddenly Steph appeared from where she'd been listening behind the door to the kitchen. She got her arm around Ben's neck and forced him to drop the cord.

Two more officers from the Leeds force, one female, came in from where they'd been hiding in a bedroom. The female officer went to Louise where she'd slumped to the floor, the other helped Steph to get the handcuffs on Morton and checked him for any more weapons.

'Ben Morton,' began Steph. 'I'm arresting you for the murders of Hugh Preston, Andrea Barnes, and Dominic Holgate and for the attempted murder of Louise Oldroyd. You do not have to say anything, but it may harm your defence if you do not mention when questioned something which you later rely on in court. Anything you do say may be given in evidence.'

Morton remained silent. Louise screamed: 'Ben? No! Oh my God!' and started to cry.

'Okay,' continued Steph. 'Let's get him into the car. I'll phone for help; she's had a terrible shock. You two get him down to the station and I'll wait here with her for the ambulance. I'll secure the building. When you get back someone needs to arrange his transfer to Whitby.'

'Okay, Sarge,' said one of the officers as Morton was led out of the flat to the police car parked in a secluded back street. Steph checked that the keys to the flat were in her pocket as she knelt by the distraught figure of Louise on the floor.

'Why, how . . . are you here?' Louise struggled to talk.

'Let's say it was an instinct,' replied Steph. 'I felt you were in danger so I had a duplicate set of keys to the flat cut and we were able to get in here to monitor what was happening.'

Louise was rubbing her neck. 'Oh my god, I've been such a fool. Does Dad know what's happened?'

'Not yet. He's still over in Whitby. He wasn't able to do anything so I've dealt with it myself. I'll be calling him soon, so don't worry. The ambulance is coming to take you in for a check-up, but I'm sure you'll be fine.'

Louise nodded and put her hands up to her face. It was all too much to take in, but she was dimly aware through the awful shock, that the terrible ordeal that had begun in the escape room was now over.

~

In Whitby, everyone was focused on the drama surrounding the arrest of Elaine Pesku.

Granger and Oldroyd had come down to the harbour to witness the stand-off between the police and the desperate fugitive. An armed officer was delivering messages via a megaphone, but there was no sign that she was showing a willingness to surrender.

'She's a tough character,' observed Oldroyd. 'I wonder what she fears most: facing judgement here or the possibility of being deported back to Romania?'

'Probably both,' replied Granger. 'Oh, looks like we're going to get some action.'

Two officers were preparing to fire tear gas into the interior of the yacht. One clung to the side of the vessel, positioned to smash a window, while another aimed the tear-gas gun. The officer with the megaphone was talking constantly to distract the target inside.

Suddenly the officer clinging to the side of the boat smashed the window with a metal pickaxe. There was a crack, and the tear gas canister flew in through the hole. Gas billowed through the broken window.

There was the sound of coughing from inside the cabin, and then a figure recognisable as Elaine Pesku appeared on deck before diving into the water without even trying to take a shot from her handgun. Two officers dived in after her. She made it across to the other side of the harbour, and out of the water.

She was running down the road when the officers caught up with her and brought her down.

'That was a plucky effort,' said Oldroyd. 'She doesn't give in easily, but now the game's up we'll see what she has to say for herself.'

On the way back he checked his phone for messages, but there was nothing yet. He tried to call, but there was no answer from either Louise or Steph.

❧

Oldroyd looked into the cold blue eyes and blank face of Irina Albesku, who was known in the case as Elaine Pesku. It was the tough, inscrutable face of a hardened criminal, which Oldroyd had seen many times before. There was no point trying to break her down; they had to appeal somehow to her self-interest. He was sitting with Granger in the interview room at Whitby police station. On the other side of the table were Pesku and a duty solicitor. Pesku had insisted on her rights.

'Okay,' began Oldroyd. 'Let's get to the main points. You're here because you were part of the plan to murder Andrea Barnes and Dominic Holgate. You were also involved in the murder of Hugh Preston and you personally shot Holgate with the gun you used to fire at police officers when you were avoiding arrest at Whitby Marina. So it's a pretty serious list of charges. Do you wish to say anything at this point?' Oldroyd could see that Pesku was calculating her next move. She looked to her solicitor, who advised her that she didn't need to say anything.

However, she turned back to Oldroyd. 'You can't prove I shot Holgate. I wasn't in the room where Barnes was stabbed.'

'Oh, I think we can. We've retrieved the gun from where you dropped it into the water and I think we'll find it's the same one that killed Holgate, which was why we couldn't find it near his body. And if you weren't guilty of any of this, why were you so desperate to escape from us?'

'I got scared you make me go back to Romania. I'm sorry I fired gun.'

'I can understand that,' said Granger, 'given your criminal record over there, but we think that Hugh Preston told you about the trick sarcophagus and so he had to be got rid of. We've also found some hairs on the hood that the figure who was supposedly Holgate was wearing when he went crazy outside the pub on Church Street. They're long hairs and we think they'll match yours. You impersonated Holgate that night. You had to do it because he was already dead. You then dressed Holgate's body, wherever you'd been storing it, in the clothing you were wearing and dumped it in the harbour.'

'We're in the process of arresting Ben Morton,' added Oldroyd. 'So it will be interesting to hear what he has to say about all this and your part in it.'

Elaine frowned and looked away. Oldroyd sensed there was more calculation going on. Eventually she turned back sharply to face Granger and Oldroyd. She appeared to have made a decision.

'Okay, I tell you everything. It was Ben's idea and he forced me to take part. He said he would tell authorities about me and I would be sent back to Romania. I didn't want to do it. I am very sorry.'

Oldroyd smiled. Her declaration of relative innocence and her remorse were not credible, but at last they were going to get a detailed account of what happened.

Oldroyd and Granger had just finished interviewing Pesku when Oldroyd's phone rang. It was Steph.

'You go on to the office,' he said to Granger. 'I'll just take this.' Granger went off down the corridor.

'Sir, there's been a major incident here in Leeds. I want to stress to you that everybody is okay, including Louise.'

Despite this reassurance, Oldroyd felt the anxiety hit his stomach. 'What the hell's been going on?'

Steph began to explain.

When Oldroyd didn't arrive at the office, Granger went to the door to look for him. She saw him in the corridor slumped over and holding on to a radiator.

She ran down to him. 'Sir, what's happened?' She helped him into the office, sat him down and made a drink of hot tea. It was some time before she could get the story out of him. She'd never seen him so shocked and fragile. Haltingly, he explained what had happened in Leeds.

'So they've got Morton . . . but Louise . . . my daughter. He nearly killed her.' He covered his face with his hands.

'My God, sir, that's terrible.'

'I was here and couldn't do anything to help. I had no idea she'd actually arranged to meet him at the flat.'

'Look, sir, it's probably better that you didn't know until it was over. Steph sounds to have done a fantastic job. And Louise is okay, remember that.'

'Yes, yes. It's just the thought of what could have happened. It's too horrible to contemplate.'

'I know, sir. But it's all over now, and she's safe,' repeated Granger.

At that moment Oldroyd's phone went again. It was Andy asking how everything was progressing.

'It's fine, Andy,' he finally managed to say. 'It's all over. We've got Pesku here and Steph has arrested Morton in Leeds. They were the murderers. Steph's done a wonderful job. I'll tell you more later. Can you send a detailed report on what you've found to Inspector Granger?'

'Okay, sir. I'll get all this stuff sent up too.'

He ended the call and felt enormous relief that they'd finally got to the end, mixed with the awful shock of knowing how close things had come to further tragedy. He'd never felt so utterly exhausted at the end of a case.

Seven

From Brig O' Dread when thou may'st pass,
Every nighte and alle,
To Purgatory fire thou com'st at last,
And Christe receive thy saule.

From the Lyke Wake Dirge

It was Sunday morning and Oldroyd and Granger confronted their captive in the interview room. He'd been brought over from Leeds the previous evening. A solicitor sat next to him and a police officer sat on a chair in the corner of the room. Morton was bedraggled and defeated but retained a sullen defiance. Oldroyd stared at him for a few moments, appalled that his daughter had almost entered into a relationship with this man and then nearly been murdered by him.

'Let's go right back to the beginning,' he said. 'This was one of the most evil and devious schemes I've ever encountered in over thirty years of detective work. It was about the shocking betrayal and murder of three innocent people, two of them your own friends, for nothing other than personal gain.'

Morton shrugged but didn't say anything.

'It all began about a year ago, didn't it?' continued Oldroyd, trying not to express the utter contempt he felt for the man in front of him. 'You were in Leeds at a conference or something and Andrea, who was also up from London, invited you to the flat she'd inherited from her aunt. She particularly wanted you to see the artwork. If only she'd known what would happen as a result. When you got there you were very impressed by the collection but you were astonished to see one painting that was extremely special.'

Morton's face lit up at the memory. 'It was a painting called "Love and Pain" by Edvard Munch. He painted six versions of it and I knew one of them was missing. I couldn't believe it. I can't imagine how her aunt ever came to possess it but there it was.'

'Of course you knew all about that because you were obsessed with vampires.'

Morton's eyes seemed to take on a mad gleam and he spoke with a terrifying enthusiasm. 'Oh, yes, the thrill of that darkness and power. That bite of love which gives you complete control. The beauty of the red blood of life spilling out and catapulting the lucky victim into the eternal glamour of the undead. Who could resist that wonderful pain? And to paint such things is an ecstasy. I've been in thrall to vampiric art since I saw my first vampire painting. It's pure joy to . . .' And so he went on until Oldroyd finally stopped him.

'I see,' said Oldroyd, shocked at the sadomasochistic rant he'd just heard. 'Why did you keep all this a secret? You had exhibitions of your work but I don't think you ever included anything of this nature.'

Morton smiled. 'This was private, you see, just for me until I'd become famous and then I would unleash it on the world in all its deadly glory, like Dracula rising from his coffin.' He stood up and the uniformed officer stirred. Morton's voice was raised. 'And all would worship the glory and power of my art!'

'Sit down!' said Oldroyd firmly. This broke a spell. Morton seemed to deflate, slumped back onto his chair and wiped his brow with his arm.

'So,' continued Oldroyd. 'You realised that Andrea had no idea about the significance of this painting and how valuable it was so you didn't say anything. It was your intention from that day onwards to get your hands on it. I suspect you had two contradictory motives. It was a painting you would love to possess, but on the other hand, with the money you could get from selling it, you could give up the distraction of having to earn a basic living through teaching and concentrate on your own art. Your talent could finally be fulfilled. You believe in your unrecognised genius. Am I right?'

Morton nodded and smiled. He seemed to appreciate Oldroyd's understanding of his motives.

'There was the painting hidden in a collection. If you could get rid of Andrea Barnes, you could remove it and even if someone noticed that a painting was missing no one would remember what it was and no one knew its worth. Then you could sell it anonymously. Lost paintings are always being discovered, aren't they?'

'Yes. I asked her questions and it was clear that there was no one around who could have known about the painting so no one would report it stolen.'

'I'm sure you did. But unfortunately you forgot that there was someone else besides Andrea who was familiar with everything in the house, even if she didn't know much about the works of art. The cleaner, Mrs Adams . . . She told Louise about the artwork that was missing and described it. That made Louise suspicious, especially when she learned that you'd been in Andrea's house. But we'll come to that later.

'The problem was: how could you get rid of Andrea? It had to happen in a way that drew all attention away from you. Suicide, accident, or being murdered by someone else. I imagine it was very difficult to think how it could be done until a number of things came together for you, which they sometimes have a devilish habit of doing for someone planning a wicked crime.

'It started with one of your students – Elaine Pesku. She was Romanian. You began an affair with her. She was very cagey about her previous life, so you decided to investigate a little. You discovered that she was a criminal on the run, and her real name was Irina Albesku. She had a violent past as part of a drugs gang in Bucharest. How did you get all that information?'

At this point, the solicitor advised Morton that he didn't have to say anything. Morton, however, shook his head. It seemed that he realised it was all over. And he wanted to talk about his plan. It appeared to Oldroyd as though he was proud of it. He smiled. 'I have a friend who's a detective; he owes me a few favours. It didn't take him long with a photograph of her to find what I wanted.'

Oldroyd nodded. 'More likely you blackmailed him over something, but never mind about that for the moment. The big break finally came over the summer. Elaine, let's continue to call her that, had come up here to Whitby for a summer job and you came to see her.'

'She was working in this escape room on a Dracula theme . . . in Whitby of all places, where Dracula himself arrived in England. She showed me round. I suddenly had this incredible idea. It was so ingenious. It was a thing of beauty. It brought everything together.'

'Your concept of beauty is a very dark one,' replied Oldroyd sharply. 'Anyway, I think by then your affair with Elaine was probably near its end, but she was a useful, tough accomplice, having a violent past and being used to handling a gun.'

'It was her who got the gun,' said Morton. 'She seemed to have some connections with the underworld over here.'

Oldroyd paused. It was time to play his card. 'We have apprehended Elaine Pesku and her account of the scheme you played out together was that it was entirely your idea and you forced her into assisting you. Is that true?'

Morton shook his head again. 'It's true that I hinted that I could reveal what I knew about her, but she was more interested in getting her share of the money from us selling that picture. She was up for it all, so don't let her play the victim. She's a ruthless woman.'

Oldroyd smiled. He would never have seen Pesku as a victim. It was interesting to play accomplices off against each other. It usually worked and they ended up telling you more than they intended in order to incriminate the other.

'Anyway,' he continued. 'The first victim was the unfortunate Hugh Preston. He made the mistake of telling Elaine about the trick sarcophagus. Having checked that he hadn't told anyone else, you killed him and hid his body in the skip.'

'Yes,' said Morton. 'We couldn't risk anyone else finding out. Of course you did eventually.' He shot Oldroyd an evil look. 'It was good practice for the main event. Elaine lured him into the escape room office when he was paying a visit one day after the escape room had closed. I stabbed him with the same knife I used on Andrea and then we went out in the night to dispose of his body. It was like a rehearsal. I never thought those bloody kids would discover the body; that was a stroke of bad luck.'

Oldroyd frowned and shook his head. 'So,' he continued, 'the main scheme depended on getting the confidence of Andrea and her boyfriend Dominic and exploiting their love of dressing up and drama. You were all coming up to Whitby for the Goth Weekend, which I imagine was your suggestion in the first place, and to add to the excitement and the horror, you suggested a practical joke. What would happen was this: Dominic and Andrea would pretend to have rows with each other and then when you were all in the escape room, Dominic would pretend to completely lose it and stab her.'

Morton seemed to relish the memory. 'Yes, everyone thought the Goth Weekend was a great idea so I booked an Airbnb and organised the escape room with Elaine. No one knew about her connection with me. Then one night I was in a pub in London with Dom and Andrea, and I suggested we should perform this trick while we were up in Whitby taking part in this vampire-themed game. It would be perfect for the Goth Weekend. We would all be dressed up in a spooky environment: perfect. They were eating out of the palm of my hand; they thought it was a fantastic idea. They both had a great sense of humour and loved jokes. Everybody would laugh about it for days. We came up to Whitby the week before without anyone knowing. I explained everything and we practised it. It all fell into place. I remembered that Dom had told us about the gun his uncle had given him, so I carefully asked him a little more and he said it was a Glock pistol. So Elaine got hold of a similar model, along with a silencer. Like I said, she has lots of contacts in the underworld.'

'They didn't suspect a thing,' continued Oldroyd. 'Why should they? It was meant to be a clever practical joke that would amuse their friends and they played their parts to perfection, even having an argument the night before to establish they were in a bad mood with each other. It turned out to be a devilish confidence trick in which they lost their lives. They unwittingly collaborated in their own murders.

'Dominic stabbed her with a false knife, one where the blade retracts inside the handle as it meets the body so it looks as if the blade is entering the flesh and then he ran out through the emergency exit. There was a bag of fake blood inside her dress and Andrea also had capsules of the same blood in her mouth, which she crushed with her teeth. She got the blood from a joke shop for use on her Dracula's bride costume but she also poured some into these capsules which she'd emptied of stomach medicine. The blood seemed to flow out of her mouth. You rushed across to help her while Dominic ran out of the room. While the attention was on him you stabbed her in the chest with a real knife and hid the false one. Both knives looked very similar.'

Morton laughed. 'She said "Has he gone out?" I didn't reply. While Maggie was in the other room I covered Andrea's mouth hard with my hand and sunk the knife in. Then I pulled the empty capsules out of her mouth and wiped away all the fake blood. The only blood left on her mouth was hers. I pulled out the empty bag from inside her dress. It didn't matter that there was fake blood mixed with her own on the costume because that was meant to look bloody. She really had been stabbed to death. It was so neatly done. I'd checked where all the CCTV cameras were positioned, and I knew the real stabbing would not be captured on film.' His eyes sparkled at the memory.

Oldroyd was appalled at the pride and relish with which Morton was describing his calculated murder of Andrea Barnes.

Ben continued. 'The plan was for Dominic to briefly hide inside the sarcophagus. Then he would burst out when Andrea came back to life to general relief and then to applause and hilarity. The perfect gothic trick: an extension of the escape room game we were playing. Elaine's role was to assist with this trick. She had rushed round from reception into the storage room which contained the sarcophagus. She was waiting behind the door and her job was to block it with a packing case when Dominic had come through. This would give them time for the next stage. Elaine was to help him into the sarcophagus, shut the lid and then get back quickly to reception.'

'But she didn't do that, did she?' asked Oldroyd.

'No, she blocked the door and got him into the sarcophagus all right, but then she shot him in the side of the head with the silenced pistol, closed the lid and turned the sarcophagus round. Dominic had no idea that the thing rotated, and he never found out. It was a marvellous trick within a trick and it worked perfectly. There was too much commotion in the room where we were for anybody to hear the thud of the silencer. She did it all very efficiently; she was no victim. She had already got Andrea's phone out of her bag while we were still in the first room and deleted any texts between us that might be incriminating.'

Oldroyd saw where this was going and intervened. 'So when Maggie finally pushed through the door, Dominic was nowhere to be seen. And you were nearly home and dry.'

Morton suddenly turned angry. 'The plan would have worked if you hadn't come over. You and that bloody daughter of yours. I tried to arrange the escape room for a time before she got to Whitby. I knew she would be trouble and there was the added threat that you might get involved: Daddy, the great detective. But she turned up in time to take part. Bloody bitch!'

Red-faced, Oldroyd got up from his chair and had to be restrained by Granger. After a moment he sat down again, struggling to control his feelings. Granger carried on the interrogation.

'So you played the part of the caring friend who tried to save the victim's life while administering the death blow, at the same time as your accomplice murdered the poor woman's partner. Are you proud of that?'

Morton shrugged again. He'd returned to a sullen silence.

'You must have been pleased that part one of the scheme had worked so well. Part two involved creating the fiction that Holgate was still alive, but in a deranged state. Was that what all that stuff with the text messages and meeting in the churchyard was about?'

Again Morton warmed to the opportunity to talk about his plans. 'I'd already planted the gun holster in Dominic's room. We returned to the escape room in the night and removed his body from the sarcophagus. There was tape across the door into the side street, but we carefully removed it and then replaced it when we left. We left the body in the back of the car. Elaine had taken Dominic's phone so we were able to send the texts to his friends. Elaine impersonated him at the church yard. She's tall, it was dark and she kept her distance. I shouted out when we arrived to warn her we were there. She left Dominic's watch to prove it was him and all that garlic stuff was meant to confuse everybody and suggest that Dominic was mad.'

'So what happened when you staged the suicide?' asked Oldroyd, who had recovered some composure. He was relieved that Morton was not only putting up no defence, but seemed eager to tell them all about what he'd done.

'It was easy. Elaine dressed as Dominic again and conducted that scene at the pub, firing the gun and causing mayhem. It created the impression that he'd lost his sanity. She ran down the alley into darkness by the harbour where I was waiting with a change of clothes. She fired the gun again and we hid behind one of the buildings. She took off the mask, cape, hood and black trousers and put on a skirt and coat. Then we carefully made our way back to Church Street and mingled with the crowd. I even walked back to the pub to see what people were saying about what had happened.'

'And you dumped Holgate's body into the harbour?'

'Yes, we'd already got his body out of the escape room and into the boot of my car, which no one knew was in Whitby. I rented a garage near to where Elaine was staying. We dressed him in the clothes Elaine had worn earlier in the evening and in the middle of the night when everything had gone quiet, we drove down and waited until there was absolutely no one around. Then we got the body into the water.'

'What about the gun?'

'We kept it. I knew you wouldn't necessarily expect to find it at the bottom of a muddy harbour. I thought by the time the body was recovered from the sea, the forensic evidence would be poor and it wouldn't be possible to tell that he'd been dead for a few days. There would not be much water in his lungs, but that would be consistent with him shooting himself first and being dead just as he fell into the water.'

'You were right about that but it was a mistake not to put his mobile phone into his pocket; that made us suspicious. Surely he would have had his phone with him?'

'I realised that later but it was too late.'

'And that was it. There was a couple who had a history of having arguments. The man went crazy and stabbed his partner, probably not meaning to kill her. He ran off into hiding but his guilt and his instability led him to kill himself a few days later. All you had to do was volunteer to identify Holgate's body. This earned you more sympathy with the group and you were already in high esteem with them because you'd apparently tried to save Andrea's life.'

'Yes . . . how ironic is that? But it worked beautifully in my favour. They were so sympathetic to me and put my tiredness down to the trauma I'd been through, whereas it was really because I had to sneak out in the night to meet Elaine and complete important tasks like getting rid of bodies and going over to Leeds.'

'With Andrea and Dominic out of the way, you were clear to remove the painting and nobody would miss it,' said Granger.

'Yes. I got the keys from their room at the Whitby flat. I'd made sure she had a set with her. I'd asked her if I could have another look at the paintings in the flat while we were up here. The plan was for us to call in Leeds before going back to London. So I went over in the night and got the painting.'

He stopped and let out a deep breath. At that point, thought Oldroyd, he must have felt the plan had succeeded.

Morton looked at Oldroyd with an expression which combined anger and admiration. 'I don't know how you got onto me.

If it wasn't for you . . .' he said again and then put his hands up to his face. The reality of his position had reasserted itself.

Oldroyd was under no obligation to explain his thinking in the case, but as Morton had been so open about his plan he felt a professional urge to explain how he had responded. With ruthless criminals like this it was like playing a deadly game of chess and they always had the first moves.

'I was never convinced by the story we were meant to believe. Neither was Louise, although she never thought you were responsible. It seemed unlikely that Holgate would kill Barnes in a row as everyone spoke of them as basically happy together even though they had arguments. Holgate apparently had a knife with him, which suggested he had premeditated his attack and not just lost his temper in the moment. Discovering the trick sarcophagus and Holgate's blood inside it led to more doubts. We were meant to think that Holgate had just blundered out of the building, but if he was hiding in the sarcophagus he must have known about it beforehand and planned to use it. Furthermore, he must also have known it was a trick, because we found his blood in the compartment that was concealed from view. We thought he must have used the mechanism to turn it but in reality he didn't know that the sarcophagus had two compartments; in fact, that was part of the way he was duped. On the face of it there seemed to have been a degree of planning on his part, which was very odd if this was indeed a crime of passion. If he wanted to kill Barnes, why choose a strange, overly dramatic method like this? It also suggested that other people were involved. When I saw the CCTV, I thought it seemed unreal. They looked like actors in a film. It was this sense that everything didn't quite ring true that was at the heart of Louise's refusal to accept what we were presented with.

'However, I have to hand it to you, the apparent facts we were still faced with – that he stabbed her in front of everybody; that there was blood; that he went out of the emergency exit door into that storeroom and that poor Andrea Barnes was dead – were seemingly inescapable whatever we felt about it all.

'The next stage was less convincing. Nobody got a clear view of Holgate either up at the church or by the pub when he apparently went mad and fired off his gun. He stayed at a distance from his friends in the churchyard that night and ran off before anybody could get near. He left a watch to prove it was him and garlic to confuse people and confirm the idea that he'd lost it. Of course we now know it was Pesku. She could easily impersonate Holgate when dressed in a goth costume and she did the same thing the night Holgate apparently committed suicide, concealing her features with a hood and mask. I wondered how Holgate had managed to conceal himself during this three-day period, from the murder of Andrea Barnes on the Wednesday through to the Saturday, especially given that he didn't know Whitby well. We now know that he was killed immediately after Barnes. Also he'd acquired a gun. You cleverly placed the gun holster in his room at the flat but no one had any recollection of seeing Holgate with a gun before, or a knife for that matter. But again: there were the text messages, his body in the harbour and that he'd been seen firing a gun. The obvious explanation for his behaviour after he'd killed Andrea was that the guilt had sent him mad. The whole thing was apparently clear.'

Morton fidgeted restlessly and scowled as these flaws in his plans were exposed by Oldroyd. He wasn't so impressed with the detective now.

'Our investigations in London had not revealed very much but when we discovered Hugh Preston's body, I was pretty sure the whole story we were meant to believe was bogus,' continued Oldroyd.

'That was just luck,' blurted Morton. 'It was those damned kids. I wish I could—'

'Maybe,' continued Oldroyd, interrupting. 'But I couldn't imagine that Holgate had got the information about the sarcophagus from Preston and then murdered him. We still had no firm leads on anyone else. The missing painting had somehow resonated with me from the beginning but I had nothing more to go on. It was Louise who found out more from Mrs Adams about the painting and then she found out from her friend that you had been to the flat. She knew you were a person with a knowledge of art who might recognise the painting and how valuable it was.'

Oldroyd paused before he went on. 'You were fortunate that she didn't tell us anything at that point because she was trying to protect you.' He stopped and swallowed. He was finding this difficult. Granger looked at him but let him continue for the moment. 'She was fond of you and it blinded her to having any idea of what you were really like. The worst she thought was that you had stolen the painting after Andrea's death and she was right. But she'd no idea that you had orchestrated the whole thing.'

'I knew she liked me,' said Morton casually. 'And I liked her, but I had much more important things on my mind. I played up my attraction to her because I knew she was less likely to suspect me if she felt there was something developing between us but she turned out to be a nuisance. She wouldn't accept what I wanted everybody to believe and she encouraged you to doubt it. When she texted me to say she wanted to talk to me about the missing picture, I knew I had to silence her for good.'

Oldroyd looked away from Morton and struggled again for self-control. He indicated to Granger that she should continue.

'What were you planning to do?' Granger said.

Morton shrugged again. 'I didn't have time to plan in any detail. I was pretty sure that she wouldn't have told anybody else we were meeting so I could kill her at the flat, put her body in the back of her car and drive off. I would dispose of the body and abandon the car. There would be nothing to link me to what had happened. The assumption would be that she'd been abducted and murdered by some random killer.'

Oldroyd got up and lurched out of the room.

Granger cast him a worried glance as he left, but continued with her questioning of Morton. 'You must have known that it was unlikely you would get away with that,' she said.

'Maybe, but things were looking desperate. She could have unravelled the whole plan. I had to do something and quickly. I didn't know that sergeant was monitoring things.'

Granger gave him a searching look. 'Did you have no feelings for any of these people who were your friends?'

A strange expression came onto Morton's face. 'I did. I was sorry I had to do it, but it was necessary for my art. I had to have the space to develop my art so it could be acknowledged.' His eyes had a faraway look. 'There is a genius in me; I can feel it and I can't ignore it. It must be fulfilled. This opportunity came and it would have been a crime not to have taken it. Have you read *Crime and Punishment* by Dostoevsky?'

'Yes,' said Granger.

'Raskolnikov, the poor student, murders an old woman to get her money because he thinks his need justifies it. I felt the same. These people would all have died for a good cause if . . .' His voice trailed off and he shrugged again. His dream was dead.

Granger said nothing. She continued to gaze into Morton's face as if looking for further answers but there were none. Mystified, she shook her head.

Oldroyd came back into the room and sat down.

'I think we're done here,' said Granger.

Oldroyd studied Morton for the last time. 'Would you have been able to sell that picture in the end?' he asked at last.

'It would have been hard, but I would have made the sacrifice.'

Oldroyd took a deep breath and then signalled to the officer. 'Take him out.'

～

'Well, sir,' said Granger, grinning as she met with Oldroyd in her office for the last time. 'I see you haven't lost your touch. We lesser mortals can only look on in awe.'

'Oh, don't exaggerate. I was very late getting there on this one and it nearly cost me, well . . .' He frowned and shook his head, remembering how close Morton had come to killing Louise. 'And don't be too hard on yourself for going with the evidence. It was a very skilful plot and had me taken in too for a while. In fact, I think I would have bought it too if it hadn't been for Louise being so insistent that she felt something was not right. She pushed us on to crack it, but she nearly paid with her life.'

It was a sombre thought and one of many ironies of the case.

'Try not to dwell on it, sir,' said Granger, and then she changed the subject. 'I thought you'd like to know we've tied up most of the loose ends. Your sergeant sent me a report. The painting was found undamaged in Morton's room in his shared house in London. I'm not sure yet what's going to happen to it.'

'Let's hope it finds its way to one of the public galleries.'

'Yes. He also found a trick knife with a retracting blade as you predicted. As you know we've got the gun which proves that Pesku, as we call her, shot Holgate. There's not much forensic evidence to link either of them to the murder of Hugh Preston, but plenty of circumstantial stuff. The thing is though, as they've both confessed, a lot of the evidence probably won't be needed. It'll be a judgement by the court as to whether Morton controlled Pesku. They're not denying that they're guilty. Oh, and by the way, the game's up for the Withingtons, too. I've got another team investigating their activities and they've uncovered a whole network of fraudulent goings on in the world of fake jewellery. I'm expecting some arrests soon.'

'Good, well, you don't need me anymore then.'

'No,' replied Granger rather sadly. 'It's been great working with you again, sir.'

Oldroyd smiled as they shook hands. 'The feeling's mutual. Although I can't say I've enjoyed it in the circumstances; far too personal.'

'I can appreciate that. Please pass on my best wishes to your daughter.'

'And mine to yours. Is she okay?'

'Yes, she'll be fine. To tell you the truth a bit of a shock might do her good and make her take life a bit more seriously. I'm hoping she'll knuckle down to her studies now. The fact is she's bright but she's just been coasting for a while. As Bill's not around a lot of the time, the responsibility for cracking the whip falls to me.'

Oldroyd laughed. 'It's only teenage angst. If it's any consolation, Louise went through a similar phase at the same age and she got over it. And I have to confess I left most of it to my wife because we were separated by then. We men still have a lot to learn, but it's not that we don't care.' He paused, thinking about Louise again. 'Anyway, keep up the good work here in Whitby. I'm proud when I see people brought up at Harrogate HQ being so successful.'

'Thank you, sir and give my best wishes to everyone back at Harrogate. I have a lot of fond memories.'

~

Andy got back to Leeds in the late morning. He'd already spoken to Oldroyd and Steph about what had happened.

'Where's the hero of the moment?' he called out as he entered their apartment overlooking the River Aire in Leeds.

'In here,' Steph replied from the living room where she was watching television.

Andy took off his coat and went in. Steph, still in her dressing gown, got up from the sofa.

'Hey, well done,' said Andy as they embraced. 'You were brilliant.'

'Maybe,' replied Steph, who was feeling drained after the excitement of the day before. 'I'm relieved it came out right in the end.'

'That's an understatement. You saved his daughter's life. You'll be permanently in favour with him now.'

'Andy! It's not about that.'

'You'll be his blue-eyed girl even more than before!' He loved to tease her about their long-running, light-hearted competition about who was most in favour with their boss.

'Stop it, it's serious. If we hadn't been there Morton would have killed her.'

'Okay, I know, I'm only teasing. I'm just jealous. The only important things we found were the knives in Morton's flat and the painting. That bloke was creepy though. He has a giant ego and he's a big vampire freak.' He told her about the series of photographs and the paintings.

'Yuck. Well, the painting was what the whole thing was about in the end, wasn't it?'

'Yeah, and I'll tell you, it's nothing to write home about. Just a picture of a woman biting a man; she's supposed to be a vampire, I think. The thing that puzzles me is why something like that is worth so much money. I wouldn't put it on my wall.'

'It's because it's by a famous artist, Edvard Munch, and it's been missing for a long time. That gets the art collectors excited, doesn't it?'

'I suppose so. Anyway, apart from finding that I've seen no real action down there, just a lot of interviews in offices.' He smiled at her. 'In fact, I'm ready for a bit of excitement myself.'

'Look at him. He's not been in the place two minutes but I'm so gorgeous he can't resist me!' she laughed.

'Something like that.'

'You'd better be a good boy then and carry me in. I'm tired after all my outstanding efforts.'

Andy scooped her up in his arms and she laughed again as he took her down to the bedroom.

~

Louise was lying on the sofa in the darkened sitting room at her mother's house in Chapel Allerton when Oldroyd came quietly into the room. He put his hand lightly on her shoulder and whispered 'Lou?' It had been his pet name for her when she was a little girl. He hadn't called her that for years.

She stirred. 'Dad, is that you?'

'Yes, love.'

She sat up and held out her arms. She burst into tears as they hugged.

'Oh, Dad!'

He waited for a while as she sobbed on his shoulder. He winced when he saw the red mark round her neck. Then she lay down again and he sat on the floor beside the sofa. She propped herself up a little.

'I'm sorry, Dad, I feel such an idiot. You couldn't get through to me because my phone was dead and I had no idea that . . .' She couldn't continue and cried again.

'Don't blame yourself. He took us all in for a long time.'

'But I should have told you what I suspected: that he'd been to the flat and seen that picture and everything. I was going to keep his theft a secret.' She put her hands up to her face. 'I don't know what I was thinking. It was just wrong. You should arrest me.'

He laughed. 'I don't think that's necessary. You were trying to correct things in, let's say, a private manner. You thought you could persuade him to act in the right way. It's not as if you said, "I know you've got that picture, how about giving me some of the spoils?"'

She smiled at this. 'But why did I think that way? And why didn't I suspect he was more involved than just stealing the picture?'

'Because you had feelings for him. It's well known, isn't it, that those kinds of emotions can affect our judgment? What's the old saying: "love is blind"?'

'I didn't love him though. I was only . . .' She stopped and shook her head.

'You were at the beginning of what could have been a romantic relationship, and at that point there's often a bit of infatuation going on. You can't see anything wrong with the person. Thank goodness you didn't get in any deeper; it would be far worse now. But the feelings you had made you not really want to consider that he might have been responsible for murdering your friends. It was at a subconscious level.'

She sighed and dried her eyes on a tissue. 'I never even considered it.'

'No, you wouldn't. And lots of other people would have been the same in your position so you're not an idiot. Often it's far worse when this tendency to overlook becomes downright self-deception. I've known people who wouldn't admit that their partners were criminals, even terrible serial killers, despite the evidence in front of them. It gets to the point where they just ignore what they don't want to see.'

She nodded. 'Yeah, I can understand that. At the refuge we used to get women who blamed themselves and wanted to go back to their abuser despite the fact that he'd assaulted them. They made all sorts of excuses for them. It was often to do with their lack of self-worth, but some just didn't want to believe that the man they cared about could do this to them.'

'And don't forget, it was you who made us think about the case again when we were all content to go with the facts as they appeared on the surface. You convinced me to continue to ask questions. We wouldn't have got to the truth without you.'

'I just couldn't believe that Dom would kill her. Something about the whole thing felt strange. Do you remember me saying that?'

'Yes, when you were very upset on the day it happened and we put it down to shock.'

'It's suddenly occurred to me what it was. Dom and Andrea were acting, weren't they? And even though their performances were very convincing, there was something not quite real about it. It was as if we were watching a play, or a horror film, but without realising it, we were in it too, dressed in those hideous costumes.' She put her hands to her face. 'It makes me cringe. And it's just kept getting worse. There's been all sorts of weird stuff going through my mind. This Dracula, vampire thing. Ben was like a vampire, wasn't he? Feeding off Andrea and Dom's blood. And Andrea wasn't dead when we thought she was. It was as if she was undead like a vampire herself, but she was about to die when Ben stabbed her in the heart. Then Dom blundered into the next room to get shot. It was as if Dom and Andrea were the stars of a horror film about their own deaths, wasn't it? It's terrible.'

'Yes, but the film is over now and you're safe. It's not surprising that your imagination's got so feverish but things will fade in time.'

Louise picked up her phone from the sofa beside her. 'Look, I found this.' She handed the phone to her father. On the screen was the picture of the group, which had been taken by Pesku before they started the game. 'I keep finding stuff like this. Look at us pretending to be evil. Most of us thought we were having fun, but one person in that picture and the person taking it were evil and were planning murder.' She shuddered. 'It freaks me out. It's going to take a long time to come to terms with it.'

Oldroyd handed the phone back. 'It will, but you'll do it. And it'll take me some time to get over the shock of what nearly happened at that apartment. I'm glad I didn't know what was going on until it was all over. I was in Whitby and completely powerless. My sergeant did a wonderful job.'

'Steph? She's brilliant; so clever and brave. She worked out what might be going on when I was taken in. I should have told her too.' She shook her head again at her own folly.

'I've trained her to follow her instincts as well as assess the evidence,' continued Oldroyd. 'She knew something wasn't right and she planned accordingly. I'm proud of her.'

'You should be.'

'Mind you, I don't think her partner Andy will be that pleased. I sent him off to London to investigate all your friends and he did a lot of donkey work down there for very little reward apart from finding the picture; then on top of that he missed all the action up here.'

'Oh dear,' said Louise faintly. She'd slowly sunk back into lying on the sofa and her eyes were closed.

Oldroyd paused and looked at her, feeling yet again the intense relief of seeing her alive and okay. 'I won't stay long, love. I can see you're exhausted.'

'I'm not sleeping at night. I get nightmares where he's got that cord around my neck.' She shuddered. 'Thank God Steph was there.'

'It's the shock and trauma of being attacked added to what you've already been through. Maybe your mum should take you to the doctor's. I assume you're going to stay here for a while?'

'I've no choice at the moment. I'm not capable of doing anything.'

'Don't worry about it. Just take it a day at a time. Your mum will look after you. I'll be over to see you and when you're a bit better you can come over to see me and Deborah.'

'That would be nice. Maggie and Mark are going to come up at some point. Mum says they can sleep in the loft bedroom.'

'Good.'

'Everyone's been so kind, but . . .'

'But what?'

'I feel everything's shattered. I've lost three friends and one of them was a ruthless murderer. I feel like I can never build my life up again and trust people. How can I trust people after Ben? I don't feel I know anyone anymore. I'm always going to be on my guard.'

Oldroyd nodded. 'I understand that, but gradually you will regain some faith in people. Remember most people are good; you were exceptionally unlucky to encounter a person like Morton. You've got some good friends.'

She sighed. 'I suppose so. Will I have to go to court? That would be awful.'

'Maybe. From the way he cooperated with us and confessed to everything, it looks as if he might plead guilty. If he does, I don't think you would have to appear. There might be some dispute between him and Elaine Pesku about the extent to which she was forced into being his accomplice, but I can't see you being a relevant witness to that. Anyway, let's not think about that; we'll cross that bridge when we come to it.'

She nodded. 'Thanks for coming, Dad.'

He leaned over and kissed her on the head. 'Bye for now. See you again soon.'

'Bye.' She closed her eyes as he left the room as quietly as he could.

Julia was sitting with a mug of coffee, her elbows propped up on the kitchen table. Oldroyd sat down opposite her.

'How is she?' murmured Julia.

'Okay. Just exhausted. I said you might take her to the doctor's; she would benefit from a course of sleeping tablets.'

'Yes.' Julia yawned. 'I'm not sleeping well myself. It's a good job I've got some compassionate leave from the college.'

'That's excellent. She knows you'll look after her and she'll recover. It looks bad at the moment, but underneath it she's a strong character. She'll bounce back.'

'Yes, but it will take time.'

'It will.'

Julia gave him a wan smile. 'Thank that sergeant of yours again, won't you? She saved our daughter's life.' Her face crumpled for a moment as she faced the enormity of what could have happened.

'I will, don't worry. I've got a brilliant team working with me. I'm very lucky.'

She shook her head and looked at him. 'I don't know how you can do this work. I never could understand it and that was always a problem.'

Oldroyd wasn't sure how to respond to this reference to their old marital difficulties.

Julia continued. 'But now, what can I say? If you hadn't got to the bottom of what was going on, not only would two killers have walked free, but our daughter would have started a relationship with a murderer. That's too awful to contemplate.' She smiled at him again. 'So thanks, Jim.'

A tear fell down her face. Oldroyd leaned over, put his hand on hers and kissed her lightly on the head. He wasn't far from tears himself.

Alice Granger got back home from work in the late afternoon, feeling satisfied that the case was wound up but very tired. The house was unusually quiet. She found Lesley writing an essay at the kitchen table on her laptop. Granger nearly rubbed her eyes and did a double take, but it was true: she was working.

'Hi,' she said. 'Where's Ian?'

'At Graham's; they're gaming I think.'

'Okay,' Granger sighed. 'What do you fancy for tea?'

Lesley looked up. 'I'll make it, Mum. You have a rest. I saw some mince; I'll make spag bol.'

Granger sat down at the table partly with the shock. 'Are you okay?' she asked.

'Me? Fine. Sorry I can't talk much. I've got to finish this essay; it's already late. I've got to hand it in tomorrow or I'm in deep trouble.'

'Right. I'll let you get on with it then.' Lesley looked up and smiled.

'I know you're thinking "what's got in to her?"'

'I am a bit.'

Lesley sat back in her chair and sighed. 'I dunno. I've started to feel different somehow after what happened last Saturday.'

'How?'

'I was shocked. When that figure – you say it was a woman dressed up?'

'It was.'

'When she fired those shots. It made me realise we were all playing around at horror – all that dressing up and stuff – but when something bad actually happens, it's not fun at all, it's nasty. I saw terror on people's faces and Mandy was crying. Then I called you to come and get me out of it.'

'Well, that was the right thing to do.'

'Maybe, but it all reminded me that I'm not as grown-up as I think I am.' She looked at her mother with admiration. 'And you deal with that kind of stuff all the time. I never understood until now. I think you're amazing. And now I'm going to be a bit more sensible.'

Granger smiled at her. 'Thanks for the compliment and that'll be really good, for you I mean. If you work hard you'll do well and get to uni and I think you'll have a great time there.'

'Yeah. There's just one thing, Mum.'

'What's that?'

'This essay is really late so I wondered if you'd write a note saying I've been upset since last Saturday and not able to work properly.'

Granger shook her head. She got up and gave her daughter a hug.

'Of course,' she said and left Lesley to get on with her work. Maybe things were looking up as Oldroyd had said they would. And anyway, after what had happened to the young people in the escape room, she felt it was time as a parent to count her blessings and to acknowledge that things could be much worse.

∾

On Monday morning things were back to normal at Harrogate HQ. Oldroyd's first task was to speak to Tom Walker. He sat in Walker's spartan office opposite his boss who was pleased to see him back. He regarded Oldroyd as a kindred spirit in the fight against managerialism and the business culture. He'd been reading a report on his monitor and he took off his reading glasses.

'Welcome back, Jim. I've been following everything and you've had a right do over there, haven't you?'

'Aye, Tom, it's took me to t'door and back as my granddad used to say.'

'Right,' said Walker, laughing, but then he went more serious. 'I don't suppose I should be laughing when your lass was in such peril.'

'Don't worry, Tom. She's safe and that's all that counts.'

'So the murderer killed his own friends in order to get possession of a valuable painting?'

'He did. He wanted the money so that he could pursue his own artwork without having to earn a living; thought he was some kind of genius.'

Walker grunted and shook his head. 'Do you know I've been in this job for over forty years and you'd think I'd have seen everything, but the depravity of some people still shocks me. Anyway, Stephanie Johnson was outstanding, I hear.'

'She was. She saved my daughter's life. It's as simple as that.'

'Well, she's always been a great asset to the force. I've thought so ever since she joined us as a young lass. With her and Carter, you've got a great team.'

'That's what I've been telling everyone.'

Walker frowned ominously as he glanced with contempt at his computer screen. Oldroyd tensed himself for what was about to come.

'This is what that fool Watkins can never grasp. It's the quality of the people in policing that matters not his bloody bureaucratic systems and stupid targets. I've just been reading his latest missive.' He jabbed at his screen. '"Artificial Intelligence: The Future of Policing?" The man's off his bloody trolley! Does he think robots will be going around arresting people? Never mind artificial intelligence, I'd like to see some real intelligence for once. He thinks he's some kind of super brain sitting in his office looking into the future. The truth is, he hasn't got two brains cells to rub together. I mean . . .'

And off he went. Normally Oldroyd would have looked for an excuse to leave, but the old boy had been so generous and understanding towards him recently that he indulged him once again.

When he was eventually released from Walker's rant, Oldroyd went straight back down to his office. The first person he saw was Andy.

'Welcome back,' he said. 'And well done.'

'Thanks, sir, but I don't think I did much to be honest.'

'Yes, you did. Never despise the more menial tasks. Policing can't be exciting all the time and every scrap of effort contributes to the solving of the case. All those people needed to be followed up; that process of elimination is important.'

'If you say so, sir,' replied Andy, smiling.

'Are we jealous of our partner, I wonder?' teased Oldroyd.

'Oh no, sir, don't worry we've talked about it. She was brilliant.'

'Where is she, by the way?'

'Round there at her desk.'

'Okay. I must have a word.'

Oldroyd found Steph at her computer in the work area. 'Steph, come in a minute, will you?'

She came in and they sat opposite each other. Oldroyd smiled at her and shook his head. She smiled back.

For a few moments he seemed at a loss for words.

'What can I say except "Thank you"? It doesn't seem anything like enough.'

'I'm pleased it all worked out well, sir, and that I played a part in it.'

'"Played a part"? It was a bit more than that, I think. You saved my daughter's life.' His voice broke and he looked away. Steph could see tears forming in his eyes.

'I was doing my job, sir, in the way you've taught me over the years. So if I got it right, you should take some of the credit.'

Oldroyd laughed as he wiped his eyes with a tissue. 'Well, that's super-modest, I must say. I'm so proud of you. You took a risk in going it alone, but it was the right decision.'

'You and Inspector Granger were too far away to be able to do anything and if I'd been wrong it would have caused you so much distress for nothing.'

'Absolutely. What put you on to what was happening?'

'Louise asked to borrow the keys to the flat, but she was very cagey about why she wanted to get in there. I just didn't like it, so I contacted Leeds police and arranged for surveillance of the flat. I had a second set of keys cut so we were able to get inside. At that point we were just going to see what happened. It could have been quite innocent. She may have just come to collect her books. But then you rang and told me about Morton coming to Leeds. We moved quickly into place and, sure enough, Louise arrived with Morton. They didn't know we were there, of course. I had to decide whether to go straight in and arrest him or not. I wasn't sure what weapons he had, so I decided it was safer to let them come into the flat. I was watching them from the door to the kitchen and when he got the cord round her neck, I knew you were right: he was the murderer and then we had to move and fast.'

There was a pause as they both contemplated that horrible moment again.

'You worked it out and followed it through extremely well,' said Oldroyd. 'You'll be pleased to know that Inspector Granger has finished everything off.' He explained how the details of the investigation had been completed.

'How is Louise, sir?'

'As well as can be expected as the saying goes. She's traumatised, obviously, and confused about herself and how she behaved. It will take some time for her to recover.'

'She will though, sir. I'm sure. She's a strong character.'

'Yes.'

'Right, I'll get back to work then, sir,' said Steph and she got up to leave. Oldroyd got up too. He came around the desk, put his arms around her and gave her a big hug.

'There, I just had to do that,' he said. 'I don't care how unprofessional it is. This is one occasion when it's called for.' He was close to tears again.

'That's all right, sir,' said Steph.

'I've never been so emotional in a case before,' continued Oldroyd. 'It all started with DCS Walker telling me how much the force owed me and how grateful he was for all my work. Well, that filled me up, and now I'm saying the same to you: thank you again for what you did. I'll never forget it.'

'You're welcome, sir,' replied Steph, and she felt tears in her eyes too.

~

Oldroyd and Deborah sat in the dark early evening in the Harrogate flat, relaxing over a glass of wine. It was cosy in the warm glow of the lamps. As the clocks had gone back, the hours of daylight had reduced and winter was approaching.

'It'll be bonfire night soon,' said Oldroyd. 'I always enjoy that. Even though it's recalling an attempted act of terrorism, it's a happy, colourful celebration. I've had enough of vampires, Halloween and gothic spookiness for the time being.'

'You like bonfire night because there's always plenty to eat,' laughed Deborah, who enjoyed teasing her partner. It was one of the things Oldroyd liked about her. 'Anyway, I had a good time over in Whitby. It was very interesting and relaxing. It's a pity you had all that work to do. It got in the way a bit for you, didn't it?' Her eyes sparkled at him mischievously. And this was another thing:

his work had always been an issue for Julia, and she showed little interest in it, whereas Deborah seemed unperturbed about the disruption his duties sometimes caused to their social life. She also seemed to find what he did fascinating.

'Well, as usual, I got some clues while we were doing things and enjoying ourselves in Whitby.'

'You do surprise me. Debrief me then. I'm always interested in how you work out the puzzle.'

'Remember when we were on the boat and I was talking about Dracula?'

'You were reminding me how, in the book, Dracula arrives in a ship during a storm.'

'And he leaps on shore in the form of a dog, which nobody realised was the terrible vampire.'

'Yes?'

'It just made me think about how things are not always what they seem to be. It was a trick Dracula performed using his supernatural powers and I began to wonder again if there was some kind of trick going on here. It had been at the back of my mind since I discovered that sarcophagus illusion and the more things appeared cut and dried, the more suspicious I became. It turned out the evil lay in the character who seemed the most harmless, who'd apparently done the most to help.

'I remember you saying that you sometimes had to remind yourself that what was happening in a horror film was only people acting. That confirmed what I was already beginning to think about the whole business in the escape room. Then when I played that trick on you at the museum and you said what if it had gone wrong, it stirred something in my mind. That evening it was Halloween and I heard "Trick or Treat" being called out by kids. I couldn't stop thinking about that phrase and it kept me awake. But the next morning I was pretty sure I knew what had happened. I remembered that the two dead people were actors and Andy Carter had reported that Holgate enjoyed practical jokes. I realised that they were performing in a trick that went wrong, at least for them. They weren't aware that there was a second, deadly trick being played out, and that this one was on them.'

'Hmm. It was an ingenious but evil scheme, wasn't it?'

'Yes, worthy of a vampire, though there was nothing supernatural about it, just the dark side of human ingenuity.'

'So, how's Louise?' asked Deborah.

'She's doing okay I think; still with her mother.'

'Do you think she'll come and stay with us for a bit? I'd love to see her.'

'Maybe. I think she wants to get back to London as soon as she can and start up her life again.'

'That's understandable.'

'Thanks for arranging for her to have those therapy sessions. She took a bit of persuading, but I think she'll benefit from them.'

'Good. It will be much better for her in the long run. She went through some very traumatic things and often people bury the pain caused by experiences like that. PTSD therapy can help a lot.'

'I'm not sure the sense of betrayal she feels isn't worse than the shock of being attacked.'

'It probably is . . . and the two go together, don't they? Someone she cared for tried to take her life after killing two of their mutual friends. She's bereaved of those friends and, in another sense, of the man who tried to kill her. He was also her friend and maybe more. It's much worse than being attacked by some random person in the street.' She shook her head. 'There's a lot of difficult stuff to work through and I'm glad Denise is helping her. She's a very experienced practitioner, but it will take time.'

Oldroyd took a sip of wine. 'What do you make of Ben Morton and his motivation? Alice Granger told me he compared himself to Raskolnikov in *Crime and Punishment*. He needed the money so that his genius could flourish. It's an extraordinary justification for what he did. Unlike Raskolnikov, he doesn't appear to have felt any guilt.'

Deborah rolled her eyes. 'There's a lot of stuff in there too. Clearly a terrible egomania where the needs of his unappreciated genius are paramount, self-delusion about his talent and a measure of psychopathy in the lack of empathy with others, even his own friends. I don't envy my colleagues in forensic psychology trying to untangle that lot.'

'No.' Oldroyd took another sip of his wine. 'You know, I often find myself comparing a dramatic case like this to a Shakespeare play. We were definitely near the world of *Macbeth* in this one: the great themes of loyalty and betrayal acted out in a dark, violent atmosphere of witches, vampires and general ghoulishness, even if the witches and so on were people dressed up and not real as in the play.'

'But not everyone is evil in that play, are they? Isn't there some light at the end?'

'Yes, there is hope in the loyalty of Banquo and later on in the young Malcolm. He brings the possibility of renewal.'

'And that's what will happen with Louise and the others who suffered. In time they will experience renewal too.'

'I think you're right,' said Oldroyd, who suddenly felt optimistic about the future as he poured them both another glass of wine.

～

But on the instant, came the sweep and flash of Jonathan's great knife. I shrieked as I saw it shear through the throat; whilst at the same time Mr Morris's bowie knife plunged into the heart.

It was like a miracle; but before our very eyes, and almost in the drawing of a breath, the whole body crumbled into dust and passed from our sight.

From Mina Harker's Journal in Dracula

∼

This ae nighte, this ae nighte,
Every nighte and alle,
Fire, fleet and candle light,
And Christe receive thy saule.

From the Lyke Wake Dirge

Acknowledgments

I continue to find help, inspiration and encouragement from the Otley Writers' Group and from my family and friends.

The twice-yearly Whitby Goth Weekend is a fascinating event. I would like to thank the organisers and all the people who put such effort and imagination into their amazing costumes!

Bram Stoker visited Whitby in the summer of 1890. He found the name *Dracula* in a book in the Whitby Subscription Library and decided to set a substantial part of the story in the town. His account of Dracula's arrival in Whitby is based on a real event when a ship ran aground in the harbour and it was discovered that very few of the crew remained alive. Some rescue workers reported seeing a black dog jump off the ship and run up the 199 steps to the abbey.

Edvard Munch painted six versions of 'Love and Pain', sometimes called 'Vampire', between 1893 and 1895. One version is missing.

West Riding Police is a fictional force based on the old riding boundary. Harrogate was part of the old West Riding, although it is in today's North Yorkshire.

About the Author

John R. Ellis has lived in Yorkshire for most of his life and has spent many years exploring Yorkshire's diverse landscapes, history, language and communities. He recently retired after a career in teaching, mostly in further education in the Leeds area. In addition to the Yorkshire Murder Mystery series, he writes poetry, ghost stories and biography. He has completed a screenplay about the last years of the poet Edward Thomas and a work of faction about the extraordinary life of his Irish mother-in-law. He is currently working on his memoirs of growing up in a working-class area of Huddersfield in the 1950s and 1960s.

Did you enjoy this book and would like to get informed when J. R. Ellis publishes his next work? Just follow the author on Amazon!

    1) Search for the book you were just reading on Amazon or in the Amazon App.

    2) Go to the Author Page by clicking on the author's name.

    3) Click the 'Follow' button.

    If you enjoyed this book on a Kindle eReader or in the Kindle App, you will be automatically offered to follow the author when arriving at the last page.

THOMAS & MERCER